What You Wish For

What
You
Wish
For

David Cray

An Otto Penzler Book

CARROLL & GRAF PUBLISHERS
NEW YORK

WHAT YOU WISH FOR

Carroll & Graf Publishers
An Otto Penzler Book
An Imprint of Avalon Publishing Group Inc.
161 William Street, 16th Floor
New York, NY 10038

First Carroll & Graf edition 2002

Library of Congress Cataloging-in-Publication Data is available.

ISBN: 0-7867-1085-3

Printed in the United States of America
Distributed by Publishers Group West

A pair of long overdue acknowledgments:

To my son, Ethan, for his willingness to share his knowledge of computer arcana and for his patience in the face of my admittedly willful computer illiteracy. I am indebted to him not only for his help in the writing of *What You Wish For* but for each of the other novels I've written over the last five years. Alas, as the knowledge he imparts does not accumulate in my technophobic brain, I'm sure to be calling for advice on the next one as well. Thank you.

And to my friend Robert Knightly, a retired NYPD lieutenant who now toils in the bowels of the criminal justice system as a Legal Aid trial lawyer. Bob's insights are unique, a view from both ends of the bridge that he has been generous enough to share on many occasions. Though Bob's insights often lead to extensive rewrites on my part, I am, nevertheless, in his debt, and it's about time I said so. Thank you.

1

I T W A S the wrong day for a murder, a day of cotton-ball clouds nearly stationary in an azure sky, of temperatures kissing seventy degrees, the first warm day in New York after a long and troubled winter. With the collapse of the towers of the World Trade Center six months before, a chill had settled over the city as the funerals came one after another, a chill and a calculated determination to endure. New York had turned a corner and the gay nineties were over and you didn't need a crystal ball to know it. Nonetheless, you were along for the ride, come what may, and you knew that as well. As you knew that spring would eventually arrive. As you knew you would be grateful when it did.

Thus Captain Julia Brennan, as she skirted the police barricade at First Avenue and 88th Street, paused for just a moment to turn her face up to the early afternoon sun. The warmth was delicious, a reward for having persevered, one she gratefully accepted.

"Help you?"

Quite automatically, Julia displayed her badge and ID card to the uniformed officer blocking her path. She watched him stiffen slightly as he noted her rank. "Who's in charge here?" she asked.

"I guess you are." The uniform was impossibly young and so pale-skinned Julia wondered if he'd remembered to use sunblock before coming on duty. "Oh," he declared when Julia didn't reply, "you mean, of our guys?"

Julia read the man's name off the ID bar pinned to his breast, then fixed him with a sardonic smile. "Exactly, Officer Carlsson. Your guys."

"That'd be Lieutenant Storm. He's over there by the stoop, in the gray coat."

Storm turned at the sound of his name. His eyes flicked from Julia's head to her feet and back to her head before he walked over to join her. "The famous . . ." He snapped his fingers and glanced at the heavens for inspiration before adding, "Captain Brennan. Here to give me the bad news. Well, easy come, easy go."

Julia nodded once, pleased to find the good lieutenant resigned to his loss. Though both were on the NYPD's payroll, Storm worked out of the 21st Precinct while Julia headed the investigative arm of the District Attorney's Sex Crimes Unit. Ordinarily, precinct detectives got first crack at a homicide, but not this time. This time the silks downtown had decided to pass the case to Sex Crimes and there was nothing to be done about it. Or to be gained by a show of temper.

Refusing the offer of Patrolman Carlsson as a guide to the crime scene (her own people were already on-site), Julia made her way up the high concrete stoop and through two sets of oak doors to a large room made even larger by fourteen-foot ceilings. To her right, a crime scene cop in a white paper jumpsuit dusted a small wooden cabinet. A tangle of wires jutted from the rear of the cabinet. There were wires jutting from a recess in the wainscoting as well.

Julia walked over, identified herself, squatted next to the tech. "What am I looking at?" she asked.

The tech opened the cabinet door to reveal an alarm box with a key pad and a panic switch, along with the logo and name STARETT HOME SECURITY SYSTEMS. "The siren's in the closet." He gestured to a door at the corner of the room.

Julia crossed the parquet floor and opened the door. She was looking for a battery that would sound the alarm if the AC was cut, but found none.

"Old as Methuselah."

Julia looked over her shoulder to find Detective Bert Griffith standing behind her. A black man approaching middle age, his expression was composed, as always. In the past, when both were assigned to Manhattan North Homicide, Griffith's colleagues had joked about his great stone face, pronouncing it worthy of Mount Rushmore. Recently, though, whether through age or the force of events, Bert's look had assumed an aspect that could only be called mournful.

"Did anyone check with the alarm company?" Julia asked.

Griffith flipped through the pages of a spiral notebook until he found the name he was looking for. "Detective Malillo, one of the locals, phoned over and spoke to a man named Rudy Green. Green claims the last time Starett Alarm received an alert was about a month ago when somebody broke in. He also says the system is twenty-five years old and if you cut the electric and phone wires, that's all she wrote. Newer systems have all kinds of backup, including cell phones if the land lines are cut, but he couldn't convince the victim to update. She didn't wanna go through the mess of rewiring, plus the intruder who broke in a month ago fled when the alarm sounded. That proved the system worked just fine."

Julia took a moment to look around the parlor. Though the paintings on the walls were modern and the expensive furniture sleek, the room had the unmistakable feel of age, as if nothing had been added, nothing removed, for many years. A woman's portrait hung over a white mantel supported by a pair of fluted marble columns. Despite the evening gown and the diamonds at her throat, Julia found something hard and calculating in the woman's expression. Her full mouth was a bit too firm, her large blue eyes a bit too fixed, her strong chin a bit too high. Nevertheless, she was stunningly beautiful.

"How old was she?" Julia pronounced the victim's name for the first time. "Adeline Rose."

"Eighty-three."

"Too old to live alone."

"There's a housekeeper." Griffith again consulted his notes. "Flora Esquival. She left after supper last night and was due to return this evening. It's her regular day off."

"Has she been located?"

"At her aunt's house in Queens. The locals went to fetch her."

Julia was in no hurry to climb up to the third floor, to where the torn body of Adeline Rose lay sprawled on her sitting room carpet. Better to stay objective at this stage, evaluate the scene as if it were a mechanical puzzle in which the act of murder played no part. "I understand," she said, "there was a forced entry."

"Downstairs, through the French doors leading into the garden."

"Let's take a look."

Griffith leading the way, they crossed the room, opened a pair of sliding doors, and stepped into a small foyer between the front and rear parlors. A winding flight of stairs to the right led them down to a formal dining room where a pair of crime scene cops were gathering physical evidence. Through an open door hanging from a single hinge, Julia viewed a wintering garden separated from First Avenue by a brick wall. The wall rose to a height of seven feet. Easy enough to scale, it had the additional benefit of providing cover to anyone in the garden.

"The door was ripped open with a pry bar," Griffith said. "The tool marks gouged into the frame are clear."

Julia nodded. No investigator in her command read a crime scene better than Bert Griffith, not even Carlos Serrano, who'd recently made detective, first grade, the highest honor the job could bestow on a detective. "The alarm," she said, "once you open the door, how much time do you get to shut it off before it sounds?"

Griffith's smile betrayed just a hint of pride, as a teacher might in the presence of a gifted pupil. "Thirty seconds," he replied without hesitation.

Julia glanced at her watch then walked swiftly up the stairs and through the front parlor to where the alarm box had once hung on the wall. Twenty-one seconds had passed.

The front door opened before she could take it any further, and a slight Latino woman, flanked by two uniformed cops, entered the parlor. The cops towered over the woman, who appeared to be in her mid-forties.

Julia flashed her ID for the benefit of the two uniforms, then said, very gently, "Flora Esquival?"

"Yes?"

"Would you mind waiting here in the parlor? We need to speak to you, but we're really busy right now."

"Sí," Esquival replied. She was holding her hands in front of her body, washing them one over the other. "This thing," she said, "it has happened to Senora Rose?"

"Yes," Julia replied evenly, "it has." She waited until the house-keeper found a seat near the fireplace, then turned back to Griffith. "Where's Betty?" Betty Cohen was another of her detectives. "I want her to handle Ms. Esquival."

"Betty's on the third floor," Griffith replied, "with the body."

For just a moment, Julia was tempted to send Griffith up with a message, but there was no point. "Alright," she said as she headed for the stairs. "Time to get on with it."

2

B UT FOR Assistant Medical Examiner Solomon Bucevski's misfortune, Julia would have been too late to view the victim's body, a turn of events that would not have overly troubled her. The nature of this misfortune was made clear as she approached the second floor by the disbelief and indignation apparent in Bucevski's voice, which echoed in the stairway.

"How you have done this?" Bucevski demanded. "How? How? How?" His thick Russian accent made it seem as though he was forcing each syllable around a wad of chewing tobacco. "This is your job to make sure equipment is in van. How you are coming to scene of homicide without body bags?"

"I. . . ."

"Cease to speak. You are idiot. In my country you would be sent to gulag for this. You would be sent to tuberculosis ward in gulag."

Bucevski quieted when Julia appeared on the narrow stairway, though his long skinny frame continued to quiver. He was positioned two steps above his tech, a burly Asian whose deadpan expression might have indicated anything from outrage to contrition to utter indifference.

"Ah," Bucevski said to Julia, "you see this what I have to deal with? It is insult to the intelligence."

"Life is hard," Julia replied as she brushed past the two men, "and you know what happens next." She halted a step above Bucevski. "If you're gonna stick around for a while. I'd like to speak to you, Solomon. Just give me a few minutes to view the body."

"For you I stay ten minutes," Bucevski declared without looking away from his tech. "And you, Mr. Hong, you are waiting for what exactly? For body bag to appear by way of miracle?"

As she approached the third floor, Julia found her way blocked by a uniformed sergeant whose name tag read Karatopolis. She identified herself yet again, then asked, "Can I get in there?"

Sergeant Karatopolis jammed himself against the wall to let Julia and Bert Griffith pass. "We're bringing a spatter expert down later," he told them, "to reconstruct the scene, but you should be able to get a couple of steps inside. It's the second door. The bathroom where the perp cleaned up is directly across the hall."

"Thanks."

At the top of the stairs, Julia entered a short hallway punctuated by four doors, the two on her left wide open. The closest of these led to a smallish bedroom filled with heavy furniture, including a four-poster bed that might have been lifted from a Victorian mansion. Though at first glance the bedroom appeared pristine, two crime scene cops in search of fingerprint evidence were busy dusting an armoire. Detective Betty Cohen was also in the room, standing next to a lacquered jewelry box. She came out into the hall when Julia made her appearance.

"The box was open," she explained, "when the first cops arrived." Although Betty Cohen was a twenty-five year veteran of the New York Police Department and a seasoned professional, between her pronounced overbite and her lopsided smile, she was often mistaken for the sort of woman who lives to please others. It was an error she generally encouraged.

"Who called them in?"

"The family lawyer, Craig Whitmore. He says he tried to reach her several times this morning before he phoned 911."

"This lawyer available?"

"On his way."

Julia nodded to herself. She expected her people to be competent and professional, and they seldom disappointed her. "The housekeeper's downstairs in the parlor. Her name's Flora Esquival. I want you to go down there, play it low key, but get whatever you can. If she's been blabbing about her rich employer to some gangster boyfriend or relative, I wanna know about it."

"Done."

THE MURDER scene was as bad as Julia had imagined. Adeline Rose had been stabbed and slashed many times, and the entire room was crisscrossed by feathery lines of spattered blood. The lines were thicker in their centers, thinner at the ends, but their collective point of origin was apparent. They could only have begun on the floor where the crumpled body of Adeline Rose lay in a small black sea of coagulated blood. At first glance, the elderly woman appeared to be naked, so shredded was the blood-soaked nightgown she'd put on before her killer arrived. The blood had matted in the lace fringe on her cap as well, and collected in every stretch mark, every crevice, every wrinkle on her thin angular body.

"The murder weapon's behind the chair," Bert Griffith finally said, much to Julia's relief.

"Lily mentioned a letter opener," she replied. Assistant District Attorney Lily Han, Julia's boss, headed the DA's Sex Crimes Unit.

"Right. The handle's ivory and carved into the shape of an angel. It matches the handle of a magnifying glass on the victim's desk."

"A weapon of convenience," Julia said. When Bert didn't argue the point, she asked, "Is it sharp enough to do that much damage?"

"I didn't examine it myself, but I'm told by the responding officers that it has an extremely sharp point and one edge is sharp enough to cut paper."

Nodding to herself, Julia looked for the magnifying glass but found herself distracted by a photograph mounted in a polished silver frame. The photo was a typical eight-by-ten glossy, a publicity shot from a time long past. The woman it depicted was standing on a stage, concealing her apparently naked flesh with a large fan covered by red roses. The pose was quite demure by new millennium standards: a cocked hip, a rounded shoulder, a sliver of thigh. The woman's expression, on the other hand, was far more provocative. The dark eyes challenged and the narrow smile was only a hair's breadth from a dismissive sneer.

"That's her," Julia said, pointing at the photo. "Adeline Rose. Her portrait's hanging downstairs."

"I saw it," Griffith said. "Hard to believe it's the same woman."

"She's older in the portrait by a good fifteen years, but the eyes are identical."

Julia looked back to the victim's body. Adeline's eyes were closed now and there was no longer any expression to read, not even fear. It was this lack of expression that begged for justice, this absence of personality, Adeline reduced to her component parts. Or so Julia thought as she finally turned away.

"I'M GOING to speak to Bucevski," she told Griffith as they retraced their steps. "Why don't you round up the lawyer, see what he has to say?"

"You don't wanna be there?"

Julia smiled. She not only wanted to be there, she wanted to brace the man herself. Unfortunately, she was the unit's commander, not a front-line detective, and her duties were primarily administrative. One of those duties, one she took very seriously, was maintaining the high morale of the cops who worked for her, a morale she could easily undermine by pushing them aside to do the work herself. That was why she'd sent Betty Cohen to conduct a solo interview with the housekeeper. Still, Julia occasionally found herself personally involved in the grunt work of an investigation. Given the way SCU worked, it was inevitable.

Overwhelmingly, by the time cases reached Lily Han's desk, the perpetrator had been arrested by local detectives and was ready for prosecution. These were the routine rapes and child molestations inevitable in a city of eight million. A much smaller number of cases, on the other hand, found their way to SCU in the early stages of investigation. One and all, they were big cases and the pressure was as unrelenting as the hours were long. But Julia could not only live with those conditions, she thrived on them, and there was other good news, too. After all, once ordered to keep a close eye on a given investigation, she could not be blamed for merely following orders.

Julia found Solomon Bucevski outside the townhouse. He was standing at the foot of the stoop, puffing on a cigarette wrapped in black paper, his face turned up to the sun.

"So beautiful," he said as Julia came down the steps. "Winter has been without end."

Though the winter, in fact, had been exceptionally warm, Julia merely nodded her assent. "When did she die?"

The question was simple enough, but the conversation it evoked continued for several minutes, with Bucevski insisting that an estimated time of death could only be established after an autopsy and Julia assuring him that he would not be held to account if his best guess proved to be inaccurate. She and Solomon had danced this little dance so many times in the past that each step came automatically with the final dip virtually assured.

"Early this morning," Bucevski finally declared, "between eleven and three o'clock. This is my estimation from state of rigor and internal body temperature."

"Thanks." Julia started up the steps, then turned back to Bucevski as if her next question had just that moment occurred to her. "Say, Solomon, did you find anything to indicate a sexual attack? Other than her torn nightgown?"

"Autopsy will establish this. There is now too much blood to make determination."

Julia sighed. "I know that. I know it's too early, but all I'm asking is if you found any positive evidence that Adeline Rose was raped. So far."

Bucevski dropped his cigarette to the sidewalk, then ground it into the concrete with a sharp twist of his shoe. "*Nyet*," he declared. "There is nothing."

Then why, Julia thought, as she passed into the front parlor of Adeline Rose's home, am I here?

3

I GNORING BETTY Cohen and Flora Esquival, who were
seated hand in hand on a long couch, Julia walked directly into the
back parlor where she found Bert Griffith perched on the edge of
a stiff side chair. Bert was facing a short man in his mid-sixties who
sat in a ladder-back rocker. The man wore a vested charcoal suit
over a starched white shirt and a silk tie.

"Don't let me interrupt," Julia said as she dropped onto a love
seat halfway across the room.

"You're Julia Brennan," the man said. "I recognize you. I'm
Craig Whitmore, Adeline's attorney."

Julia nodded once, then took a spiral notebook from her purse
and pretended to flip through it. Whitmore's smile was as cold as
his slightly protruding eyes which measured her through wire-
rimmed glasses. When he spoke, his tone was matter-of-fact and

his posture relaxed. If he cared at all about his client, he wasn't showing it. He didn't appear even to be shocked.

"Should I start over, detective?" he asked Griffith.

"Why not?" For once, Bert's face was animated. He was smiling and his chin was tilted a bit to the right as he nodded encouragement. The message was clear enough to Julia. As long as the lawyer was willing to talk, Bert was prepared to listen.

Whitmore adjusted his glasses then dropped his hand to his lap. "Adeline Rose claims to have been born eighty-three years ago and she claims to have no blood relatives. I use the word *claimed* because nothing is known of Adeline's early life. She has always refused to speak of it except to say that she was born in New Jersey and that no record of her birth was made. Personally, I don't believe she would have volunteered even that much if it hadn't been necessary to explain why she had no birth certificate."

"So she just appeared out of the blue?"

"Yes, on the burlesque circuit at the height of the Depression. She was billed as the Wild Jewish Rose."

Griffith's smile expanded. "Now I get it. She did a dance with a fan, right? And the fan was covered with roses?" He leaned back and tapped his knee. "There's a publicity shot upstairs. You know, in the room where she was stabbed to death."

Whitmore didn't even blink. "I've never been up there," he said as he again straightened his glasses. "Generally, we conducted business in the parlor or in my office. In addition to her legal affairs, I managed Adeline's portfolio and her real estate investments."

"I see." Griffith pulled at his lower lip with his thumb and forefinger, as though trying to suppress a smile, then said, "Tell me something, when I was upstairs I kept lookin' at the photo, but I couldn't decide one way or the other. Were the roses real?"

"Paper, I'm afraid."

"Not even silk?"

"Paper."

"Figures." Griffith signaled the lawyer to continue.

"If you accept Adeline's date of birth as accurate, she met Herschel Liebman in Cleveland when she was twenty-one, then married him two years later. Mr. Liebman was a widower at the time and very rich. He'd inherited a fortune estimated to be in the tens of millions from his father, then managed it well, despite the Great Depression. He also had two children from his prior marriage, Hannah and Stephen, ages four and three respectively when their father married for the second time."

"How did the family react? You know, when Liebman got involved with a stripper? I mean, they musta went crazy, right?"

"Wrong, detective. The family wasn't the problem. There were only a few scattered cousins, poor relations one and all, whose opinions counted for nothing." Whitmore's hands went to his glasses again, then he smoothed his thinning white hair. "This part of Manhattan, it's usually called the Upper East Side, but it's also known as the Gold Coast."

"I've heard that."

"Have you also heard that there are two kinds of money here, old and new?"

"I have."

"Well, you were misinformed. There are three kinds of money on the Gold Coast- old, new and aging. Before he married Rose, Herschel's second-generation money was aging. After he married Rose, his money went back to new. This did not please his children who were third generation, but, of course, they were too young to complain at the time. Later on, however, they became . . . resentful."

"What about Herschel? How did he feel about returning to square one?"

"Herschel was in his mid-forties when he and Rose fell in love. For the next twenty years, until he died of a heart attack, they were devoted to each other. I began working for the Liebmans some years before Herschel passed away, so I bear personal witness. They were made for each other, which is why the children were unsuccessful when they challenged the will. Herschel left small trust funds to each of his children, but the bulk of his holdings, almost seventy million dollars, went to his wife."

Julia continued to stare down at the notebook on her lap. Two things were already clear: Craig Whitmore had come prepared and he didn't give a damn who knew it. At some point, he'd decided to point the finger at Herschel's kids, who must by this time be senior citizens.

"How much do they get, from their trust funds?" Griffith asked.

"Seventy-five thousand a year."

"Each?"

"Each."

"So, they're not rich."

"They own small cooperative apartments in the same down-town building. They pay their bills."

"But that's it."

As Whitmore drew a breath, his eyes grew even colder and his skin, already pale, became chalky. "Adeline Rose was not a good person," he said. "Aside from her husband she only had one pur-pose in life and that was to move her money from the new to the aging pile. She belonged to every civic organization that would have her, gave lavishly to dozens of approved charities, endured thou-sands of slights. In the end, she succeeded. In the end, she was tol-erated by those she considered her betters."

"Does that mean she had a lot of friends?"

"Once upon a time, Adeline employed the full regalia: butler, chauffeur, chef, and three full-time housekeepers." Whitmore leaned back and for the first time the rocker moved slightly. "About fifteen years ago, when she turned seventy, she gradually eased back. For the last few years, Adeline's been almost reclusive. She still donates, of course, but she no longer attends the balls and the parties."

Griffith raised an eyebrow. "No friends at all?"

"The Gold Coast Glitterati." Whitmore's fleshy mouth jerked into a semblance of a smile. "Five rich old ladies who alternate hosting a lunch every Thursday. The girls wear their best gold jewelry and some article of gold clothing. They come with their chauffeurs and their home health aides, pushing walkers, in wheel-chairs. I suppose it's all very inspiring, especially when you con-sider what they have in common."

"I can't wait to hear."

"They've all, by dint of hard work and persistence, raised the status of their fortunes from new to aging."

"God bless 'em. Myself, I'm still bending over to pick up quar-ters on the street. But what about you, Mr. Whitmore. Which are you? Old, new or aging?"

"Neither. I'm petit bourgeois, at best."

"And the children? What would you call *them*?"

Whitmore lifted his chin slightly, but his mouth remained immobile, his eyes blank. Julia, no longer even pretending to have other business, watched with undisguised curiosity. Whitmore's lips parted only slightly when he spoke and his words seemed to come from the back of his throat.

"The children? Well, after their father's death, they simply became poor relations. Tolerated, though not encouraged. I called

Steve and Hannah, by the way, and told them what happened. They asked me to give you their phone numbers."

"But they're not rushing over."

"Afraid not."

"Tell me, do they do anything, these kids? Besides hate their wicked stepmother? Do they work, for instance?"

This time the lawyer's smile was genuine. "Steve Liebman failed at everything he tried to do and he tried to do many things."

"And Hannah?"

"Hannah never tried."

4

As PETER Foley crossed Sixth Avenue at 10th Street in Greenwich Village, he glanced to his left, not at the oncoming traffic which had stopped for the light, but at the patch of sky once obscured by the towers of the World Trade Center. The gesture had become a ritual for him, like a Roman Catholic making the sign of the cross when passing a Catholic church, or a Jew touching a mezuzah when entering or leaving home. Foley knew what he wanted, admit it or not, was for the towers to reappear. He wanted to return to the affluent optimism of the nineties, to the years when tourists poured in from around the world, when the restaurants and the hotels and most of all the streets were packed with celebrants.

The irony, which Foley both anticipated and accepted, was that his glance did not produce a miraculously restored World Trade Center. Instead, two distinct images—of the many thousands presented in the week following September 11, 2001—rose to his consciousness. The first was of smoke rising, day after day after day. The second was of a clear blue sky as beautiful as it was merciless.

Foley's very brief reverie was interrupted by a furiously pedaling bicycle messenger who passed within inches of his body. Thus chastened, he hurried on to the corner of Hudson and Perry streets where he took a table at an outdoor café. It was one o'clock in the afternoon and the day was warm enough to draw him into a small patch of sunlight at the very edge of the restaurant.

Though Foley was thirty minutes early for his appointment with Toshi Matsunaga, he was more pleased than annoyed by the necessary wait. These days, Peter Foley's greatest joy was his lover, Julia Brennan, and her family, but his attachment to New York City, of much longer duration, followed only a short distance behind. At one time or another, as cop and as civilian, he'd hiked through virtually every neighborhood in its five boroughs. He wasn't hiking now, of course, but that really didn't matter. By taking his place upon the stage, in full view, he was playing his part. He was announcing a bottom-line truth shared by every city resident. The show must go on.

The young woman who came to take his order was young, slender and very attractive. She approached to within a few feet of his table before speaking with a distinct Australian accent. "What can I do for ya?"

Foley ordered a cappuccino and a cannoli, then waited for the woman to leave before checking the contents of the shoulder bag he carried. The bag had been designed to hold and cushion a laptop computer, but Foley had taken to using it for whatever came to hand, including the pistol he, as an ex-cop, had the right to carry. Inside, in a zippered compartment, he found the two DVDs he'd put there an hour before. DVDs were hot items in the narrowly circumscribed world of child pornography. Hot enough to lure Toshi Matsunaga to the corner of Hudson and Perry.

On his second cappuccino when Matsunaga arrived, Foley rose to his feet and took the smaller man's hand. Matsunaga, a third-generation Japanese American, had been advertised as a small-time collector of kiddie porn, an easy mark,

"Goober," Matsunaga said as he laid his leather backpack on the ground beside his chair, "we meet at last."

Foley smiled at the use of the cyber name he'd established as web master of little_love.com. Though the site had been down for almost a year, he was still using the information and the evidence he'd gathered while it was up and running. He'd been a cop back then, with at least semi-authority to pursue his obsession. Now he was on his own.

The waitress made an appearance at that moment and Matsunaga, his thin smile still in place, ordered green tea. As the waitress walked back into the restaurant, he fixed his eyes on her swaying buttocks. "Too bad," he said, "they don't invent a regression pill. You knock ten years off that babe, she'd be alright."

Foley laughed dutifully. He'd long ago realized that it was simple lust that drove his prey, lust that drew them into the open where they risked all. "I've got what you want," he said. "DVDs. Digital audio, digital video, all original. There's even a story line. Something about two little children who become lost in the woods and the wolf who befriends them."

Matsunaga rubbed his hands together. In his thirties, he wore silk trousers, a sweatshirt with the sleeves cut away, and penny loafers without socks. Foley assumed Matsunaga had donned the sweatshirt in order to add a masculine touch to his outfit. In fact, the sweatshirt only emphasized the man's thin arms and wrists.

"I brought what you asked for." Matsunaga reached into his backpack to produce a pair of DVDs. "Top of the line," he announced. "Cutting edge. They coulda been shot at a major studio."

They chatted for another twenty minutes, mostly in general terms about the local pedophile scene. At one point, Matsunaga expressed his outrage at the continuing persecution of pedophiles, insisting the sexual relationship between adult and child sprang from love, not exploitation. Then he casually contradicted himself by describing his personal predilections. On those rare occasions, he explained, when he had access to a living child (girls, always girls), he liked to dress them in the flimsiest lingerie and personally apply the sort of makeup generally associated with street prostitutes.

"Face it," he told Foley, his dark eyes inflamed with passion, "deep down, they're all whores anyway."

For his part, Foley contented himself with an occasional nod of agreement. There was an FBI agent named Raymond Lear eager for the material Matsunaga had so casually swapped, but Lear could wait. With its crooked streets and superb townhouses, the West Village was one of Peter Foley's favorite neighborhoods and he fully expected to remain exactly where he was until the sun dropped behind the nearest buildings, to lose himself in the strollers passing within a few feet of where he sat.

As Matsunaga droned on, Foley began to divide the pedestrians into two groups, the cautious and the bold. The cautious were bundled into their winter wardrobes. They wore thick coats and tightly knit watch caps, gloves which they now carried in their hands or shoved into their pockets. The bold were already flaunting navel rings.

"I gotta go." Matsunaga stood, reached into his back pocket, withdrew a thin leather wallet.

"Hang on a minute, Toshi. I want to show you one more thing."
Pete waited until Matsunaga resumed his seat before withdrawing
a 4×6 photo from his shoulder bag. "You ever see this girl? I lost
her about a year ago and I'd give a lot to find her. She was great."

Matsunaga took the photo and stared at it for a minute. The little girl posed with her arm around Foley's neck was about eleven
years old. She had a very wide, very innocent smile, a smile certain to warm the heart of any pedophile. In fact, she was Peter
Foley's daughter who'd vanished from the Little Kitty Day Care
Center five years before. Foley had been showing the photo to the
pedophiles he hunted for years, hoping against hope that his
daughter was still alive. As a cop, he knew the odds were all against
him. He knew that she was more than likely dead, that once the
monster who'd stolen her grew bored, he'd tossed her away like a
broken toy.

"So?" Foley said.

"So I think I know her." Matsunaga continued to stare at Patti
Foley's likeness. "I think I got her on a video." He turned his face
up to meet Foley's eyes. "I mean, a smile like that, how could you
forget it?"

5

THOUGH FOLEY tried to maintain his generally relaxed posture, along with an expression denoting keen interest, he could not control his heart which skipped several beats, then snapped back into action with a nearly audible thump. Nor was he able to sort through the rush of thoughts and emotions which galloped from one ear to the other like lemmings in search of a sea. He might have remained in this state indefinitely if Matsunaga's own expression hadn't changed from one of mild amusement to concern.

"Hey, you alright?"

For some reason he couldn't begin to fathom, Matsunaga's question banished all the little demons prancing through Foley's mind to some inner dungeon. Even as it evoked the boss of all bosses, a cold purposeful rage that knew exactly what it wanted.

Foley allowed his smile to fade. He dropped his chin and his eyes, assuming the posture of a supplicant. "You think," he asked, "I could get a look at that video? The girl—her name was Marsha—well, she meant a lot to me." Foley could not bring himself to use his daughter's name.

"I gotta dig it out first, but sure, Goober. Absolutely."

"I mean, like now. I was hopin' we could do it now."

"Hey. . . ."

Foley raised his eyes to meet Matsunaga's. He winked, then smiled. "I've got this ninety-minute video, Toshi. It's hot and it's very, very rare. Three little girls trapped in the clubhouse of a black motorcycle gang. One little white girl, one little Asian girl, one little Puerto Rican." Foley gave it a few seconds before allowing his smile to expand. "Let's make a deal."

Matsunaga's eyes jigged to the right and the left as he imagined the various combinations to be found in the scenario Foley described. In fact, no such video existed. Foley was working Matsunaga the way he'd worked hundreds of suspects when he carried the gold badge, cueing off the man's very predictable reactions, feeding that rope. At the same time, Foley was acutely aware of the semi-automatic pistol tucked inside his shoulder bag. Toshi Matsunaga was going to produce that video before the afternoon was over. There was simply no room in Foley's mind for any other possibility.

"Where is this tape?" Matsunaga asked.

"Uptown, in my apartment. Look, here's what we do. First, we go to your place, see if you can locate Marsha's video. Then we cab it up to my place and make a copy, at which time I'll give you the tape I described. Simple, right?"

Matsunaga looked at his watch for a moment, then took a cell phone from the outer pocket of his backpack. "Give me a minute," he said. "I gotta put something off."

THE SMALL townhouse Toshi Matsunaga owned was only two stories high and had once been a stable. Utterly unpretentious, its brick facade, painted a glaring white, had all the allure of a sugar cube. That was, of course, irrelevant. The townhouse was located on Charles Street in the heart of the West Village. That made it valuable, that made it charming.

Matsunaga led Foley directly to the second floor, to a room at the rear of the building where he'd arranged a long couch to face an enormous HD-ready television surrounded by a forest of speakers. The room's single window was covered by maroon drapes heavy enough to prevent sound from escaping, while the track lighting was soft and indirect.

"Hang out here for a few minutes," Matsunaga said. "I'll dig up the tape."

"Sure."

When Matsunaga closed the door behind him, Foley jumped to his feet and began to pace. Some careless jailer had apparently forgotten to lock the door to the dungeon and the prisoners were on the move. Foley held them off by using his cell phone to call Julia Brennan.

"Gotta make it quick," she said at the sound of his voice, "I'm really jammed here."

"Just wanna let you know I won't be able to make dinner tonight. Something came up and. . . ."

"Call me soon. Bye."

That done, Foley resumed pacing. There are certain realities here, he told himself, that you have to face. For instance, the photo you gave to Matsunaga? That's not Patti. That's a five-year-old snapshot of Patti aged by a computer that gets it wrong forty percent of the time. Patti might be thirty pounds heavier and four inches taller; she might look entirely different. Plus, Matsunaga's relying on his memory of a tape he watched so long ago he isn't even sure where it is or if he still has it. Most likely, he won't even find the damn thing, so don't get your hopes up.

But Foley's hopes were indeed up, a fact made entirely clear when Matsunaga reentered the room and Foley's heart did another doubleskip.

"Hey, Goober, I got the goodies," Matsunaga proclaimed, a salacious grin firmly in place. "Let's take a look."

THOUGH FOLEY knew he was expected to watch the video right to the end, he viewed less than thirty seconds of the tape before pressing the VCR's stop button. Not only was the little girl who appeared on the TV screen nearly identical to the girl in the photo he'd shown to Matsunaga (right down to the spray of pale freckles across the bridge of her nose), the video's title left no room for doubt: *Patti's Dance.*

"Where'd you get this?" Foley asked.

"Uh-uh. Can't go there. I might ask around, though, find out if she's . . . available."

Without making any conscious decision to do so, Foley smashed his fist into Matsunaga's mouth. As Foley was six inches taller and forty pounds heavier, the force of the blow drove Matsunaga to the carpeted floor and left him stunned. Foley nodded in satisfaction, then walked to the drapes, cut a length of the draw cord, finally wrapped the cord around Matsunaga's throat and drew it tight. Although he grunted twice while Matsunaga fought suffocation, Foley did not speak.

When Matsunaga lost consciousness, Foley loosened the cord, allowing the man to fall straight back. Matsunaga's head bounced once as it hit the carpet, his arms and feet twitching as though jabbed with cattle prods. None of this alarmed Foley. In fact, as he waited patiently for Matsunaga to recover, the emotion he felt was as close to joy as he'd come in many years. This was what he'd always wanted, the gloves off, the battle joined, to be the giver and not the receiver of pain. He knew he'd have to regain control at some point, but for right now, for just these few self-indulgent moments, the intensity of the elation that curled his lip could be reasonably equated with that of a man just told his lung biopsy had proven negative.

When Matsunaga recovered sufficiently to roll onto his stomach, Foley dropped a knee to the small of the man's back, then tightened down on the cord still wrapped around his neck. This time, however, Foley eased the tension before Matsunaga passed out.

"Look at me," he demanded as he rose to his feet.

Matsunaga sputtered for a moment before he was able to draw a breath. Then he turned his head and vomited onto the rug.

"Look at me."

Slowly, Matsunaga pulled himself to a sitting position, his legs sprawled out before him, head wobbling slightly. When he finally turned his head up, his stiff unruly hair had fallen forward to cover his eyes.

"You understand what's at stake here?" Foley asked. "You see where this is going?"

"I understand."

"Swear you do. Swear on the Holy Bible."

"I swear."

"On what?"

"On the Holy Bible."

"That's good."

Almost without effort, Foley wrapped his hands in Matsunaga's sweatshirt and hauled the man to his feet. He said nothing for a moment, content to trace the inflamed ligature mark that encircled

Matsunaga's throat with the tip of a forefinger. "So tell me, Toshi," he finally asked, "where'd you get the tape?"

"Charlie Terranova." Though Matsunaga spoke in a near-whisper, his voice contained just a touch of satisfaction. "Charlie's connected."

Foley dumped Matsunaga on the couch. He knew who Charlie Terranova was, had done business with one or another of his boys from time to time. He also knew that Terranova, though he ran a tough crew, was not connected to what was left of the Italian mob. Terranova was an opportunist, a striver to his bones. He dealt in stolen goods, drugs, porno, whatever came to hand.

"When did you get the tape?"

"A few months ago. It's nothin', a kid doin' a strip tease. Charlie threw it in."

"A freebie?"

"That's right."

"Like a party favor. Or a two-for-the-price-of-one sale."

"I didn't mean—"

"Tell me where you were when the exchange took place, Toshi. Tell me how much you paid. Tell me what you ate for breakfast that morning." Foley raised an index finger, pointed it at Matsunaga's chest. "You wanna get the details right," he warned. "Because if I think you're lyin' to me . . . ?"

FOLEY WORKED Matsunaga back and forth until there was nothing more to gain. Then he looked at the cord still wrapped in his fist.

"Don't," Matsunaga whispered.

"I gotta. Toshi. I can't leave you alive to warn Charlie. Besides, you don't deserve to live."

Foley circled the couch, taking his time, wondering if he'd get away with it. He'd been careful not to touch anything in the house, had only blown it the one time when he pushed the VCR's stop button which could be easily wiped. Of course, Matsunaga might have bragged to one of his porno buddies that he was meeting Goober, the famous web master. But that really didn't matter because Raymond Lear of the FBI already knew that Peter Foley and Toshi Matsunaga had a date. The point was to buy time and the best way to do that was to not leave any physical evidence behind.

Matsunaga began to cry when Foley came up behind him. Though he sat with his clenched fists pressed against his throat, he did not resist when Foley pulled his arms down. In fact, Matsunaga's fear was so great he was beyond resistance. Nevertheless, he managed to save his own life when he lost control of his bladder as Foley eased the cord around his throat.

The acrid stench of urine instantly filled the room and Foley jerked his head back as though struck. Then he looked down at the cord in his hands, the loop around Matsunaga's throat, and shuddered. For a long moment, he did nothing more than listen to the sound of his own breath. His lungs were pumping hard, the air rushing deep into his diaphragm, then hissing out between his teeth.

"Toshi?"

"Yes?"

"You want to live, right?"

"Yes."

"And you don't want to see me again, do you?"

Matsunaga's head whipped back and forth. "No."

"And you're not gonna tell anybody, are you? You won't tell a single person that I was here?"

Even as he spoke, a decision having been made, Foley cursed himself for being a fool. Once he was gone, Matsunaga would make an effort to restore what was left of his ego by warning Terranova, the only revenge open to him. And that was if they weren't already business partners.

"I won't tell." Matsunaga had turned on the couch and was looking directly into Foley's eyes. "I swear."

Foley ran his fingers back and forth over Matsunaga's cheek for a moment before leaning forward to whisper in his ear. "Later on, Toshi, when you're feeling safe again, remember that you don't know my name or what I do or how to find me. You only know how very close you came to dying this afternoon and that you'll never see me again if you're a good boy. That's what you want, isn't it? Never to see me again?"

"It is." Matsunaga spoke with the fervor of a newly departed soul petitioning St. Peter before the pearly gates. "And I'm sorry for whatever I did to you."

6

JULIA BRENNAN, now she'd gotten past viewing the body
of Adeline Rose, was thoroughly enjoying herself. She was sitting
at the head of Adeline's dining table, Betty Cohen to her right.
Ahead, on the opposite wall, Herschel Liebman's severe portrait
hung in an elaborate gold frame. Julia was staring at the painting,
trying to imagine Herschel arm in arm with Adeline Rose in her
nymphet mode. Between his high collar, narrow tie, and double-
breasted suit, Liebman was clearly out of another time. No great
shock; if alive, he'd be 104 years old.

"What do you think," she asked her detective, "about Herschel
over there?"

Betty looked at the picture for a minute, then shrugged. "He
might have been my grandfather." Betty was closing in on fifty. "A

hard man in business, soft as putty around the little woman. Her beauty was the only miracle in his life and he naturally clung to it."

"Are you talking about Herschel Liebman or your grandfather?"

"Both."

Mildly amused, they turned back to the portrait. The dome of Liebman's head was round and very prominent, overpowering small features made smaller by a generally pinched expression. His blue eyes were barely visible between fleshy lids, while his mouth formed a ruler-straight line above a receding chin. In fact, the lower part of his face, from the eyes down, seemed to be retreating before the onslaught of his forehead.

"Coffee's on." Bert Griffith walked into the room, set a paper bag on the pad protecting the table. He looked from Betty to Julia, then asked, "What?"

"We were admiring Herschel's portrait," Betty explained. "Trying to imagine him with Adeline."

Griffith did no more than glance at the painting. "Money," he announced as he distributed the coffee, "changes everything."

Though Julia found the explanation overly macho, as well as incomplete, she let the matter drop. "Bert," she said, "why don't you summarize your interview with the lawyer?"

THE SUMMARY clearly being for Betty Cohen's benefit, Griffith addressed his remarks to her, describing the history and the various relationships revealed by Whitmore, then concluding with Adeline's will and the non-alibi Whitmore had provided without being asked.

"According to the lawyer, there are twenty-two charitable bequests in Adeline's will, totaling four million dollars. The rest of the estate is divided between the kids, Hannah and Stephen. The lawyer gets a fee as executor but nothing else."

"How much do the kids get?" Julia asked. "In round numbers."

"Approximately one hundred and twenty million dollars."

Betty Cohen grinned, her lower lip practically disappearing beneath her overbite. "Bert," she said, "when you're right, you're right. Money does change everything."

"Not for Craig Whitmore. He not only got shafted in the will, he stands to lose his job once the money is split up. Didn't seem all that upset, though. And he wasn't upset about Adeline's death, either."

"Not a guy," Julia said, "who wears his heart on his sleeve."

Griffith corrected her without hesitation. "Not a guy, the way I see it, who *has* a heart. But the point is that he came prepared. When I didn't ask him where he was last night, he made sure to tell me."

Whitmore's explanation had been simple enough. He'd worked until nine-thirty, reviewing a prospective real estate purchase, then driven to his home in Port Washington, an upscale town on the north shore of Long Island. It was close to eleven when he'd arrived to find his wife and housekeeper settled in for the night. With no wish to disturb either, he'd made himself a sandwich, watched the nightly news and Jay Leno, then let the dog out for a quick run before going to sleep in a guest bedroom.

When Griffith finished, Julia turned to Betty. "You get anything from Flora Esquival?"

Betty Cohen took over without hesitation. Flora Esquival, she explained, was a legal alien who'd come to New York from Guatemala a decade before. Within days of arriving, she'd gone to work for Adeline Rose, having in fact been sponsored expressly for that purpose.

"You wanted to know who she might have spoken to about her employer," Betty said to Julia. "For the record, she claims to have only one relative in the country, an elderly aunt who lives in Queens. That may or may not be true, but I have to say the woman was devastated. She never stopped crying the whole time I was with her."

"That doesn't mean she didn't run her mouth to somebody with bad intentions."

"About how to disable the alarm system? She's a housekeeper, captain, not an electrician." When Julia failed to challenge her reasoning, Betty continued. "I took Flora upstairs and let her look through the jewelry box in Adeline's bedroom. She thinks there's a diamond pendant and several strands of black Tahitian pearls missing, but they could be in a safe deposit box at the local Citibank with the rest of the family jewels. She's not a hundred percent positive."

"That it?"

"One other thing. The first cops on the scene claim the television was playing at top volume when they arrived. According to Flora, her boss was nearly deaf and the volume on the TV was often turned up loud enough to draw complaints from the neighbors."

THEY TOOK a break, then, as they separately considered the facts already gathered. Julia got up at one point to examine the broken door leading to the garden. She was hoping to find some evidence that Adeline's killer had come in through the front, then faked a forced entry from the garden, but the glass on the carpet inside and the tool marks on the door indicated otherwise.

"Did Flora Esquival say who else has keys?" she asked Betty Cohen. "Besides Adeline?"

"She does."

"Not the kids?"

"Liebman's children only visited on the the holidays, Passover, Rosh Hashanah, and Thanksgiving."

"But they might have keys." When Betty replied with a shrug, Julia moved on. "Alright, anybody think we're dealing with a burglary gone wrong?"

"Do I look like a schmuck?" Betty replied.

"Damn insulting is what it is," Griffith said an instant later. "Swear to God, cap, I'm takin' it personal."

Julia smiled. "Insulting?"

"We're professionals, right? All of us?" Griffith's mouth tightened slightly and his eyes grew hard. "So it pisses me off when some damn amateur thinks he can make a fool out of us."

Though she didn't see why Adeline's murderer couldn't have been a woman, Julia didn't correct her detective. Instead, she instructed him to make the case anyway. "Assume we're looking at a botched burglary and go from there."

Griffith took a moment to consider Julia's request, then dropped his hands to the table and leaned forward. "Best case," he announced, "is for a professional thief. No way some junkie busted in through the garden, then got upstairs to disable the alarm in thirty seconds. All agreed?"

"Agreed," Betty said. She was sitting back in her chair, legs crossed, totally at ease.

"Agreed," Julia echoed.

"Okay, so we got ourselves a professional, let's say his name is Morty."

"Morty? Where did that come from?"

"When I was a kid, I had me a dog named Morty, a natural thief. You left your plate unguarded for ten seconds, your dinner was history. So, anyway, Morty targets Adeline Rose. We don't know exactly how, maybe an article in the papers gets his attention or maybe he's wandering through the neighborhood one day and notices that her townhouse hasn't been divided into apartments, that it's single occupancy." Griffith leaned forward as he warmed to the story. "Next move, he stakes the place out, learns that it's just elderly Adeline and middle-aged Flora, and Flora stays in Queens from Wednesday after supper until Thursday evening, regular as clockwork."

"You add in the loud TV and Morty's a happy boy," Julia said. "Except for the alarm. He still has to get past the alarm."

"No problem at all," Griffith said. "Remember that burglary last month? When the intruder was scared off? That was Morty scoutin' the terrain." Griffith shifted on the chair to face his boss. "From there it's simple enough. He breaks into the house, disables the alarm by ripping out the wires, goes upstairs in search of the family jewels. Adeline surprises him, so he kills her."

"And what's wrong with that?" Julia addressed her question to Betty Cohen.

"Three things. First, Morty doesn't need to go upstairs because there's a large Degas and a small Picasso hanging in the front parlor. All you have to do is cut the canvases out of the frames and roll 'em up. Second, even if Morty specialized in jewelry, there was no reason to kill Adeline. Morty's a professional, remember, so he'd definitely have a plan ready in case he was confronted. It wouldn't have to be much of a plan, either. Considering her advanced years, a ski mask and a roll of duct tape would do nicely. Third, no professional kills like that. Adeline Rose was slaughtered. Whoever did it, hated her."

* * *

JULIA RETRIEVED her cell phone and punched in her boss's number. She was still enjoying herself, the sort of mystery she faced in the Rose townhouse very different from the serial rapists and child molesters she spent most of her time pursuing.

"Julia, how's it going?"

Although Assistant District Attorney Lily Han's tone was friendly enough, Julia knew there was trouble brewing down the line. According to Deputy Chief Bea Sheperd, Lily resented the deference paid to Julia by the New York media and was contemplating a change.

"I'm in the Rose townhouse," Julia said, "and right now I'm ninety-nine percent sure we're not looking at a sex crime. I'm calling to ask if you want to hold on to it. If you do, we'll need a subpoena for the Rose financial records and a copy of her will."

They went back and forth for a few minutes, until Han cut the discussion short. "I'm due in court," she explained, "in fifteen minutes, so I gotta run. But I think what we'll do, at least until the autopsy results are in, is stay with it. There were a number of charitable bequests in the Rose will, and the mayor's getting calls from the various foundations involved. They want the matter cleared up fast so the will can be probated."

"Got it."

"Good, just be sure to keep a close eye on things, make certain the wrong feathers aren't ruffled. What I hear, the kids stand to inherit a bundle."

Julia hung up, then turned to her detectives. "The case is ours until the autopsy comes in, maybe four or five days. You think we can nab the bad guy in that time?"

Betty sneered. "If we don't, you can bust me back to patrol."

"Then let's rock and roll. Bert, I want you to stick around, get whatever you can from CSU. We're also gonna need fingerprints from the housekeeper and the lawyer to compare with any prints found in the house. Make arrangements with the locals to take them at the precinct."

"Anything else?"

"If you get a spare minute, call the housekeeper's aunt, check the alibi. Betty, grab your coat. We're gonna have a little talk with Hannah and Stephen Liebman. See what they were up to last night."

Julia read just a trace of disappointment in Griffith's eyes. He was getting the scut work and he knew it. But he had only himself to blame. Bert was going to work the crime scene because that was his strength. As for the soon-to-be-rich Liebman *Kinder*—well, how could it ever be said that two demure females the likes of Betty Cohen and Julia Brennan even had the capacity to ruffle their gilded feathers?

7

IT TOOK Julia all of three minutes to abandon the kid gloves she'd pulled on at her boss's request. The process began with mild annoyance as she and Betty Cohen emerged from the elevator, to find Stephen Liebman glaring at them from a doorway at the end of the hall, then quickly intensified as he responded to Julia's introduction with a grunt before leading them into his living room. Finally, when Liebman took a half-smoked cigar from an ashtray and blew a series of near-perfect smoke rings in her direction, the need to make clear their relative positions erased even the faintest memory of Julia's conversation with Lily Han. If Liebman were allowed to control the interview, he'd reduce Detectives Brennan and Cohen to beggars within a minute. While she couldn't speak for Betty, supplicant was not a posture Julia Brennan relished.

"Can we get on with this?" Liebman asked. "I've got an appointment in half an hour. With my lawyer."

Julia continued to meet Liebman's stare for a moment, then nodded once and turned to Betty Cohen. "Kojak, right?"

"Kojak?"

"What he's doing." Julia flicked her wrist in Liebman's direction. "The shaved head, the flattened nose, the pursed mouth, the oval face. Even the wrinkles on the forehead and the hard-ass look. I tell ya, the jerk's doing Kojak."

Betty stared at Liebman, examining him as she would a used condom at the scene of a rape. Finally she burst into wholehearted laughter. "You're right," she admitted between whoops, "he *is* doing Kojak. Only with a cigar instead of a lollipop."

"As long as he's sucking, he's happy." Julia watched Liebman's face redden as she echoed Betty's laughter.

"Can we cut the shit?" he asked.

The remark brought forth renewed peals of laughter. Julia let it go on for a moment, then pulled herself together with a sigh. Taking her cue, Betty pulled a tissue from her purse and wiped her eyes.

"Sorry, Mr. Liebman," Julia finally said. She crossed her legs and laid her purse on the rug beside the chair. "But I'm just not used to receiving hard stares from white senior citizens, especially rich ones. You'll have to excuse me."

"You think this is rich?" Liebman waved his hand in a half circle as he sat on a couch facing the two detectives. "What's rich about it?"

In fact, the living room in Stephen Liebman's apartment was nicely, though not richly, furnished. Besides the leather couch and chairs, a long oak cabinet supported a Sony TV and a Bose stereo. The cabinet appeared to be custom made and fairly expensive. On the wall behind the couch, prints of old maps hung in a ruler-straight line. Though signed and numbered, they were not originals.

"If you don't mind my saying so," Betty declared, ignoring Liebman's question, "you don't seem upset by your step-mother's death."

"Sue me."

"That mean you didn't like her?"

"I hated her."

"But you went over to her house last Thanksgiving, right? You ate the turkey, drank the wine?"

"Yeah, I went. You wanna know why?" Despite his prep school education, Liebman's speech was right out of Brooklyn. Julia understood it to be an affectation, part of the act.

"If you don't mind," Betty said.

"I went because I hoped she'd part with a few of her millions, being as I'm her beloved Herschel's only son."

"And not for the will? You weren't contemplating your inheritance?"

Liebman shook his head. Though he was still glaring, his eyes were fixed on his hands. "I won't say I never gave a thought to Adeline's will, but I never got my hopes up, either. I knew the old bitch was as likely to will her fortune to Saddam Hussein as to me or my sister. Adeline loved—" Liebman blew on the coals of his cigar, then flicked the ashes into a metal ashtray "—she loved the power of money. That's the best way to put it. When you've got as much money as Adeline, the only thing left to buy is the right to be arbitrary."

"So what you're telling us," Betty said, "is that you don't know what's in your stepmother's will?"

"That exactly what I'm saying."

"Then you're not friends with the lawyer?"

Liebman shook his head. "Craig Whitmore doesn't have friends. He has encounters."

"What does that mean?"

"It means Whitmore is well known at the more extreme S&M clubs in Manhattan."

"He pitch or catch?"

"He pitches."

"Hmmm." Betty ran her fingers through her short stiff hair. "Tell us a bit more about the lawyer. How did he become Adeline's attorney and her financial adviser? Wouldn't she want to separate those jobs, let 'em look over each other's shoulder?"

"Adeline hired Whitmore decades ago. As far as I know, she trusted him completely. He's definitely smart enough for the job, by the way. Got a law degree and an MBA, both from Harvard. The diplomas hang on the office wall behind his desk."

"So, you've been in Whitmore's office?"

"Sure."

"But you never discussed the will? Never even brought it up? That's what you want us to believe? Gimme a break."

The question caught Liebman off guard, as it was meant to do, and Julia took the opportunity to join the conversation.

"You don't wanna lie to us, Mr. Liebman."

"Unless he did it," Betty instantly corrected.

"That's true. If he murdered his step-mom, he's better off lying. Otherwise. . . ." She turned back to Liebman. "So, did you and Craig Whitmore discuss the contents of Adeline Rose's will? Yes or no?"

"Not in the last five years." Liebman rubbed his hands across his thighs. "That's when I finally decided Adeline would live forever."

"But she didn't live forever, did she?"

"No, she didn't."

"So what did Whitmore tell you? When you discussed the will five years ago?"

Liebman turned his still-ferocious gaze on Julia, who didn't so much as blink. "That the bulk of Adeline's fortune was to be divided between me and my sister. I suppose that gives me a motive for killing her."

Although she would have liked to provoke Liebman for a while longer, Julia was nearly certain the man was on the verge of demanding his lawyer and there were still facts to be established. "About a month ago, somebody attempted to break into Adeline's townhouse. Did you hear about that, maybe from Craig Whitmore?"

"No."

Julia let the word hang there for a moment, then continued. "What about Adeline's alarm system?"

"What about it?"

"It was very old and easily defeated."

"News to me." Liebman glanced at his watch. "Can we wrap this up, say before the next millennium?"

"Just one more item. Would you mind telling us where you were last night?"

"Home."

"Alone?"

"Home alone." Liebman smiled.

"Did you speak to any of your neighbors, get any phone calls, send any e-mails?"

"Afraid not."

"What about your sister? She lives on the floor above you, but you never spoke to her last night?"

"Nope."

Julia sighed. "Means, motive and opportunity," she told him. "You're a suspect now and I have to make you aware of your rights."

"I know my rights."

"And you want to continue?"

Liebman ran a forefinger along the length of his nose. "I didn't want to speak to you in the first place."

Julia stood. "When you meet with your lawyer, tell him to get in touch with us." She dropped her card on the coffee table. "Just in case we need to talk with you again before we make an arrest."

8

"THIS BUILDING," Betty said to Julia as they walked up a flight of stairs on their way to Hannah Liebman's apartment, "there's no doorman and no security cameras."

In fact, the eight-story building on East 29th Street where the Liebman's resided was utterly nondescript. Aside from a large oil painting in the lobby that might have been lifted from a doctor's waiting room, the public areas were featureless: painted hallways, fluorescent ceiling fixtures, tile floors, blank anonymous doors. Unless you lived in Manhattan, you'd never guess that the cooperative apartments behind those doors sold for upwards of $300,000.

"And Liebman has no alibi? That's what you're getting at?"

"More like, why did he want us to know it? You'd think, if he had the smarts to make an appointment with his lawyer, he'd have the smarts to keep his mouth shut."

Julia filed the information away, then changed the subject. "Tell me something, Betty. Do you think a woman could have murdered Adeline Rose?"

"I suppose it's possible, but the murder weapon, the letter opener, doesn't have a real sharp edge. You'd have to be pretty strong to slash someone as deeply as Adeline. On the other hand, if you were in a rage, if the adrenaline was up . . . who knows?"

"But you think it's unlikely."

"I don't think Flora Esquival has the strength for it. As for Hannah, she's gotta be well into her sixties. Unless she's been lifting weights all her life, I wouldn't look at her too hard either."

But the woman who answered the door at the end of the hall had clearly been up to other things besides physical fitness, as the scarred veins on her forearms amply demonstrated. The scars were old and gray and long-healed, but the ravages of drug addiction were still apparent. Though only a year older than her brother, she might have come into the world a decade earlier. Her back was bent, her body spectral thin, her dark eyes haunted.

"I'm Captain Brennan," Julia said, flashing her badge, "and this is Detective Cohen. We'd like to talk to you about your stepmother, Adeline Rose."

"Of course." Hannah led them into a living room identical in its dimensions to her brother's. The furniture was older, though, and mismatched, the walls dominated by bookcases, the books lying flat on the shelves. "Won't you sit down?"

Betty and Julia sat on a love seat draped with a worn Indian blanket. The cushions were very soft and the women sank nearly to the floor.

"Shall I make coffee?" Hannah asked. Her speech was very precise, in marked contrast to her brother's.

"No thanks." Julia waited until Hannah took a seat in a wing-back chair. "We're here about your stepmother," she said.

"Yes, I'm sorry."

Though she wasn't sure if Hannah Liebman was sorry that Adeline Rose was dead, or that two cops were now sitting in her living room, Julia continued. "We have reason to believe your stepmother was killed by someone who knew her, Ms. Liebman, so—"

"Hannah, please. Hannah will do."

"Right, so anything you can tell us about Adeline Rose would be helpful."

"Well, I don't like to carry tales."

"Your stepmother was murdered, Hannah. Don't you want to help us find her killer?"

"I suppose I'd better."

"Better help us?"

"Yes."

Julia looked over at Betty who was trying to repress a smirk. Hannah Liebman was the sort of passive-aggressive citizen detectives dread. Not even the tiniest shred of information would be volunteered.

"Did you have a good relationship with your stepmother?" Julia finally asked.

"That depends."

"On what?"

"Well, there were times when I did and times when I didn't."

"They have anything in common? These times when you did and times when you didn't?"

Hannah eased back in her chair and contemplated her hands for a moment. Then she sighed and looked up, a bit of a quizzical smile playing at the corners of her mouth. "It was better when I was stoned," she finally admitted.

"And when was that? How recently?"

"Since I got along with Adeline?"

"Since you were stoned."

"Oh, I see what you mean."

"You don't have to answer if you don't want to."

Hannah shook her head. "I have an arthritic back, and my physician prescribes OxyContin to ease the pain. So I guess you could say that I'm stoned all the time."

THE INTERVIEW went on for nearly two hours. Julia made every attempt to pose her queries simply, but Hannah, though she never refused to answer, managed to resist at every turn. Nevertheless, the essential facts were eventually elicited.

Hannah had spent the prior night at home, as usual. Like many elderly people in New York, she almost never left her apartment after seven o'clock in the evening. This was in marked contrast, she noted, to her brother who generally stayed out until the "wee hours."

Steve's propensity to gallivant was why Hannah was so surprised when she called him to ask for a loan.

"You found him at home?" Julia asked.

"Yes, I did."

"And what time was that?"

"When I called or when we hung up?"

"Both."

"Midnight."

"When you called *and* when you hung up?"

"Stephen was quite abrupt."

"I see." Though puzzled about the lie told by Liebman, Julia decided to change the subject. "Tell me about Craig Whitmore. How well do you know him?"

"Craig and I had an affair, once upon a time."

"How long ago?"

"Very long ago."

"And how long ago is very long?"

"Thirty years." Hannah waited for Julia to begin another question, then said, "No, make that thirty-five years ago."

"This affair, can I assume it's over?"

"Oh, yes."

"How long did it last?"

"Not long."

"How long is not long?"

"Perhaps a month."

"Well," Julia said, her most professional smile firmly in place, "I'm sorry it didn't work out."

"Most people," Hannah for once volunteered, "when they play . . . sexual games, they can turn it on and off. Craig was always on."

At Julia's urging, Hannah freely admitted that she and Craig Whitmore had remained on friendly terms over the years. Not only had they had dinner together a month before, he'd been kind enough to discuss the contents of Adeline's will, the break-in at Adeline's townhouse and the antiquated state of her alarm system.

"Who brought up the will?"

"Craig."

"Why?"

"Because I asked him to."

"And was your brother present for this conversation?"

"Of course. I never do anything without Stephen."

JULIA AND Betty were at the front door, preparing to leave, when Julia stayed Hannah Liebman's hand as Hannah reached for the lock above the doorknob. "One more question," Julia said. "If you don't mind." She was standing within inches of Hannah, so close she was able to whisper her request.

"All right."

"Tell me which one killed Adeline Rose. I know it wasn't you because you're too old and weak. So was it Stevie? Or the lawyer? Or is there some other scumbag out there we haven't heard about?"

"You're being very crude, captain."

"Don't give me that bullshit. You're a junkie and a former prostitute and you know all about crude." Julia shifted her weight from one foot to the other before leaning even closer. "So just answer the question. Who do you think killed Adeline?"

Forced into a corner, Hannah's arms dropped to her sides and her eyes to the floor. "I've been thinking about that ever since Craig phoned," she admitted.

"And what did you decide?"

"I didn't."

"Didn't what?"

"Didn't decide."

"Fine, I'll settle for the terms of the debate."

"Well, there's a problem. They're so much alike."

"Whitmore and your brother?"

"Yes."

"You'll pardon me, Hannah, if I say that your brother seems a bit more volatile."

"That's true."

"So how are they alike?"

"They're both naturally cruel. They like to hurt."

"Then they must have had it real tough dealing with Adeline. From what I hear, she did all the hurting."

Hannah smiled and again reached for the lock. "Yes," she said, "there is that."

9

FROM JULIA Brennan's point of view, the conversation at her dinner table had two essential virtues: It was spirited and it didn't involve her. It was spirited because Julia's fourteen-year-old daughter, Corry, and Julia's uncle, Robert Reid, the *Daily News* columnist, were discussing Corry's budding career in journalism. Encouraged by her great-uncle, Corry had long shown an interest in writing for a living. That interest had expanded into near obsession after the attack on the World Trade Center six months before. A sophomore at Stuyvesant High School (a bare quarter-mile northwest of Ground Zero), Corry had been sitting at her homeroom desk when the attack began, wondering just what she was going to wear to an off-Broadway play she and Julia planned to attend later in the week.

For reasons known only to the Board of Education, the school had not been fully evacuated. Thus Corry and her classmates had watched from a fifth-floor window as the second plane hit, as men and women leaped from the upper windows to escape the flames, as the towers collapsed.

Like many Stuyvesant High students, the horrors profoundly affected Corry Brennan. She seemed to grow up overnight, to become more purposeful and to toughen. At times, to Julia, the firm set of Corry's mouth and chin demonstrated powerful determination. At other times, however, Corry appeared merely grim.

Julia had done everything she could to help her daughter cope, even though she herself didn't sleep through the night for weeks afterward. One of her detectives, David Lane, who happened to be in the neighborhood when the first plane struck, had run into the north tower and up the stairs. He was still inside thirty minutes later when it collapsed. Coarse David Lane. Foul-mouthed David Lane. David Lane the bully, the intimidator. A cop to his bones.

"YOUR WORK is improving," Reid told Corry as he toyed with the pasta primavera on his plate. "You've become better at compressing language and separating relevant from irrelevant facts. But you need to work on your style. If not, you won't be noticed, even if you land a job."

Having heard these exact words before, Julia tuned out, her thoughts drifting back to Lily Han as she faced the reporters a few hours before. "Because at this time we have no reason to conclude that anything was taken from the apartment," she'd told them, "we think it extremely unlikely that Adeline Rose was a robbery victim. At present, we're concentrating our attention on individuals who knew her, although we'll continue to pursue the burglary angle."

It was a masterpiece of Clintonese. The missing jewelry was only possibly missing and SCU could hardly be faulted for not *concluding* that items were stolen from Adeline's home. Meanwhile, Lily had effectively turned up the heat on Adeline's killer—Craig, Hannah, Steve or all three—on notice. The first line of defense had been easily breached. It was time to worry about the second and the third.

"You don't want to be naive about this, Corry," Robert Reid continued. "You're in a brutally competitive business with dozens of well-qualified applicants for every available position. Plus, as a rookie reporter, you're expected to do your job and keep your mouth shut."

"You make it sound impossible," Corry complained. "If you stick to the facts, nobody notices you. If you get too fancy, you're a showboat." She sighed dramatically. "What's a girl to do?"

"What a girl, *or* a boy, should do is employ a very few telling details to elevate her or his prose."

"You're telling me to slide under the old radar screen?"

Reid grinned. For some months, he'd been wearing a testosterone patch prescribed by his doctor. As result, his energy level had skyrocketed even as his back straightened and his arms thickened. His liver and heart, on the other hand, were as damaged as ever. "We don't have to slide under radar screens anymore," he announced. "We have stealth bombers that can't be seen by radar. We can fly as high as we want."

THE REMARK was sufficiently cryptic to produce an extended silence, during which Julia reviewed the assignments handed out to her team just before they broke for the day, searching for some detail left unaddressed. Stephen Liebman was the first link in the chain. He'd lied about not having discussed Adeline's will in the past five years, at least according to Hannah, whom Julia believed to be telling the truth. Stephen had also lied to them, according to Hannah, about his knowledge of Adeline's alarm system and the abortive break-in a month before. Finally, he'd lied about his lack of an alibi.

The last was the most telling, or so Julia believed. Suspects in criminal investigations often lied in an attempt to create an alibi, but this was the first time someone had lied to her about a genuine alibi. True, the phone call from his sister didn't cover the entire period in question, from eleven until three in the morning. Steve Liebman lived only ten minutes away from his stepmother. But Julia had posed the question directly: Did you speak to your sister last night? What was his reason for denying it?

When Julia raised the issue with her detectives, Betty Cohen's response was sobering, though less than helpful. "We worked the poor bastard over pretty hard, Julia. You know, with the Kojak bit. Could be, Steve was getting himself a little payback by making our lives harder."

Bert seconded the possibility, adding, "When you get right down to it, people lie to us all the time, sometimes for no reason whatsoever. In fact, some folks lie all the time to everybody."

There was no arguing with those observations and Julia didn't try. Instead, she assigned Betty to draw up a subpoena for Steve Liebman's phone records. If he had an ironclad alibi, she wanted to know it as soon as possible. Betty was also charged with interviewing the girls in the Gold Coast Glitterati, Adeline's luncheon club. Hopefully, the gossip exchanged at their weekly meetings would shed some light on the odd collection of personalities involved in the case. . . .

"Yo, Earth to Mom, Earth to Mom."

Julia shook her head. "Sorry." Her daughter was standing beside her, cradling an armful of dishes.

"Are you finished eating?"

"Sure."

Corry picked up her mother's plate, added it to the stack. "When you get through meditating, you'll tell us about the case, right?"

"The Wild Jewish Rose case," Reid added.

Julia turned to her uncle. Only a few months before, his bearded face and haunted eyes had seemed to her ravaged. Now he bristled with energy. "You saw the press conference?"

"I did and you were great. Han tried to take credit, but nobody bought it for a hot New York minute. Face it, honey, you're a star."

10

BUT JULIA Brennan was not a star, not even a leading light, at least according to her mentor, Deputy Chief Bea Sheperd. Julia had phoned Bea immediately after the press briefing. She'd personally done nothing, she'd explained, to draw the attention of the reporters and was merely a victim of her own celebrity.

"It doesn't matter if I stand at the back of the platform and look down at my hands. The reporters want to quote me and the papers want to run my picture."

"You're right about one thing," Bea responded without hesitation, "it really doesn't matter. Lily Han's just looking for an excuse to get rid of you."

Always ambitious, Julia had come to the Sex Crimes Unit, at least in part, because of the networking opportunities the position offered. Now it appeared she was about to retire with her reputation tarnished.

"What kind of excuse?"

"Any kind."

"Give me an example," Julia persisted. "I'd like to see it coming."

"What I heard, Julia, you don't put this case down before the autopsy, Lily's gonna give it back to Homicide Division, then blame it on your incompetence."

To her surprise, Julia's first thought on receiving this tidbit was that she'd call Bucevski and attempt to buy few extra days for the cost of a midtown lunch. She was nearly certain her squad would make an arrest within a week, that Griffith was right: Adeline's killer was a delusional amateur who'd decided to go head-to-head with professionals. He could not prevail.

"Any way I can get out of this, Bea?" Julia finally asked. "Maybe retreat with honor?"

"Ah, now you're talking sensibly. I'm in the process of working out a compromise even as we speak. Still, it'll make my job a lot easier if you clear the Wild Jewish Rose homicide."

"And that's it? Make an arrest and I'll get a deal I can live with?"

"That's the way it looks."

"Then we have nothing to worry about," Julia said. "Not a thing."

"THERE'S REALLY only one other suspect," Julia told Corry and Robert Reid. They were seated in the living room, dipping ginger snaps into mugs of cocoa. Julia had just finished describing her confrontation with Steve Leibman. "And that's Craig Whitmore."

Corry instantly demurred. "I think the sister hired a hit man."

"Just like in the movies?" Julia teased.

"Alright, it's a long shot. I mean, how would she even find a hit man? It's not like there's a listing in the Yellow Pages."

"No, it's not. And it's not like Hannah Liebman is mobbed up, either." Julia looked at her daughter for a minute. Corry had matured physically, as well as psychologically, in the last eighteen months. Her breasts had enlarged, her face narrowed, her hips rounded. Julia could see it in the greedy stares she drew. Men riveted their eyes to Corry Brennan's charms, coming and going, and most of them made no attempt to disguise their interest. "But Hannah could still be working with her brother."

"Or the lawyer," Reid declared.

"Or both," Corry added.

There were times when Julia regretted her decision, made about a year before, to let Corry into her professional life, but this was not one of them. She felt entirely comfortable surrounded by her family, all but Peter Foley. For just a moment, she stopped to wonder why he hadn't called her back. Had she been too abrupt? She could be very short, she knew, when she was sharply focused on a case.

"The question I kept asking myself," she finally said, "is why Craig Whitmore, without being asked, told us he doesn't have anyone to back up his alibi."

"And what's the answer?"

"That he *does* have an alibi and wants us to think he doesn't."

"The same conclusion," Reid pointed out, "you reached about Steve Liebman."

"Curious, no? But I'll get a better fix on Whitmore tomorrow morning when Bert and I serve a subpoena for Adeline's will and her financial records. Whitmore could challenge the procedure, hold us up for weeks."

"He won't do that," Corry declared.

"Why?"

"Because if he was stealing Adeline's money, the last thing he'd want is for her to die. For sure, the Liebmans' accountants will be all over her records. And if there's a penny missing, they'll be all over Craig Whitmore."

"Out of the mouths of babes," Reid declared. "Look, Julia, how far do you want me to go with this? What part of this tale is for attribution?"

Julia knew the question was coming and had her answer prepared. "Let's confine it to something like: Investigators believe killer knew victim. Burglary gone wrong seems unlikely."

"Ah, turning up the heat, are we?"

"Out of the mouths of senior citizens," Julia replied.

IT WASN'T until two hours later, after she'd put out the light and pulled the covers up under her chin, that Julia again thought about Peter Foley. Of all the elements that had slowed her once-rapid rise in the NYPD, Foley, as Bea Sheperd had pointed out, was the most easily removed. The celebrity that had come her way after the Little Girl Blue case refused to dissipate, though she'd turned down all requests for one-on-one interviews.

Julia's blond good looks were also a part of the problem; she was photogenic and editors knew it, a problem compounded by her very position. The cases that came her way often drew media attention and the press had to be courted. If they wanted Julia Brennan, Lily Han wasn't about to disappoint them, not while Julia still headed the unit.

The situation with Foley was fundamentally different because Foley was a problem within her power to correct, at least in theory. A half-rogue cop who'd crossed an invisible line years before, Foley was simply the wrong choice for a captain with a serious career

plan. Yes, he'd suffered great losses: his daughter first, then his
wife to suicide two years later. One and all, the bosses genuinely
pitied him. But that didn't mean they cared to spend time in his
company. He was not the man you brought to the wedding of a
Chief's daughter. When they saw you with him, they thought,
Maybe Julia Brennan's not serious, after all.

"The guy's seriously attractive," Bea had explained. "I'll give
him that. But for a weekend, Julia, not for life." Bea Sheperd's own
boyfriend was a cellist with the New York Philharmonic.

Julia turned on the light, then dialed the number of Foley's cel-
lular. When she got his voice mail, she left a brief message.

"Hey, honey, sorry if I was a bit shitty this afternoon. Hooked
a big one. Can't wait to talk about it. Love ya."

Impediment or not, Peter Foley wasn't going anywhere. Julia
had long ago accepted the irony of their relationship. Virtually the
whole of her life had been invested in a struggle to maintain control, but not only couldn't Peter Foley be controlled, she had no
desire to control him. She was content, for some unfathomable reason, to love him.

As she turned out the light and settled her face into the pillow,
Julia smiled, remembering that she wasn't the only one in the family to have a crush on Peter Foley; Corry, too, was smitten. Which
certainly made things easier, because Julia Brennan and Peter Foley
were long past pretending that their relationship was chaste.

11

PETER FOLEY spent the first three hours following his confrontation with Toshi Matsunaga in flight. His flight took him, on foot, due north along Eighth Avenue, through Greenwich Village and Chelsea, then past the back of Penn Station and the front of the Port Authority bus terminal. It was five o'clock and the sidewalks were packed with commuters walking virtually shoulder to shoulder. Though impatient, Foley was compelled to accept their slow, relentless pace.

A few feet away, the traffic on Eighth Avenue was barely moving and the cabs had to fight their way to the curb in order to discharge passengers. Some didn't try, stopping two or even three lanes out whenever traffic ground to halt. As often as not, they were still there, with a door hanging open when traffic began to move again. Behind them, the drivers of the cars and buses headed for the Lincoln Tunnel were driven to levels of rage that could only be resolved by curses and uplifted fingers heaved from the windows like bombs.

The crowds began to thin once Foley crossed 42nd Street to enter the theater district. It was too early for the shows and tourism was always down in March, a month judged to be without charm in New York. Foley picked up the pace as soon as he was able, swinging around an elderly man wearing a black cashmere overcoat despite the warm afternoon. As he passed, the man's head turned. "What's the rush?" he demanded. "What's the rush?"

At another time, Foley might have responded that this particular segment of the working day was commonly called rush hour, a misnomer since it wouldn't end before seven o'clock. But Foley was preoccupied by two very strident voices that had begun their debate while he was still in Matsunaga's townhouse. Though Foley believed that the issue in question was essentially meaningless and nothing was to be gained by resolution, he could not stop them. As it turned out, though, he was wrong on both counts, and wrong to try.

The first voice insisted, as it had from the beginning, that Charlie Terranova's crew were hardened veterans of the New York crime scene. Peter Foley could not attack them directly; the element of surprise was his one and only advantage. Thus, leaving Matsunaga alive was simply unacceptable, given what was at stake. And then there was the obvious fact that Toshi didn't deserve to live. He was a short-eyes, a child molester who would continue to molest children until stopped. Children like Patti Foley.

As if cued by an unseen director, a second voice, different in tone and pitch but equally assertive, interrupted. A man, it declared, cannot freely murder, in cold blood and without remorse, and remain fully human. If you choose that path, you will become something else, some other kind of being, and no degree of repentance (even if you attain forgiveness in the eyes of God) will restore your humanity.

And then there's Julia Brennan, and Corry, and the love you feel for them, and the possibility of a normal life due solely to their taking you into their family. Down the line, when the going gets tough and you need backup, will you give your lover a call, play on her family loyalty? It wouldn't be difficult. Julia Brennan is as committed to you as you are to revenge. If you call, she will come.

As these thoughts alternately berated him, Foley crossed the southern edge of The Park and headed north to Holy Savior, a Roman Catholic church on East 81st Street in the heart of the Upper East Side. Whenever possible, Foley attended mass at Holy Savior. Father Jean Lucienne, the church's pastor, was a personal friend.

The church was closed when Foley arrived, but he rang the rectory's bell without hesitation. It was fully dark now, dark enough so that Father Lucienne's elderly housekeeper, Josefina Zeppo, refused to open the solid wooden door.

"Who's there?" she shouted.

"Peter Foley!" Foley shouted back.

"Father eats his dinner. Come back later."

"I need to speak to him, Josefina."

"Why?"

"I want to confess," he said.

The door finally swung open and Foley stepped inside to confront the housekeeper's baleful stare. Josefina Zeppo was a woman out of another time. A widow for several decades, she wore a black wool dress that fell to her ankles, black stockings and black shoes with laces. Her short gray hair was held in place by a black net.

"I see your predicament." Father Lucienne was sitting in a high-backed chair mounted on wheels. He rolled the chair back until his knees cleared his desk, then swiveled to the right and to the left. "If your analysis is correct, you have to use brutal methods. "

"Jean, I've already used brutal methods to achieve lesser ends." Foley sensed that he was returning to some sort of equilibrium, a state in which he could at least think. It was what he'd come for, though he hadn't known it when he set out for Holy Savior. "What I'm talking about is far worse."

"Then you're not asking God's forgiveness for what you did this afternoon?"

"No, not for what I did. I need to be forgiven for what I wanted to do. I need to be forgiven for what I might do."

"Afraid not, Pete." Father Lucienne continued to swivel his chair from side to side, though his eyes never left Foley's. "As you already know, one of the elements of a true confession is a sincere resolution not to reoffend. Until you make that resolution, you cannot be forgiven." The priest leaned forward. "Nor can you be forgiven for sins you expect to commit in the future."

"Then it's my soul for hers, right?"

"Say again?"

"My soul for Patti's." Foley stood up. "Makes sense when you think about it." He extended his hand. "Tell me, is it a sin to kill a child molester in order to free a child?"

"You're not freeing a child," the priest replied evenly. "You're freeing *your* child."

12

FOLEY WENT directly from Holy Savior Church to the offices of Joseph Grande, Private Investigator, in Long Island City. A retired cop, Grande had broken Foley in to the realities of policing in New York, advising him to forget everything he'd learned at the Academy, to keep his eyes open and his mouth shut, and to always have a story ready for the brass.

"And you defend that tale to the death, kid. It doesn't matter if they got a video tape shows you buck naked in the back of a Cadillac with a pre-op transexual. You just tell 'em *That's my story and I'm stickin' to it.*"

When Foley walked into Grande's outer office it was almost seven-thirty. Grace Cowell, Grande's office manager, was long gone, as was his computer specialist and partner, Alonzo Johnson. Grande was in the back office, on the phone. He waved to Foley through the open doorway, then said, "I gotta go, baby. See you in a few."

The baby in question, as Pete knew, was the woman Grande had married forty years before. Foley's envy of their relationship was one of the reasons he didn't see Grande more often. That and the fact that he'd been using the man for years.

"So whatta ya want, Pete? What's so important I had to leave Caroline's roast drying in the oven?" Grande's appearance was perfectly ordinary, his smallish brown eyes neither bright nor dull, his near-perpetual smile neither fawning nor threatening. Closing in on sixty and thirty pounds over his best weight, his full cheeks ran down either side of his face, then curled across his throat to form a soft loop.

"I've got a lead on Patti," Foley announced. He was pleased to find his tone steady. "A video tape."

Grande's smile dissolved. "You sure?" he asked.

"The tape's got a title: *Patti's Dance*." Foley hesitated before yanking on the hook. "She still has her freckles."

"Shit."

"I have a lot of work to do, and I need some help here."

"Name it."

"Right now, I'm looking hard at two men. If either or both decide to run I have to know where to look for them."

"They have any special options?"

"I don't think so. I think if they decide to bolt they'll be in too much of a hurry to plan an itinerary. They'll go to ground in some familiar place where they won't have to use credit cards. I need to find that place in advance."

Grande nodded agreement. As a private investigator, he'd traced dozens of fugitives, from husband or wives who'd run off with the kids to felony bail jumpers. Mostly they either did as Foley suggested or made the supreme error of using their credit or bank cards. Only a very few had the foresight to accumulate enough cash in advance to start a new life.

"It's a challenge," he finally declared. "Something different."

"How so?"

"In the past, I always had to give the target a head start." Grande scratched his head, his smile now back in place. "Seems like more fun this way."

"Fun? The first man's name is Toshi Matsunaga. The second is Charlie Terranova."

"Charlie Banana? Well, well, well."

Gangster lore had it that Terranova's street name derived from one of two possibilities. The first was simple enough: Charlie Terranova's temper was the stuff of legend; he was given to fits of uncontrolled anger and periodically went bananas on some unsuspecting subordinate. But it was the second (which Terranova encouraged) that was generally considered more likely. Because Terranova was never called Charlie Bananas but always Charlie Banana, his nickname could only refer to the size of his sexual organ.

Foley stood up. "You want to keep this from coming back on you, Joe," he said. "Don't leave any fingerprints on the ether net."

"If you remember, I'm the one who taught you how to do it." Grande failed to return Pete's smile. "Can I give you a piece of advice?"

"Sure."

"Don't get too crazy, Pete. You and I both know that tape could be sixth generation. It might have come from anywhere and passed through any number of hands before it got to Matsunaga. You don't wanna throw your life away until you have your daughter in sight."

Foley began to move toward the door. "I hear what you're saying, Joe, and I want you to know that I agree with you. Play it slow, play it safe, that's my best chance. Only it's Patti out there, and she's eleven years old now, and the monsters have her." Foley took a step back toward Grande. His eyes became distant, his tone nearly apologetic. "I'm her father," he explained.

B Y   T H E   time Foley walked into Royal Video, a triple-X porn shop in the Sunset Park neighborhood of Brooklyn, some three hours later, he was well prepared. The man he'd come to see was at the back of the store, rearranging videos on a shelf. He turned when the door opened behind him. His expression, at first apprehensive, quickly relaxed when he recognized his visitor.

"Whatta ya say, Pete?"

"Nothin' to it, Philly."

The son of Syrian immigrants, Philly Habib's real name was Habib al Rif'at. He was a tall man, some five years younger than Foley, and quite handsome. Though Habib liked to think of himself as a tough guy, there was a feminine tilt to his good looks. His mouth was full and soft, his large eyes round and shaded by dark lashes.

"So what could I do ya for?" he asked. Habib knew Foley as Pete Stearn, a sometime buyer of the kiddie porn that produced the bulk of Royal Video's profits.

"I got somethin' you want to take a look at."

"C'mon, Pete. I'm not a buyer. I'm a seller."

In fact, as Pete knew, Habib's kiddie porn was supplied by his protector and silent partner, Charlie Terranova. It was this protection, and the false sense of security it inspired, that explained why Habib was alone in the store. On weeknights, he sent his assistant home at nine o'clock in order to save a few bucks.

"It's not about my selling you something," Pete said as he took an envelope from the inside pocket of the light coat he wore. "It's something else." He opened the envelope to reveal a thick sheaf of bills, then riffled through them to prove they were all hundreds. Finally, he returned the envelope to his pocket, then declared, "So I'm still a buyer."

Habib thought it over, his tongue flicking across his lips. The man, Pete knew, was not motivated by lust. Habib was in it for the money. The tapes on his shelves went for between twenty and fifty dollars apiece. The kiddie-porn tapes stored in his office sold for a grand and up.

"Hey," Habib finally said, "I got nothin' to lose. Just give me a couple of minutes to close the store. Then we'll go into my office, take a look." He grinned. "I may not know much about art," he declared, "but I know what I like."

13

PHILLY HABIB watched the first minute of the tape—until Foley shut off the VCR—without changing expression. As a reasonably adjusted adult, he was not attracted to the children who performed in the videos he peddled. But he was not repelled either, their predicament being of as much concern to him as the origins of a Sierra Leone diamond to a Fifth Avenue jeweler.

"So whatta ya want from me?" Habib asked when Pete returned the tape to his bag.

"You ever see this tape before?"

"Why do ya wanna know?"

As Foley's hand dipped into his bag in search of the photo he'd shown Matsunaga, his fingers brushed the .22 Colt automatic with its stubby suppressor. He'd confiscated both on the street following Kirstin's suicide and held on to them ever since. The Colt was of no use to him in his day-to-day life. It was an assassin's weapon, pure and simple, and would only be of value in the event that he got within striking distance of his daughter.

From time to time over the years, he'd been tempted to rid himself of the pistol and the silencer, to fully embrace his professed belief that Patti was dead. Why, he'd asked, should he expose himself to any risk? All he had to do was take a walk by the river, toss the .22 into the water, be done with it. He hadn't, though, carrying it instead from apartment to apartment, one step ahead of the ghosts, real and imagined, who haunted his days.

Foley extended the photograph and the tape. "This really explains it."

Habib glanced at the tape, then stared down at the man and the girl in the snapshot, at Peter Foley and his daughter. "Cute kid," he observed.

"Yeah, she is. I really miss her, Philly. I've been missing her for a long time. Anybody helps me get her back is gonna be taken care of. There's five grand in the envelope. That'd be a down payment."

Habib lifted his eyes from the photo to stare at Foley. His manner was frankly speculative, but Foley had no insight into the issues under debate. "I handled the video for a while," he finally admitted, "but I started gettin' complaints. No action. So, where'd you get it? And what made you come to me?"

"I got the tape from somebody you don't know, Philly, who I since lost track of. I came to you because you're in the business and you're hooked up. I figured, if anybody could help me, it'd be you."

Though Habib seemed to be flattered, as Foley intended, he returned the photo and shook his head. "You figured right, ordinarily. But the way it is right now, I can't help you. Like I said, I'm not a buyer, so I don't know where it came from. I got a silent partner, whose name will not be mentioned, who does the buying."

"Charlie Banana," Foley said.

Habib winked. "You didn't hear it from me."

"So why not ask Charlie? From what I heard, Charlie likes money."

"Because the gentleman in question got popped by the Feds two days ago and he's not talkin' to anyone but his lawyer."

Foley took a moment to process the information, recalling Father's Lucienne's observation that a man in fear of his life is as likely to lie as tell the truth. Habib had handled the tape and that meant it had come through Charlie Terranova, as Matsunaga claimed. But Matsunaga must have known about Terranova's arrest and that Terranova would be unapproachable until (and unless) he was released on bail.

"Anything else I can do for ya?" Habib asked.

"Two things, actually. First, you remember when you got the tape? When it came in?"

"Let's see." Habib scratched his chin for a moment, then snapped his fingers. "I remember now. It came in with the Christmas order. What's the second thing?"

"What were the charges against Charlie?"

"Distribution of child pornography."

"And you're still in business?"

"Only for my regulars." Habib raised a finger. "I ain't worried about it, though. What I heard, some Jap ratted Charlie out. The Jap don't know me and Charlie would never give me up. I'm an earner."

"Good, good," Foley replied as he took the little Colt from his bag and pointed it at the center Habib's forehead. "But I'm afraid you're gonna have to earn for a new boss now. Anything else you want to tell me?"

Habib's eyelids, top and bottom, retreated into his skull as if abandoning ship. "Holy shit," he said. "You don't wanna do this. What's the point? Some little kid?"

"Philly, you don't answer the question, what I'm gonna do, right now, is kill you."

"What question?"

"Do you have anything more you want to tell me?"

"No."

"You never, in all the time you and Charlie have been associated, discussed the origin of the tapes you sold?"

"Never."

"You swear it, Habib? You swear on the Koran?"

"My family's Christian, but I swear anyway. On the Bible, the Koran, whatever the fuck you want. Look, Pete, I—"

Foley silenced his prisoner with a wave of the .22. "What I'm gonna do now is search your office. And what you're gonna do is keep your mouth shut and be a good boy. *Comprende?*"

Habib raised both hands, palms out. "You got the gun," he admitted. "You're the boss."

Foley began his search with a closet on the wall farthest from Habib where he found a padlocked trunk. He dragged the trunk into the room, then said, "What's in it?"

"Product. Your kind."

"The combination?"

Foley spun the dial as Habib called out the numbers. He handled the lock gingerly, aware of every surface he touched, his movements precise. If he felt anything at all beyond the hope of discovering some bit of information that would lead him to Patti, he wasn't aware of it.

Inside the trunk, he found columns of neatly stacked video tapes: *Tammy Has a Party, Cathy's Communion, Peter Goes to Camp.*

"How much are they worth?" Foley asked.

"What are you gonna do, steal 'em? Charlie Banana will not like that."

Foley looked over at Habib, wondering if the man understood the implications of what he'd just said. But Habib's gaze revealed only mild defiance and Foley soon turned away to rummage through a three-drawer desk. In the center drawer, he found a ledger and a Palm Pilot which he brought to the top of the desk before examining each. The ledger contained both debits and credits, with the principals identified only by letters. The Palm Pilot was password-protected.

"Talk to me, Habib."

"About what?"

Foley discharged a round into the wall a few inches above Habib al Rif'at's head. The impact released a small cloud of white dust that settled on the man's face and shoulders like dandruff. "No more bullshit. The time for bullshit is over. I got a mystery here which I expect you to solve."

Habib surprised Foley by clinging to his only certainty. "Charlie's gonna kill you when he finds out."

"Last chance to live, Habib. No more threats. No more warnings. It's life or death and you get to pick."

Not surprisingly, al Rif'at chose life. "Those things, Joey Cadillac brought 'em over on the day Charlie got busted. Charlie thought they'd be safer here."

"But you examined them, right? You checked them out."

"I did," Habib admitted, "but I couldn't figure out the Palm Pilot and I don't know the code for the ledger." After a brief hesitation, he added, "And I don't know anything about that girl you're after. I swear it."

Foley lowered his weapon, then opened the bottom drawer. As he bent to look inside, Habib dropped to one knee and yanked his right pant leg high enough to reveal a snub-nosed .38 in an ankle holster.

"Don't do it!" Foley shouted. "Don't be a jerk."

But having apparently understood the implications all too well, Habib al Rif'at was beyond Foley's good advice. He grabbed at the handle of the revolver and yanked, realizing only after the fact that he'd failed to release the little strap securing the weapon.

"Oh, shit," he said as Foley leveled the automatic and squeezed the trigger.

The .22 made a little burp, and a round hole opened just above al Rif'at's left eye. He brought his palm to this small hole, his mouth opening as if there were something he wanted to say but couldn't remember just what it was. Then he fell over backward, his life gone before his head struck the floor.

For just a moment, Foley stared down at Habib, wondering what he was supposed to feel. Remorse and regret? Or maybe their opposites, rage and satisfaction. But he felt none of these, or very much of anything. He did note, however, that the debaters who'd plagued his afternoon and evening had vanished without a trace.

As he began to wipe down the surfaces he'd touched, Foley wondered if his bad and good angels, equally unsatisfied with the ambiguous turn of events, were still slugging it out somewhere below the radar of his consciousness. Then he imagined himself on the witness stand, arguing self-defense to a jury, and laughed out loud. In his own mind, he was fairly certain that he would have killed Habib al Rif'at even if the man hadn't resisted, but there was no way to be sure. Until the next opportunity for murder presented itself.

14

JULIA MADE a beeline for her office when she arrived at nine-fifteen on the following morning, pausing only long enough to nod to the detectives and shake off her umbrella before vanishing. Inside, she fell into her chair and picked up the phone. Her first call went to Peter Foley. When she got his voice mail, she hung up, wondering if she had his number wrong. It'd been a long time since Pete had a land line and he switched cellulars often enough for her to be a switch behind.

Well, he would call her soon enough. In the meantime, there was work to do. Julia punched in Solomon Bucevski's number and was gratified when he answered on the second ring. Given the deadline imposed by Lily Han, phone tag was a game to be avoided whenever possible. That was another reason she hadn't left a message for Peter Foley.

"Julia Brennan here," Julia announced. "I—"

"I presume you are not calling to ascertain autopsy results," Bucevski interrupted. "I presume you are not thinking that all work in Medical Examiner's office has stopped for victim in your case."

"Perish the thought," Julia replied. "My motives in this instance are beyond reproach."

It took Julia ten minutes to work her way around Solomon's bluster and secure the postponement of Adeline's autopsy from the following day until after the weekend. The price of the favor was a lunch at a restaurant of Bucevski's choosing. As Solomon had become something of a family friend (he was a special favorite of Robert Reid), it was a bargain Julia would have no problem keeping.

"Till we meet again, Captain Brennan," Bucevski said, once the deal was made, "over caviar and champagne."

"Lunch, Solomon. We're doing lunch. If it gets any fancier than that, my boyfriend'll have to kill you."

"Ah, Mr. Peter Foley. Him I should not like to cross."

Julia rang off on that note, then went into the squad room to gather Betty Cohen, Bert Griffith and a third detective she'd added to the case, Harry McDonald. McDonald was a steady, competent cop, normal in every respect except one. The look in his eyes suggested that his main goal in life was to remove a suspect's kidneys with a nail clipper. As Julia and McDonald's fellow detectives knew, this effect was a trick of nature. One of Harry's blue eyes, the left, was set noticeably higher than the right, and both eyes were slightly crossed. When excited, he appeared absolutely demented.

From Julia's point of view, Harry was the perfect interrogator. He could add the proper physical tension necessary to successfully conclude certain interviews without her worrying about his actually going off. At her suggestion, he'd learned to arch the eyebrow above his right eye. What with the goatee and the slash of a mouth, his mere presence was enough to rattle the nerves of the most ferocious hoodlum.

Julia led her detectives to a small conference room where she waited only long enough for them to sit down before announcing the results of her conversation with Bucevski. "Since we're all agreed that we're not looking at a sex crime, we can expect to lose the case after the preliminary autopsy results come in. That'll be Monday afternoon or Tuesday morning, the latest. Anybody think we can't do it in that time?"

Bert Griffith was the first to respond to Julia's challenge. He looked down at his watch. "I was hopin' for an arrest by noon tomorrow, maybe get a head start on the weekend. I got a hot date with a charter boat sails out of Sheepshead Bay. First time fishing this year."

"Then why don't you lead off?"

Griffith lifted his spiral notebook and quickly reviewed his notes. He touched the tip of his finger to the tip of his tongue as he turned the pages. "Okay," he said, "I talked to the blood guy from Crime Scene. He's not ready to swear under oath, but he thinks the scene is consistent with one attacker on one victim. Preliminary testing shows all samples taken at the scene to be type A positive, so most likely we're outta luck there and our perp didn't cut himself. As for the rest of it, the DNA and the trace evidence, we're looking at weeks in the lab, if not months."

"Anything from the neighbors?"

"The locals ran a canvas, including shops and restaurants open Tuesday night after eleven. Nobody saw anything, and there are no video cameras that reach into the back garden. But her closest neighbors did confirm what the housekeeper told us. Adeline played her TV loud enough to be annoying."

When Griffith lapsed into silence, Julia turned to Betty Cohen. "What did you get, Betty?"

Betty Cohen smiled her chipmunk smile, then very deliberately touched her tongue with her right forefinger before turning a page in her notebook. The parody drew a laugh from all except Bert

Griffith who feigned indifference. Finally, Betty laid her notebook on the conference table and leaned forward. "Flora Esquival told us that Adeline kept the bulk of her jewelry in a safe deposit box. Well, with Flora's help, I found the key after you left. It was in a little compartment on the bottom of Adeline's lingerie drawer."

"You get the name of the bank?"

"Citibank on Third Avenue."

Julia smiled. "Good work. I'll get Lily to write up a subpoena which I want you to serve right away. Maybe we'll get lucky. Maybe we'll get hold of a branch manager who doesn't have an attitude."

In theory, individuals lost the presumptive right to privacy upon their deaths. That was why Julia needed only a subpoena, not a search warrant, to examine Adeline's financial records or the contents of her safe deposit box. But the facts on the ground were a bit different. Subpoenas can be resisted, at least for a time, and banks often chose this route to protect the imagined constitutional rights of the dead.

"I also," Julia continued, "want you to interview the members of that club Adeline attended. What was the name of it again?"

"The Gold Coast Glitterati."

"Right." The assignment made, Julia turned to the last of her detectives. "Harry, what have you been up to?"

Though Julia's manner was abrupt, her detectives, as far as she could see, were unoffended. More than likely, they were used to her style. Julia had twelve detectives under her command and time was at a premium under the best of circumstances. At that moment, her people were all working active cases and she would have to review them before she could devote herself fully to Adeline Rose.

"Rap sheets, Cap," McDonald replied. "On the Liebman kids. Whitmore came up clean." He fumbled in his battered leather briefcase for a moment, then pulled out a pair of arrest records. "Hannah was busted for felony possession of heroin three times between 1980 and 1995. The charges were eventually reduced to misdemeanors in each case, and she was sentenced to probation with drug treatment. Also, she was arrested twice for prostitution, but that was back in the 1960s. Stephen Liebman was arrested and charged three times, the last in the mid-1990s. He went down twice for third-degree assault, once for second-degree assault."

Julia was impressed. Second degree assault is described in Article 120 of the penal code as a battery resulting in serious physical injury. For arresting officers, serious injury was usually defined as multistitch lacerations or a broken bone. "He do time?"

"'Fraid not. The third degrees were dismissed, and the second degree was plea-bargained to a misdemeanor. Mr. Liebman received a year's probation." McDonald sipped at his coffee for a moment, then bit into a jelly doughnut. "I pulled up photos of all three suspects," he mumbled. "I'm thinking maybe we oughta show 'em in restaurants around Whitmore's offices, see how chummy they were."

"Where did you get the photographs?"

"There were mug shots for the Liebmans. A little out of date, true, but good enough. Whitmore submitted a photo in January when he renewed his license to practice law. As his application is a matter of public record, I lifted the photo off the New York Bar Association's computer."

"That's very good, Harry. I thought you'd be playing catch-up, and here you are carrying the flag." When McDonald accepted the compliment with a nod and a thin smile, Julia continued. "Go ahead with your idea. Check out the restaurants near Whitmore's office and Liebman's apartment. But let's add the S&M clubs in Manhattan. Steve Liebman claims the lawyer's an aficionado."

"The clubs won't open before eight or nine o'clock tonight."

"True, so in the meantime get hold of the Liebmans' and Whitmore's phone records. Draw up a subpoena, get it signed, serve it."

"Done."

Julia paused just long enough to take a breath. "Bert, it's down to me and you. Myself, I'm gonna be busy for a couple of hours, but after that I plan to visit the lawyer and, serve a subpoena for Adeline's financial records and her will. I want you to do the talking."

Though Griffith maintained his graven-image posture throughout, Julia knew he was pleased with the prospect of reinterviewing Craig Whitmore. Like any good homicide detective, he craved confrontation. "What I'll do until you're ready," he said, "is touch bases with the locals and CSU, see if anything new surfaced overnight. And if you don't mind, I'll talk to the housekeeper again. She should be a lot steadier by now."

Flora Esquival was Betty's witness, as Griffith apparently knew. He looked directly at Betty Cohen, though he spoke to Julia who read a neat tit-for-tat into the exchange. Bert was repaying Betty for her little impression by poaching on her turf.

Julia was intimately familiar with the games detectives play. To a certain extent, she encouraged them. A little bit of rivalry never hurt any operation. The trick was to prevent the little bit's spilling over into backbiting animosity.

Her attention already turning to her next task, Julia rose abruptly. "Okay," she announced, "we're done in here. Let's go to work. Anybody see Carlos Serrano out there, send him in." Without waiting for a reply, Julia walked to a telephone at the end of the table, then punched in Lily Han's number. Perhaps, by the time Serrano made his way to the conference room, she could arrange to retrieve the subpoena for Adeline's financial records and request a new subpoena to examine Adeline's safe deposit box. If not, her detectives would just have to wait.

15

SEVERAL HOURS later, Julia and Bert Griffith tracked Craig Whitmore down, not at his office, but at his suburban home on Long Island Sound where Bert nosed a department Caprice up to a wrought-iron gate blocking the lawyer's winding driveway. It was one-thirty in the afternoon.

As Griffith shut down the engine, Julia whistled appreciatively. Though she could only see the upper floor of Whitmore's home above the trees blocking her view, the length of its multilevel slate roof and the six Tudor chimneys fairly screamed money. As did the home's waterfront location on the North Shore of Long Island in the town of Port Washington.

"Don't I remember," Julia asked, "Craig Whitmore describing himself as petit bourgeois?"

"I believe he used those exact words. So where do you wanna go with that?"

Julia ignored the question. She pointed at a plaque mounted on a brick pillar to the right of the gate: PROTECTED BY TRANQUILITY ALARMS. "There's Craig's alibi," she declared.

"Say again?"

"Whitmore claims he got home around eleven, but there's nobody to confirm his story, right?"

"Right."

"He also claims he went out to walk the dog later on."

"Around one-thirty."

"Well, I got fifty bucks says this alarm system makes a record each time the system recycles and the record confirms the lawyer's story. You wanna take the bet?"

Griffith smiled. "Not even if you gave me odds."

JULIA WASN'T surprised when she reached Whitmore through the intercom mounted on the gate and found him in a cooperative mood. Nor was she surprised when a shaggy golden retriever bounded toward the car, its tail wagging madly, as Griffith pulled to a stop in front of the house. Behind the dog, Whitmore emerged to stand on a small porch. The lawyer's gray complexion seemed to exactly match the drizzly skies above. Or so Julia thought as she stepped out of the car.

"I thought you'd call first," Whitmore said as he pushed his glasses up onto the bridge of his nose. "To arrange an appointment."

"Your personal assistant, Ms. Kerkorian, told us you were working at home," Griffith replied evenly, "so we figured we'd drive out to the country, see how the other half lives."

The comment was meant as a rebuke for the misleading information Whitmore had supplied on the prior day, but the lawyer wasn't taking the bait. Instead, he led them through a paneled foyer to a large office overlooking Long Island Sound. The view was impressive, the gray waters melting into the mist and fog at a distance that might have been fifty feet or fifty miles. Julia's attention, however, was elsewhere. At the edge of the property, a short pier led to a shingled boathouse that hung over the water. A smaller structure, also shingled, clung to the wall of the boathouse closest to her like a barnacle to a wooden piling. The two, half-inch plastic pipes feeding into this little room made its purpose clear enough. It was an outdoor shower.

"I've got everything ready," Whitmore announced. "In those cartons by the door. I knew you'd be coming."

"What made you lug Adeline's records out here?" Griffith asked.

"I work from my home most of the time. When you only have a single client, carrying documents back and forth to meetings at the office is no problem at all."

Whitmore paused when a middle-aged woman stepped into the room. Perhaps a decade younger than Whitmore, she stood by the door as if uncertain of her welcome. Her makeup was perfect, every hair in place. Her wool sweater and skirt appeared soft enough to have been spun by caterpillars.

"Captain Brennan and Detective Griffith," he said, "this is my wife, Margaret. Margaret, this is Captain Julia Brennan and Detective Albert Griffith. Would you tell them where you were last night when I came into the house?"

"In bed, asleep."

"What time did you go to sleep?"

"At ten-thirty."

"Do you ordinarily take sleep medication before you retire?"

"I take an Ambien every night."

Whitmore turned to Julia and Griffith. "Any questions for Margaret?" he asked.

"Not a one," Bert admitted.

"Margaret, would you please ask the housekeeper to step into the office?"

"That won't be necessary," Griffith said. "If you don't mind, Mr. Whitmore, we'd like to speak to you alone."

Before Whitmore could say *Run along, dear*, Margaret ran along. She backed out of the room, smiling, then turned and vanished.

"Now, what can I do for you?" Whitmore retreated to the window behind his desk where he stood looking out over the water.

"Adeline Rose had a safe deposit box," Griffith said. "Do you have access to that box?"

"I do," he said, "and the key is in the top carton." When the lawyer turned to face her, Julia half expected to find him sneering at the softball question, but his face remained expressionless.

"You recall the last time you saw the contents of that box?"

"Maybe three weeks ago."

"Could you tell us what was in it when—" Griffith scratched his head and smiled. "What am I talkin' about? There's gotta be an inventory, right? In fact, if I remember correctly, when you rent a safe deposit box, they give you an inventory form so you can make a list of what's inside." He hesitated just a beat, then repeated himself before lapsing into silence. "Right?"

Whitmore leaned on the edge of his desk, then pushed up his glasses before replying. A hairline crack in the armor? Julia couldn't be sure, but she was nevertheless encouraged. Bert had yet to show the lawyer his best stuff.

"If there's an inventory of the contents of Adeline's safe deposit box," Whitmore said, his voice steady, "I'm not aware of it."

Griffith shrugged. "Guess not everybody uses the form. So, what were you doing in Adeline's box three weeks ago?"

"Adeline was heavily and profitably invested in New York real estate. At her request, the original deeds to her properties were kept in her safe deposit box. I added the deed to a commercial lot in Ozone Park, a recent purchase." On firmer ground now, Whitmore straightened. "You might want to speak with Menachem Levi, Adeline's accountant at Ferrer, Levi, and Simpkins. In addition to preparing Adeline's taxes, he conducts a semiannual review of my work. Anything else?"

Griffith took a half step to the right, placing himself in Whitmore's line of sight. "Well, there is one other item you could help us with. See, after carefully evaluating the evidence from every conceivable angle, we just can't make the burglar thing work. You heard there's nothing missing from Adeline's apartment, right?"

"It was on the news this morning."

"Okay, so what kind of burglar, who just killed someone to get to the swag, is gonna then ignore the swag. You got paintings worth two million dollars in the living room, for Christ's sake. And what kind of burglar comes prepared to clean up after stabbing someone to death? You know, we worked every inch of the house and garden and found only a couple of traces of blood on the wall. If it had just happened by accident, a burglary gone bad, we coulda followed the blood trail all the way to the perpetrator." Griffith shook his head firmly, his mind apparently closed on this question. "Nope, we're certain she was murdered by someone who knew her, and what I've been actually dying to ask you is which one of them you think did it? Steve or Hannah?"

Whitmore's mouth tightened slightly as he absorbed the subtext. Julia and Griffith had decided to pursue this line of questioning on their way out to Port Washington. Given the Monday deadline for putting the case away, it was time to stir the pot.

"I'm sure I don't know," Whitmore said after a moment.

"But it couldn't be you, right? Because you don't have a motive."

"Enough, detective—"

Griffith ignored the interruption. "But it couldn't be Hannah, either, because she's too frail. And it couldn't be Stephen, because Stephen has an alibi." The last part was a bluff. Whitmore could not know what Liebman had told them, not for sure, not even if they were co-conspirators. "I tell ya, counselor, this case, it's got me turnin' in circles. The two suspects with a motive didn't have the opportunity while the suspect with the opportunity didn't have a motive. I feel like I'm out of my element."

Again, Whitmore straightened his glasses before replying. "If you believe you can lure me into wanton speculation," he finally said, "you're mistaken. You are also mistaken if you believe that I'm going to allow you to mock me. Unless you have a pertinent question, it's time we adjourned this interview."

"Your privilege," Griffith acknowledged with a little salute. "So if you'll just tell us what you were doing in your office until nine-thirty on Tuesday night when you work mostly from your home, we'll be on our way."

"I was reviewing documents."

"What kind of documents?"

"A proposed contract for the purchase of an apartment complex on Castle Hill Road in the Bronx."

"Why not review it at home?"

"The contracts were delivered to my office at ten o'clock in the morning. I went in to receive them."

"Your assistant could have sent them out to you by messenger."

"I suppose she could have, but I'd been away from the office for more than a week and I wanted to come into the city anyway. I took advantage of the opportunity to have lunch with Menachem Levi. We discussed Adeline's pending deal."

"What time was that?"

"We had a one o'clock reservation at the Blue Water Grill, which we kept. We left the Blue Water shortly after two. I went directly back to my office."

Griffith winced. "Lemme see if I get this right. You came into the office at ten o'clock in order to receive a routine proposal that a messenger service would have brought to your home by noon. Since you were in the city anyway, you decided to have lunch with Adeline's accountant which you finished at two o'clock. Then. . . ." Bert hesitated long enough to catch his breath. Again, he shook his head in disbelief. "See, this is the part that bothers me. And I mean I'm actually insulted when I think about it. You want me to believe that at two o'clock in the afternoon, when traffic is at its lightest, when you could jump into the Midtown Tunnel and be gone in fifteen minutes, you chose to go back to your office where you studied this routine proposal for the next seven hours."

Whitmore's face reddened, the contrast with his customary pallor ample evidence that Griffith's little speech had found its mark. "I believe I've had quite enough for one day," he announced. "I'll see you to the door now."

Having done all they'd hoped to do, Bert and Julia walked directly to their car and drove away. As they passed through the gate at the end of the drive, Julia, who hadn't spoken during Whitmore's interview, could contain herself no longer. She stretched forth her arms and made her approval known. "God," she told her reflection in the windshield, "I love this game."

"Don't ya just?" Bert declared. "Don't ya just?"

Twenty minutes later they stopped at a 7-Eleven on Northern Boulevard where they tapped Styrofoam coffee containers together while Griffith made a toast. "To Adeline," he proclaimed.

"To Adeline," Julia responded. "The Wild Jewish Rose."

16

THEY CAME back over the Triborough Bridge, the East River crossing farthest from SCU's offices, because Julia was in a hurry and she judged the Triborough to be the crossing least likely to be choked with traffic. She was right. There were very few cars on the Grand Central Parkway leading up to the bridge. There was, however, an emergency repair crew working the entrance to the ramp leading down into the Manhattan toll plaza. As a result, traffic was backed up into Astoria on the Queens side where she and Bert Griffith came to an abrupt halt.

"You know what we oughta do?" Julia asked. She was sitting in the backseat, her notes and her cell phone in her lap.

"Tell me."

"What we oughta do is ignore the Manhattan ramp, take the exit for the Bronx, drive straight up the Deegan to the George Washington Bridge, then make a left and keep on going until we find a city that functions. And don't blame it on the terrorists. People haven't been able to get around in Manhattan for a hundred and fifty years."

Griffith met Julia's eyes in the rearview mirror. "You feel better now?"

"Much, thank you." Julia leaned back. "Tell me again about your interview with Flora Esquival this morning. Was she certain about the date Steve Liebman visited Adeline?"

"Thursday of last week. She's positive because that's the day Adeline gets together with her girlfriends for lunch. It seems Adeline had a few too many glasses of chardonnay with her Dover sole. She was still sleeping it off when Liebman arrived without warning at eight o'clock that night."

"How long did he stay?"

"Less than an hour. According to Flora, they argued, but she can't supply any specifics."

Julia made a note to call the Crime Scene Unit, have them work the back parlor where Adeline and Steve Liebman had their heart-to-heart. "Flora happen to mention where Steve was sitting?"

"In the club chair closest to the fireplace."

Julia added the information to her notes, then glanced to her left. They were at the apex of the bridge and the skyline of Manhattan lay to the south, from Harlem to the Battery.

At sunrise and sunset, on clear days, the effect was stunning, as if the slanting yellow light had been deliberately sent to cleanse the city. But there was no slanting yellow light when Julia looked down into Manhattan on that day, though the sun was indeed setting. Instead, her view was limited by a gray mist that became progressively more dense. The lights on the superstructure of the 59th Street Bridge, a bare three miles away, wavered like candle flame, while the hi-rise apartment houses on the Upper East Side had lost the sharp edges of their relentless geometry. To Julia, they now seemed tattered, like the weathered battlements of a long unoccupied castle.

Satisfied with her observation and somewhat refreshed, Julia turned her attention back to her work, silently reviewing what she'd done and what she had to do. The details were beginning to accumulate and the job of keeping them sorted was becoming rapidly more difficult. At the earliest opportunity, she would get behind a computer and list them all, no matter how trivial, then re-arrange them until they made sense.

Julia's first call from her backseat office had gone out to the offices of Whitmore's home security service, Tranquility Alarms, where she'd found one of the partners to be a retired cop and fully cooperative. The information he gave was another nail in a coffin she hoped to close within twenty-four hours. Julia wanted a confession, not a web of circumstantial evidence that might or might not convince a jury. The little bits and pieces were weapons she would apply to her suspect's most vulnerable points. It was the kind of psychological pain-compliance technique nobody taught you at the Police Academy. You had to receive it as a gift from those who'd gone before you.

Just as her daydream was getting to the good part, the part where the suspect announced his guilt to the world for the first time, Julia's cell phone began to trill. She answered to find Betty Cohen on the other end.

"I'm with Mrs. Dorothy Farber of the Gold Coast Glitterati," Betty announced. "Mrs. Farber only wants to speak to you."

"To me?"

"That's right."

"How does she know I exist?"

"Mrs. Farber tells me you're a kind of role model to the club members. You killed three people and they were all men."

"Get real, Betty."

"They don't come any realer than Dorothy Farber. She told me, 'I'm eighty-two years old, richer than Donald Trump, and I get what I want.' What she wants, captain, is you."

Julia shook her head in annoyance, even as Betty chuckled into the receiver. "Does she have anything to say worth hearing?" Julia finally asked.

"I can't be sure, but she claims she's known Adeline for fifty years, so there's bound to be plenty of dirt."

"Alright, bring her downtown. If you arrive before me, put her in my office." Julia hung up, then turned to Bert Griffith who'd already slapped the bubble onto the roof and flipped on the siren. As Julia spoke, he began to force his way through traffic.

"When you drop me off," she said, "I want you to go up to Whitmore's office to interview his assistant. If there's a security guard in the lobby after business hours, speak to him too. Let's see how long its been since Craig worked late at the office."

"Looks like I'm gonna get my wish," Bert responded. "We should put this one away tomorrow morning."

"Afternoon," Julia replied. "I won't be able to assemble the whole cast before tomorrow morning."

"Afternoon it is, then."

As Bert cleared the toll booths on the Manhattan side of the bridge, then accelerated around a sharp curve leading to the FDR Drive, Julia called Harry McDonald. She found him in the office, having already completed two of the three jobs she'd assigned him. First, he'd shown photos of the Liebmans and Craig Whitmore to a number of shop owners and gotten a hit at a restaurant on Third Avenue called Anselmo's.

"Steve and Hannah eat there often," he told Julia, "separately and together, on occasion with Craig Whitmore."

"What about recently."

"Steve and Craig had dinner there last Friday."

"Alright, what else?"

"I served that subpoena on Verizon and we should have the Leibmans' and Whitmore's phone records tomorrow morning. As for the S&M clubs, they won't open before eight or nine o'clock, so if you don't mind, I'd like to head home, say hello to the wife and kids, then go back out around midnight."

"Fine, see you in the morning. Bright and early."

Julia didn't respond to McDonald's answering groan. Instead, she hung up, packed her notes and the phone into her shoulder bag, finally settled against the seat. To her left, the lights of Bird Coler Memorial Hospital on the northern end of Roosevelt Island wavered for a moment, then winked off as a burst of rain splattered against the Chevy's hood and the sea of vehicles around them glided to a halt.

17

ᴇxᴄᴇᴘᴛ ꜰᴏʀ the wheelchair and the behemoth of a health aide standing behind it, Julia found Dorothy Farber much as Betty Cohen had described her. Dorothy's eyes were indeed sharp, and so dark it was hard to separate iris from pupil. Her gaze was only a millimeter from a confrontational stare.

"Traffic on the Drive," Julia explained as she dropped her bag onto her desk and sat down. "Sorry I'm late, Mrs. Farber."

"Dorothy, please. I feel like I know you."

"And why is that?"

"Because of what you've done." Dorothy waved away Julia's attempt to respond. Though her arms were stick-thin, she moved with an undeniable authority. "I know what you're going to tell me. That there's no glory in killing another human being. But I consider myself part of the last generation of women to be fully shafted by the patriarchy. I see what women are able to do now, without the aid of a man, and I admit to being frankly jealous. Jealous and angry that I'll never get my turn."

When the health aide standing behind Dorothy Farber's wheelchair nodded agreement, Julia decided to accept her role. If playing the hard-ass cop would get the interview up and running, so be it.

"Now exactly what is it you want to say, Dorothy, that requires my personal attention?"

"What do you want to know?"

"Who killed Adeline Rose."

Dorothy clasped her hand to her breast, though her gaze didn't waver. "I'm hardly in possession of that knowledge."

"Then I repeat my question. What information do you have that's so important it couldn't be entrusted to Detective Betty Cohen?"

"I know the secret of Craig Whitmore. I know *where* he came from." Dorothy's lips parted in a smile that revealed a smear of lipstick on her right front tooth. "I know *what* he came from."

"From Harvard Law School right into his current job is what I heard."

"That's essentially correct. Adeline made him an offer he couldn't refuse."

"What was that?"

"Fifty thousand dollars a year. This was in 1954, when that kind of money bought you a very respectable living. There was, however, one proviso. That Adeline Rose remain Craig Whitmore's only client."

"A kind of servant."

"Ah, but not just any servant. Craig Whitmore was the result of her long-term investment in a ragamuffin of a child. Like most of Adeline's investments, he paid off handsomely."

Julia offered up a silent prayer to St. Michael, patron saint of New York cops. Give me a motive, she beseeched. Please, please, please.

"The Craig and Adeline story begins in the years leading up to World War Two," Dorothy continued, "shortly after Adeline married Herschel. Adeline was in quite a charitable mood in those days. And why not? She was snubbed at every turn and charity was the only road open to her. I can speak frankly here, Captain Brennan, because I've traveled that road myself and I'm too old to deny it."

Dorothy paused long enough to turn and accept a tissue from her aide. Neither woman spoke during the exchange and Dorothy merely clutched the tissue between long bony fingers. "In the late 1930s, New York society embraced what amounted to a charitable fad. For ten years, we'd been funding organizations that served ordinary working folk made poor by the Great Depression: soup kitchens, shelters, job programs. Now we decided to become personally involved by sponsoring an orphan child. The idea was to guide the boy or girl through childhood and adolescence into productive adulthood."

"Adeline chose Craig Whitmore? That the way it went?"

"Adeline more than chose him, captain, she created him. Understand, the boy had absolutely nothing. His father was unknown and his mother abandoned him when he was an infant. Adeline brought Craig into her home at least once a month. She took him to the theater, the opera, the museums. She bribed Choate Preparatory School to admit him, then paid his tuition. She paid his way through Harvard as well, as an undergraduate and a graduate student. Finally, she gave him a cushy job when he received his degree. No matter how Craig may have described his duties, Adeline's properties are managed by Invictus Management Solutions and her portfolio by a senior vice president at Peterson, Tolk. Craig managed the managers."

Julia pushed her chair back. "While Adeline managed him?"

"Exactly. I suppose I'm playing amateur psychologist, but I think Adeline was Craig's only hope for a family. I think he lay there at night in the orphanage, a lonely six-year-old boy, and imagined Adeline to be his mother, the only mother he would ever know. But Craig was never more than a plaything for Adeline. When she favored him, it drove Herschel's children crazy, and that pleased her. When he excelled at school, she held him up to be examined by her social betters: Here, look what I've done. Motherhood was never her intention. I saw them together many times without ever witnessing a display of physical affection on her part."

Dorothy used the tissue to wipe her mouth, though as far as Julia could tell there was nothing to wipe. "So what's the upshot?" Julia asked. "Why do I need to know this?"

"Because Craig Whitmore, when he finally realized that he would never be Adeline's son, that he would always and only be her servant, came to hate her."

"You're sure of that?"

"I am, because Adeline told me so. She found Craig's animosity as amusing as Steve Liebman's."

"What about Hannah Liebman? She didn't hate her stepmother?"

Dorothy Farber sighed. "Poor Hannah," she said. "Hannah didn't have a chance."

Julia barely listened to what followed, a description of Adeline's perverted relationship with her stepchildren already established. There was, though, a fact and an opinion offered by Dorothy Farber that caught Julia's attention. The fact was that Adeline Rose had bailed her stepchildren out of jail when they ran afoul of the law. She'd paid for their attorneys, too. The opinion was that Steve and Hannah never married because they lacked the sort of fortunes needed to attract a man or woman who befitted their wholly imagined social status.

J ULIA RETURNED to her office to find her daughter, Corry, sitting in a chair next to the desk. On the desk, a copy of the *New York Post*, evening edition, lay with its front page facing up. The headline was a guaranteed attention grabber: KIDDIE-PORN KINGPIN KILLED IN BROOKLYN.

"Is this for me?" Julia asked as she picked up the paper to glance at the one-page story. Almost without effort, she extracted the relevant details from the page: the name of the victim, the address of the store in South Brooklyn, the manner of death, the discovery of a large trunk filled with child pornography.

"I just stopped by," Corry said without raising her eyes from the book in her lap, "to see if you were leaving soon. I was hoping to catch a ride up to Uncle Bob's."

"As a matter of fact, I'll be leaving in less than an hour. So what's with the *Post*? I thought you were more or less committed to the *Times*?"

"They give it away free," Corry responded. "So I took one. Is that a big deal?"

The big deal, as both mother and daughter knew, was Peter Foley. Caught up in the chase, Julia had passed the afternoon without a thought for her lover. Meanwhile, though she did not associate Pete with the murder of Habib al Rif'at, the headline had conjured him as if from a Tarot card. Worse still, now that he was comfortably settled at the forefront of her attention, he wasn't prepared to return to the shadows. Not without a struggle.

Thus Julia carried Peter Foley through an uptown dinner with Robert Reid and then a two-hour session with her computer during which she listed every lie or inconsistency told to her by Craig Whitmore and Steve Liebman, lining them up like rifles along the wall of a stockade. Thoughts of Foley even managed to survive a long hot shower that relaxed her just enough to make sleep a possibility.

As Julia left the shower and walked down the hall toward her bedroom, she was already composing the message she would leave on Foley's voice mail. Something about her being worried, and if he didn't call she would just have to track him down. She was passing Corry's bedroom when her daughter called out.

"I'm worried about Pete," Corry said through the closed door.

It was an invitation that could not be refused and a moment later Julia was sitting on the edge of her daughter's bed, wishing she'd never shared Foley's tragedy with her daughter even as she explained why there was no reason to worry. Habib al Rif'at, the kiddie-porn kingpin, was undoubtedly connected to a mob because the entire porno business was run by one mob or another. There were Lebanese and Russian and Italian crews out there, and there was the Armenian crew that SCU had broken up only a few months before. The money was just too good to resist.

"You don't make it in the porn trade," Julia concluded, "if you're a straight shooter. And that's even if all your merchandise is legal. The child pornography takes it to a whole other level. The way Habib was killed, a single shot from a small-caliber weapon— that's page one in the organized crime handbook."

"I get the point, Mom."

"Not yet, my daughter, because we haven't considered the possibility that Habib was killed in the course of an ordinary robbery by some junkie desperate for a fix. In New York it happens a couple of hundred times a year."

Corry was smiling now. "Is that all?"

"Nope, because we haven't talked about family members yet, or jealous lovers, or the husbands of jealous lovers, or the admittedly remote possibility that Habib committed suicide and some mope stole the gun."

Julia left Corry a few minutes later, having convinced her daughter there was no real cause for alarm. She did try to call Foley, though, leaving the message she'd composed after her shower when he didn't answer. Then, as she switched off the lamp beside her bed and settled onto the pillow, her thoughts shifted back to Steve Liebman and Craig Whitmore. The scenario she'd arranged for the following day was the food and drink of a detective's working life. This is what you lived for, to corner your prey in a little room, to break him, to do justice. From Julia's point of view, Liebman and Whitmore's being educated and fully aware of their rights under the constitutions of New York and the United States only the raised the bar. She really couldn't wait to get at them.

18

PETER FOLEY'S day was as unproductive as his lover's was productive. It began at six o'clock in the morning when two FBI agents showed up at his door to request that he accompany them to an undisclosed location. Taken completely by surprise, Foley's initial reaction was embarrassment. He was subletting a small apartment in northern Manhattan, paying his rent in cash. As far as he knew, he was not on record anywhere; even the phone, electric and cable were in the name of the legally registered tenant. All of which had deluded him into believing that his whereabouts could not be easily discovered.

"You know something?" he told special agents Henderson and Prescott as he took a raincoat and a wide-brimmed hat from the closet, "if you guys were as good at finding terrorists as you are at finding ordinary citizens, New Yorkers would feel a lot safer."

It was the most provocative taunt in Foley's arsenal, but the agents failed to respond. Instead, they put him in the back of an unmarked Crown Victoria and drove him to a private house on Staten Island where they dumped him in a back bedroom. The bedroom had two windows on the wall farthest from the bed, but Foley didn't bother to check them. He knew they wouldn't open, just as he knew the glass in their frames wasn't glass but high-impact plastic. He was in an FBI safe house, a mini-jail for unreliable informants who might flee the jurisdiction rather than testify.

In a way, it was a blessing. Driven by a rational fear of the visions awaiting him should he close his eyes, Foley had been up all night working with Charlie Terranova's ledger and Palm Pilot. The ledger contained entries on both the debit and credit sides, with vendors and buyers identified only by initials. That left Terranova's Palm Pilot and the distinct possibility that one of its files held a key to the entries in the ledger. If not, there would have been no reason for Charlie to pass the organizer to Habib for safekeeping.

The Palm Pilot, unfortunately, was password-protected and though Foley's computer held software designed to test commonly used passwords, he had no way to apply that software to a handheld device. Instead, he was forced to print a list of those commonly used passwords, then enter each by hand. As the list contained more than a thousand words, the process was laborious in the extreme.

Nevertheless, Foley persevered, his mind drifting this way and that as each word he entered produced an identical result: PASSWORD INCORRECT/PLEASE TRY AGAIN. It was only by merest chance that in the course of all that drifting he recalled the last time he'd seen Habib al Rif'at before that evening. They'd met at a topless bar in the Sunset Park neighborhood of Brooklyn prior to Foley's making a buy. Charlie Terranova had been there as well, standing off by himself, mooning over a blond dancer with silicone-swollen breasts. Though

Foley was in a hurry, Habib had insisted they stay to the end of her performance as a show of respect. The dancer's name was . . .

Foley jumped up and began to pace, the name of Terranova's love object skipping through his mind like a bird flitting through the branches of tree. Every attempt to grab the name failed and he was close to giving up when it settled softly into his consciousness: Cynthia Submissive. That was how the emcee had announced her. "Cynthia Submissive, the kinda girl, at the end of the first date says, 'You can do anything you want to me.'"

The acronym CYNSUB finally opened the Palm Pilot's magic door, whereupon Foley's persistence was rewarded when the unit's phone book linked phone numbers and addresses to the initials found in the ledger. Adding names to those phone numbers and addresses was all that remained, a task easily accomplished through the on-line search of a national database, one of many that matched names to addresses and/or phone numbers.

It was four-thirty in the morning when Foley completed the task, but he didn't go to sleep. Instead, he composed an e-mail listing the recovered data, sent it off to a web site where he could retrieve it at his leisure, finally wiped all trace of the e-mail from his computer. Then he disposed of the ledger and the Palm Pilot, the ledger pages by way of a shredder and the Palm Pilot by way of dismemberment. Both were, of course, evidence in a homicide investigation that would begin the minute Habib's body was found. That was also the case with the .22 which was already hidden behind a pipe in the basement laundry room.

When the FBI appeared on Foley's doorstep fifteen minutes later, Foley understood their appearance to be a harbinger of good fortune, a confirmation of the essential rightness of his mission. Though Agents Henderson and Prescott did no more than glance into the apartment, Foley knew his rooms would in all likelihood be thoroughly searched before he returned.

OVERALL, FOLEY regretted the loss of his time but was not terribly resentful. He'd played similar games often enough when he was a cop. It was about who had the juice and who didn't; it was about putting the scum in their place. Peter Foley would stay put until his keepers saw fit to unlock his cage.

Curiously, after an hour alone in that cage, when it became apparent the feds were going to let him stew in his own juices for an extended period of time, Foley did what many criminals do when faced with similar predicaments. He quite involuntarily fell asleep.

Foley awakened six hours later, at four o'clock in the afternoon, when Agent Henderson entered the room carrying a small tray. Henderson set the tray on a pine writing desk, then left without speaking. The tray contained a plate with a single egg nestled in a puddle of grease and a mug of coffee. Foley settled for the coffee, which though cold was at least strong enough to bring him to full alert before Special Agent Raymond Lear strode into the room and shut the door behind him.

"Agent Lear," Foley declared. "Am I glad to see you! A pair of absolute thugs kidnapped me this morning. They brought me to this hovel, where I've been imprisoned all day. Thank God you've come to save me."

Raymond Lear's slash of mouth did not so much as quiver. "Shut up, Pete, and don't speak again until I tell you to speak."

"Okay."

Lear sat on a wooden chair set beside the desk. He stared down at the cold egg for a moment, then shuddered. An average-looking man in his early forties, his most imposing feature was a full head of inky black hair which he plastered with enough hair spray to create a fire hazard. "You wanna play the smart-ass," he declared, "I'll bust you right now for assault with intent to kill."

Peter Foley had been working with Agent Lear for several years, providing evidence used by Lear to close dozens of cases. Though their relationship was not without difficulty, Foley didn't believe Lear would sacrifice so valuable an asset as himself. Nevertheless, he kept his mouth shut and waited for Lear to get to the point.

"You really fucked up big-time," Lear announced after a moment, "with Matsunaga."

"Is that right?" In fact, Foley's meeting with Matsunaga had been at Lear's request.

"Yeah, Pete, it is. Matsunaga was working with us. He was an important witness in a very important case."

Foley's eyebrows shot up. "And you sent me to him without telling me? Not too sharp, Agent Lear. Not too sharp at all."

"We were testing him."

"You wanted to know if he was staying clean?"

"Yeah."

"Because if he wasn't staying clean and it got out, say in the course of his testimony at time of trial, your case would be blown for good and forever."

"Look—"

"Well, Agent Lear, he wasn't."

"Wasn't what?"

"Wasn't clean."

Lear ran the palm of his hand over his hair. "Tell me why you did it," he demanded. "Forget about Matsunaga and just tell me why."

"I suggest you ask Toshi. Assuming you haven't already."

"You know I'd sure like to, Pete, but when I spoke to him on the phone, he was very accusing. His position was that the FBI had failed to protect him and he could only save his own life by taking a powder. And that's exactly what he did."

"Sorry to hear that. But Matsunaga's not much of a witness now. Not against your target, whoever he is, or against Peter Foley."

Lear smiled for the first time. "This is about your daughter, isn't it? About that photo you pass around?" When Foley didn't deny the charge, Lear continued. "I know all about that photo. The way I see it, only news of . . . of Patti . . . could penetrate the Foley cool. The *famous* Foley cool." Again Lear paused and again Foley refused to reply. "This case we're running, it's against Charlie Terranova. Did you know he was arrested two days ago?"

"I didn't." Foley shifted his position on the edge of his bed. A year before, he'd suffered a compound fracture of his right leg and from time to time his thigh ached as though worked over with a sap. "I take it that's your problem, that you've already made the arrest."

"Yes," Lear admitted, "and without Matsunaga we don't have enough to convict. So what we're gonna do, Pete, is take the prick into custody, then present him to a jury as a warts-and-all bad guy. And what we absolutely don't need is you finding him first and killing him. You could see, right, how that would mess up our plans?"

Foley hesitated long enough to compare the conviction of Terranova to the release of Patti Foley. In the greater scheme of things, which was more important? And why didn't he care?

"I can see your problem," he said, "but if you'd been straight with me, it wouldn't exist."

"Admitted. Now, what I can do for you is this." Lear spread his hands apart, the gesture of a reasonable man. "Once we have Matsunaga in custody, I'll arrange a meet. And I'll make it clear to him, before you get together, that I expect him to cooperate." Lear smiled. "I'm not unsympathetic here," he declared. "I've got children of my own. If Matsunaga has any information that'll help you find your daughter, I guarantee you'll get it. Remember, we're holding eighty years in a federal prison over the little prick's head."

19

FOR REASONS he kept to himself, Lear extended Foley's involuntary detention by several hours, releasing him at 7:30 P.M. with a lecture similar to the one delivered by Joe Grande on the prior day. "Don't go off the deep end," he advised, "unless you know for certain there's water in the pool. You crack your skull, it's not gonna help your daughter."

"Thanks for the advice."

"Think nothing of it." Lear opened the door to reveal a cold steady rain. The gutters in front of the house were already flooded, the water backing up onto the lawn. "Now, if you walk to the corner, then take a left and walk seven blocks, you'll find a bus stop. The bus will get you to the Staten Island ferry. Can I assume you know your way from there?"

Foley was tempted to declare that he would resist the next time federal agents showed up at his door unannounced. He was further tempted to illustrate the quality of that resistance by smashing his fist into Agent Lear's mouth. Instead, he donned his raincoat and hat, then headed off into the night.

At the bus stop on Richmond Terrace, he found an intact plexiglass shelter. Though only three-sided, the shelter offered enough protection from the rain to allow him to use his cell phone. Foley's initial call went to Joseph Grande at his home. When Grande answered on the second ring, he got right to the point.

"Any luck on those searches?"

"I put Alonzo on it right away," Grande said. Alonzo Johnson was Joe Grande's partner. "It seems Charlie Banana has a thing for south Florida. Goes there three or four times a year, always stays at the same hotel."

"Forget Terranova, Joe. He's in a federal lockup."

"I'm sorry to hear that because Alonzo came up empty on the other one, Matsunaga."

"You're saying he never goes anywhere."

"The opposite, Pete. Matsunaga flies all over the country, been in six different cities in the last eight months. The problem is where he stays when he's in those cities."

"No hotels?"

"Not on his credit card. Of course, he could be paying cash, but I can't see how that helps you."

It didn't and Foley hung up after a quick thank-you. The phone was folded and in his pocket before he admitted there was more to be done. He retrieved it quickly, then punched in the number of the cell phone he'd been using before his meeting with Toshi Matsunaga. It was the only number Julia Brennan had for him.

A moment later, he was listening to Julia's recorded voice tell him that if he didn't return her calls, she was going to come after him. Though Julia's tone was light, Foley knew she would carry through on her promise and that he would have to speak to her soon.

As the bus approached and he fumbled for his Metro card, Foley became aware of a penetrating irony. Julia Brennan was extremely disciplined, a woman who knew what she wanted and the shortest path to it. Foley had often wondered what she would become if free of the obligations that bound her. He could sense a wildness about her, a contained ferocity; he had seen evidence of it one cold night in a New Jersey suburb. The irony was that now, when opportunity again presented itself, he was going to do everything in his power to keep her on the sidelines. That was because he would tear out his own heart before he'd compromise her.

Foley's virtuous resolution sustained him on the ferry ride across New York Bay, from Staten Island to Manhattan. The rain was coming down harder now and the ferry, enveloped by mist and fog, slid across the waters as if through a tunnel. It was only as the skyline swam into view and the boat slipped into the dock that he finally turned his thoughts to the work at hand.

According to Habib, the *Patti's Dance* tape had come with the "Christmas delivery," so the December entries on the debit side of the ledger would be an obvious place to start. There was one problem, however. Overwhelmingly, kiddie porn was produced by amateurs who swapped videos and still photos through pedophile networks—that was clearly the case with *Patti's Dance*. But there were also a small number of professionals who shot top-quality video. These men were in it for the money and Terranova's Christmas delivery was likely to have come from one of them, even if it included some amateur material. All of which meant that uncovering Terranova's supplier would not bring him to Patti. There would be at least one more obstacle to overcome, another choice point, life and death at the tip of a finger.

As Foley entered the Fulton Street subway station, he experienced a sudden fantasy, an unbidden daydream that danced through his consciousness, as alluring as a woman behind a veil. He was killing them all, one after another, a demon summoned from the bowels of the Earth for no other purpose, implacable, unrelenting.

"Hey, you goin' through or what?"

Foley awakened from his fantasy to find himself poised before a turnstile, Metrocard in hand. Behind him, an elderly woman awaited his passage. The woman wore a gray jacket over a white skirt. The jacket was wet and she seemed, to Foley, unbearably tired.

"I'm going through," Foley said, as if he'd just made the decision. "Definitely."

The woman cocked her head and looked into his eyes. "Today or tomorrow?" she asked.

IT WAS just after ten o'clock when Foley entered his apartment to find that nearly everything in it had been disturbed, but nothing removed. His computer was still on his desk and its fire wall had not been breached. *Patti's Dance* was right where he'd left it in a box loaded with other collected evidence. Lear, apparently, had been content with a display of his authority, a decidedly unveiled threat with which Peter Foley was unconcerned. Tomorrow morning, he would abandon the apartment for the duration, a move he would have to make in any event because he and Julia had passed a number of steamy afternoons in its little bedroom. If she decided to come after him, the apartment would be the first place she'd look.

Foley smiled as he sat down before his computer. He wasn't supposed to be thinking of those steamy afternoons. That wasn't the virtuous way. He should be considering Julia's spiritual qualities and how he would miss those qualities, not of them slavering over each other like deer at a salt lick. Not of them. . . .

The IBM beeped once to signal that it was ready to go and Foley settled down to work, quickly retrieving the data he'd secreted shortly before agents Henderson and Prescott rang his doorbell. Though he had to go through several web sites to reach the computer holding his little cache (a maze designed to frustrate anybody working toward him from the other direction), the collated entries from Terranova's ledger appeared on the monitor in less than three minutes. Fueled by the fastest DSL line Verizon had to offer.

There were two entries on the debit side of the ledger for last December, neither large enough, in Foley's estimation, to qualify as Habib's Christmas delivery. An entry for November 25, on the other hand, for $10,780, was more promising. The shipment was from a company, not an individual, Proximate Services, Inc. Proximate's address was in the Brooklyn neighborhood of Sunset Park, just a few blocks from Habib's store.

Foley pulled up a web site that offered a satellite mapping service and typed the street address of Proximate Services into its search engine. A few minutes later, he was staring at an aerial photo of the building where Proximate rented space on the third floor. It was one of dozens of industrial loft buildings constructed on the Brooklyn waterfront at a time when New York's harbor was among the busiest in the world. The largest structures were truly enormous, with each floor offering three acres of billable space.

Although the piers and dry dock jutting into the bay along First Avenue were now infrequently used, the industrially zoned blocks extending from the water's edge still hummed with activity, the goods warehoused throughout the neighborhood arriving by truck instead of ship. Here and there, signs in Chinese or Spanish not only announced the arrival of new competitors but of new markets as well.

Competition had also come from an unexpected source, one with which Foley was quite familiar. Forced out of Times Square by a law that confined it to industrial neighborhoods away from schools and churches, New York's sex trade had established a beachhead along Second and Third Avenues in Sunset Park. A dozen triple-X video stores, three or four topless bars, prostitutes working the shadows under the elevated Gowanus Expressway— the process had been so gradual that except for a few neighborhood associations with no influence in city government, the infiltration went unremarked. Now, apparently, the stakes had been raised.

On a whim, Foley dialed Proximate's phone number. He expected, given the hour, to reach an answering machine. Instead, a digitized voice told him, "The number you have dialed, 555-1651, is not in service or temporarily disconnected at this time."

F OR THE next three hours, Foley explored web sites devoted to the interests of pedophiles, scanning photos and streaming videos for any sign of Patti. He'd performed this search many times in the past, but now the task seemed more urgent. There was a reasonable chance that *Patti's Dance* video was now for sale at one or another of the commercial sites or had been posted to a noncommercial site by an aficionado willing to share.

Foley had spent years cultivating the web masters who ran the pedophile sites, had even run his own site at one time. Eventually, he'd become so trusted that his cyber name, Goober, had been enough to lure Toshi Matsunaga to a meeting. Thus, if he found the tape posted somewhere, web masters could be approached and their cooperation secured. One way or the other.

As he'd typed the address of the first site he intended to visit, Foley had been entirely comfortable with this rationale. It stood the test of reason, forwarded the investigation, was a step that could not be omitted. But somehow, as the search continued, he found himself unexpectedly moving backward, toward the early days of his quest, when he was still fumbling around, running off in all directions as he searched for a path.

Foley's initial effort to uncover the underground web sites catering to pedophiles had taken hundreds of hours. Along the way, he'd attempted to steel himself against what he would find. After all, he was a cop and he'd arrested pedophiles with extensive pornography collections. This was nothing new.

And it might have come out that way, no big deal, if the sites he eventually found hadn't contained thousands of photos, if tens of thousands of pedophiles didn't visit those sites, if those pedophiles didn't openly brag of their exploits. As it was, Foley had discovered himself unprepared for a hurricane of images that cut right to the bone. For a time, he'd even considered chucking the whole business. But eventually he'd toughened. It was that or grief counseling.

When did I pass over, Foley asked himself, from enraged and horrified onlooker to hardened veteran?

The question produced a comment that could only have come from his good angel, now resentful and mean-spirited. You ceased to be affected by images of adults having sex with children, it informed him, when you finally gave up on your daughter, when you pronounced Patti dead because that's the way you wanted her. After all, when you're dead, nothing more can happen to you.

This is the worst, Foley told himself; this is as bad as it gets. But that was not the case. Later, when he finally shut down his computer, turned off the lights and settled into bed for what he hoped would be a few hours of uneventful sleep, his thoughts turned of themselves to the time before Patti disappeared. This was a door he'd learned not to open. It'd been years, in fact, since he'd even found the courage to peek through the keyhole. Perhaps that was why, because he was out of practice, the first memory caught him so completely by surprise.

HER RED hair woven into thick braids that whip from side to side, Patti tears from her bedroom, pudgy legs churning madly as she crosses the living room to jump into his arms, a leap of pure faith, knowing absolutely that her father, her protector, will be there to catch her.

"Daddy, Daddy, Daddy!"

Seated behind a Formica table in a small alcove to the left, Kirstin is smiling that perfect smile inherited by her daughter.

FOLEY COULD have gotten out of bed at that point; he could have broken the spell. Instead, he remained on his back as the memories came faster and faster—jumbled tableaus that suddenly burst into action, a phrase here, a gesture there—until he could no longer deny the obvious. Until the weight of the accumulated evidence proved the point not merely beyond a reasonable doubt, but to a moral certainty. Though he might rescue his daughter, he would never get Patti back.

From somewhere deep in the recesses of his mind, in a little fold of his convoluted brain, he could hear both his good and bad angels. They were laughing at him.

20

J ULIA B RENNAN passed the ninety minutes between her
arrival and the arrival of Craig Whitmore at SCU manipulating a
list of relevant facts she'd created the night before. The exercise
was purely futile. Bert Griffith was going to conduct most of the
Whitmore interview, with Harry McDonald there to play the bad
cop whenever necessary. Julia would be outside, in the squad room,
watching through the one-way mirror with Betty Cohen for company. It would be the same when Steve Liebman arrived at noon,
accompanied by Seamus Fowler, his attorney. Betty Cohen and
another SCU detective, Carlos Serrano, would interview Liebman.
Julia's role, until (and unless) the presence of a senior officer was
judged necessary, would be limited to observer.

The door to Julia's office opened and Betty Cohen stuck her
head inside. "Whitmore's on the way up."

"He bring a lawyer?"

"Nope."

Julia took a deep breath as she forced down a smile and walked to the door. McDonald and Griffith were sitting at their desks fiddling with paperwork, as if Whitmore's arrival was of little consequence. Julia was not fooled. The tension that swarmed through her own body was magically intense. Of itself, her concentration had narrowed until it seemed there was nothing in all the world but this room in this moment of time. Julia knew Bert was feeling that same excitement. Harry, too. And what made it all the more delicious was that their lawful prey was stepping into their den. As wrapped in his ego as a slumbering larva in its cocoon.

BERT ROSE from his seat when Craig Whitmore finally arrived. "Mr. Whitmore," he said, "I'm glad you could make it." His tone betrayed no hint of the sarcasm he'd employed yesterday afternoon. Whitmore had been invited to SCU's office in order to clear up a few details and had no idea what was coming.

"Anything to help."

"Great. That's just what cops need. Cooperation." Griffith gestured to McDonald. "This is Detective McDonald. He's gonna be workin' with me today."

Though Whitmore's eyebrows rose in mock surprise, the rest of his face remained utterly immobile. "I no longer rate the attention of Captain Brennan? Have I sunk to such depths?" He turned to gaze at Julia from across the room. When she continued both to stare at him and to maintain her silence, he looked back to Griffith. "Well, shall we get this done?"

Griffith led Whitmore to a small room tucked into the corner of SCU's offices. To do so, he had to pass two other interview rooms, both with their doors open. These rooms were far larger than the one intended for the lawyer, and far cleaner.

"You wanna sit down over there?"

The metal chair Griffith offered was bolted to the floor. A pair of handcuffs dangled from a cleat riveted to its right arm. In front of the chair, a small table, also bolted down, was scarred with graffiti. There was graffiti scratched onto the wall behind the chair as well. Overhead, a brown water stain snaked out from a corner of the drop ceiling like the tentacles of an octopus.

"First thing," Griffith said, "we gotta review your constitutional rights."

"I'm an attorney. I know my rights."

Griffith raised a hand. "I know you know 'em, Mr. Whitmore, but we're makin' a record of the interview, so—"

The door opened and Harry McDonald stepped inside. He was carrying an open carton which he laid on the table. "Coffee is served," he announced as he set an extra-large Styrofoam container in front of Whitmore. "And we got sugar and cream, too."

Craig Whitmore, after a moment's hesitation, opened the container and added a packet of sugar. Standing outside, Julia nodded to Betty. The coffee was meant to stimulate the lawyer's prostate-compromised bladder until he acknowledged his dependency on the detectives by asking permission to go to the bathroom. It was a small point, and ordinarily done with cigarettes, the average mutt being a committed smoker.

Griffith read Whitmore his rights exactly as printed on an NYPD form that he had the lawyer sign. Then he tucked the form into a battered attaché case before removing his notebook. As he began to turn the pages of the notebook, Griffith carefully wet his right index finger with the tip of his tongue.

"I've allotted an hour's time to this interview," Whitmore said, "and ten minutes have already passed. Just in case you're keeping track."

"Okay." Griffith laid the notebook on the table. "Let's get down to business. We brought you here, Mr. Whitmore— say, can I call you Craig?"

"Can I call you Albert?"

"No, Craig, you can't." Griffith's expression was as composed as Julia had ever seen it. "Anyway, we brought you down here because there's a few things we need to go over."

"Specifically?"

Griffith settled back in his chair. "Let's start with you leaving that restaurant on the day Adeline was murdered. What was the name?"

"The Blue Water Grill."

"That's it. So, let's go from there. Lunch is over. What came next?"

"I went directly to my office."

"No, I mean *exactly* next. Did your companion"— Griffith wet his finger, then flicked through his notebook "—Menachem Levi, that's it. Did Levi take off first? Or did you? Or did you leave together?"

"I don't see what this has to do with Adeline's murder."

McDonald spoke for the first time. "Just answer the questions," he said.

"Craig doesn't have to answer any question he doesn't want to answer," Griffith interjected. "You know that, Harry."

"Gimme a break," McDonald replied. "I got a date with Monica tonight and I'd like to get to her place on time. For once."

"Tonight?" Whitmore's lips flicked into a narrow smile as he consulted his watch. "Gentlemen, you've got forty-six minutes left."

"Then we better get to it." Griffith nodded once, as if they'd reached agreement. "So, who left the restaurant first? Or did you leave together?"

Julia TOOK a step back as Griffith led Whitmore through a maze of detail. Did you walk back to your office? Did you take a taxi? Do you remember the driver's name? The number of his hack license? The cab's medallion number? The make of the cab? Was the taxi a minivan or a common sedan? What route did the cabbie take? What was the fare? How much did you tip the driver? Did you get a receipt?

"Bert's doing his iron-man thing," Julia declared.

"Time for a bathroom break," Betty replied. "He could be at it for a week."

Though Julia knew this wasn't true, that the issue would be forced whenever Craig Whitmore tried to leave, she nodded assent. Stamina born of long experience was one of the big advantages detectives had over suspects.

Nevertheless, Julia made her trip to the ladies' room as brief as possible. When she came back out, Betty was on the phone. "Okay," Betty said, "see you then." She hung up and turned to Julia. "That was Liebman's attorney, Seamus Fowler, confirming their noon appointment."

"Perfect." Julia walked to the door of Whitmore's little jail and knocked softly. Griffith and McDonald emerged a moment later and she quickly relayed the information. Timing, after all, was everything. "I'll give you a heads-up as soon as Liebman enters the building."

When THE hour Whitman had reserved for the NYPD was up, his watch gave a little beep, only the one note which hung in the small room. Griffith had just begun to inquire into the real estate deal Whitmore was reviewing for Adeline's benefit.

"So," Whitmore said, "that's it." His expression remained life-less. "I'll be on my way."

Suddenly, McDonald began to laugh. "I swear to God, Bert," he declared, "these white boys, they don't have a fuckin' clue." He placed a hand on Whitmore's shoulder when the lawyer started to rise. "You're not goin' nowhere," he declared. "No-*fucking*-where."

"Am I under arrest?"

Griffith pushed McDonald's hand away, then drew his chair close to Whitmore's. "Let me be up front with you, Craig, so there's no bullshit between us. The simple fact is that we have enough on you to get an indictment right this minute. Now I admit that most of it's pretty circumstantial, but that's why we're givin' you this opportunity to erase any false impressions we might have. Otherwise, it'd just be off to Central Booking."

"False impressions?"

"Yeah, some discrepancies."

Again, Julia nodded to Betty Cohen. Driven by a very rational fear of incarceration, Whitmore had nibbled at the bait, at the hope of freedom on the tip of Bert Griffith's hook. No surprise. At present, he was imagining that he could talk his way out of jail without revealing anything he didn't want his interrogators to know, that he could avoid the traps. Little did he realize that the odds now favored the cops. More than likely, if guilty, he would confess.

Many reasons had been offered for this counterintuitive outcome. The theory Julia favored was generally subscribed to by mainstream forensic psychologists. It claimed that a violent criminal act produces a psychological tension that lies outside the boundaries of the perpetrator's normal personality. In an effort to relieve this tension, criminals often admit their crimes to wives, lovers, and friends. They will also admit it to cops in the course of an interrogation if properly encouraged. You begin by ratcheting up the tension, then gradually convince your suspect that release can only be accomplished by confession.

Had Craig Whitmore been a criminal defense attorney, he would have been familiar with the technique. Just as he would most likely have brought a criminal defense lawyer with him had he known he would be threatened with arrest. But he didn't have an attorney and he didn't have an inkling of what was about to happen to him. He merely glanced at his watch, then asked, "How much longer?"

"I'll make it as fast as I can." Griffith, of course, had no interest in theories, especially theories concocted by psychologists. He knew what worked and what didn't, and that ordinary citizens, unprepared as they were for the rigors of a police interrogation, were easy prey. If they were guilty.

"Alright," Whitmore finally said, "I'll give you one more hour. What do you want to know?"

"Well, about that contract. You remember, Adeline's real estate deal?"

"What about it?"

"You said there were eight buildings involved and they were each ten stories high, right?"

"I don't get the point of this."

"Well, it's not exactly on the point, Craig, but I was just wondering, what with New York's rent regulations, how Adeline could hope to make a profit on her investment?"

21

B Y THE time Bert Griffith proved willing to discuss the discrepancies in Whitmore's earlier interview, the lawyer had twice requested to use the bathroom and twice had his request put off. Though his one-hour time limit had long ago expired, he'd made no further effort to conclude the interview.

"Alright, Craig, let's get down to business." Griffith was sitting with his legs crossed, leaning back, comfortable and content. "You know it's been bothering me about you happening to stay late at the office on the night Adeline was killed. I made that clear yesterday, right?"

"You did." Whitmore had wilted noticeably, a man who desperately wanted to end an experience far more unpleasant than any he'd anticipated. That he didn't have the courage to accept the consequences was equally clear.

"Well, I spoke to your office manager, Ms. Kerkorian, after me and Captain Brennan visited you in Port Washington. Ms. Kerkorian told us she can't remember when you worked late before last Tuesday. She says you used to have a co-op on West Seventy-fourth Street, but you suddenly gave it up six months ago and she hardly ever sees you in the office these days."

Whitmore responded a bit too quickly and it was apparent to Julia that he'd anticipated the question. "I'm getting older," he said, "and so is my wife. I simply decided to spend more time at home and that's what I've been doing. There's nothing mysterious about it."

Harry McDonald leaned into Whitmore's blind side. "Don't bullshit us about spending time with the little woman," he commanded, "and don't take us for dummies. You make the rounds of the clubs—the *S&M* clubs—twice a week. The bartenders and the regulars, they all know you. One guy, he told me, 'Craig's got a way with hot wax that borders on the sublime.'"

Whitmore jerked his head away, the gesture so sharp his chair would have gone over backward if it wasn't bolted to the floor. He started to say something, but McDonald cut him off by slamming his fist on the table. "Don't lie to us, you pitiful creep, or I swear to Christ I'll take photos of you spreading your cheeks and send 'em out as Christmas cards."

"I don't have to take this," Whitmore finally declared when he realized he was not going to be attacked. He looked to Bert Griffith for relief, but Griffith just shook his head.

"Detective McDonald has a point, especially about you taking us for dummies. Remember, cops have feelings too." When the lawyer failed to respond to this point, Griffith went on. "The plain fact of the matter is that you stay in town all the time, not to work at the office but so you can satisfy your perversions. I think a jury would find it very strange that you picked the day Adeline Rose was murdered to review a routine contract in your office."

"You're forgetting something, detective. I stopped working and left my office at nine o'clock. Adeline wasn't killed until a good deal later."

"How do you know that?"

"I read it in the *Times* this morning."

Griffith laughed. "Good for you, Craig, but even if the *Times* is accurate, it's not gonna help you because you can't prove you went straight home. Nobody saw you."

"But there's the alarm," Whitmore said.

"What about the alarm?"

"The alarm makes a record, including time and date, whenever it's shut down and reactivated."

"Is that so?"

"It is."

"Well, if you don't mind my askin', how come you didn't tell me this yesterday? Or the day before?"

"It slipped my mind."

Whitmore folded his arms across his chest and settled back. He'd flung it out there now, his alibi, and Julia was sure he felt better with his cards on the table.

"Captain?"

Julia turned to find Betty Cohen hanging up the telephone. "Yes?"

"Liebman's on his way up."

"With his attorney?"

"Yeah."

Julia knocked on the door of the interrogation room. When McDonald's head popped out, she told him, "Three minutes." Behind McDonald, Griffith's soft tone belied the import of his words.

"That alarm system you got, it's a great system," he said. "It was smart you had it upgraded six months ago, right after you sold your co-op. You can't have too much protection when it comes to home and hearth. Adeline never got that message which is most likely why she's dead."

Whitmore drew in a long breath, sucking the air between pressed lips, the hiss clearly audible in the room. He did not speak.

"Nothing to say?" McDonald asked as he closed the door. He was smiling now, the smile of a cat with its claws extended. "Well, we called that alarm company you hired, Tranquility Alarms, and they told us something very interesting. Your alarm can be programmed from outside the home via telephone. So the fact that Tranquility registered an entry at eleven o'clock, which they did, doesn't mean squat. Not when you set up the system six months ago. Not when you walked into the showroom demanding the best of the fucking best."

As THEY'D butted heads in the past, Julia Brennan needed no introduction to Liebman's attorney, Seamus Fowler. A former prosecutor, Fowler was generally rated among the top five criminal defense lawyers in the city. He was prim in appearance, with a decent head of light brown hair and smallish green eyes obscured by wire-rimmed glasses. His most engaging feature was a reassuring smile, complete with dimples, that he displayed for Julia Brennan.

"Captain Brennan, it's good to see you again."

Fowler offered his hand which Julia took readily before introducing him to Detectives Cohen and Serrano. Betty Cohen was already on her feet, but Serrano remained at his desk for a moment before sauntering over. He was shaking Fowler's hand when the door to the corner interrogation room opened and Craig Whitmore was led out for his bathroom break.

The contrast between Liebman and Whitmore was marked. Whitmore appeared disheveled. His pinstriped suit hung on his bony frame as if the past few hours had aged him by that hard decade between the mid-sixties and the mid-seventies. Liebman, on the other hand, stood erect with his hands in his pockets. Perhaps because tough guy was the only role open to him, or perhaps because he'd dealt with cops in the past, he looked at Whitmore and said, "Hey, Craig, I hope you're havin' as much fun as I am."

Whitmore glanced from Liebman to Seamus Fowler without apparent emotion, then, flanked by Griffith and McDonald, continued on his way.

22

SEAMUS FOWLER'S expression was notably glum as he took a seat beside a thoroughly relaxed Steve Liebman. He'd almost certainly counseled against his client's acceptance of Lily Han's invitation to clear a few things up. Good advice, under normal circumstances. But Leibman's circumstances were anything but normal. His inheritance, all those millions of dollars, was now in the hands of a Surrogates Court probate judge who would never release a single dime while Stephen Liebman was a viable suspect in Adeline's murder. As it stood, Liebman wouldn't be able to pay his lawyer unless he convinced the NYPD that he was innocent.

"I'm going to be straightforward with you," Betty Cohen said to Seamus Fowler. "First, your client had the means, the opportunity, and sixty million reasons to kill his stepmother. Second, when we interviewed him on Wednesday, he lied to us about facts material to the investigation. Third, right now is Mr. Liebman's last and final chance to mend his ways. He doesn't, we're gonna put him under arrest."

"I'll be sure to let him know."

Seamus Fowler's smile was now slightly bemused, as if he'd guessed their strategy. The harsh approach taken with Craig Whitmore had been closed when Liebman hired a lawyer. A bullying attitude on the part of his interrogators would not be tolerated.

"Is there a question in that speech?" Liebman asked. He was staring hard at Betty Cohen.

"You told us," Betty said, unperturbed, "that you last visited your stepmother on Thanksgiving. Was that the truth?"

The question was neatly put. In order to set the record straight, Betty's suspect would have to admit that he lied in the first place.

"I saw her last week," Liebman replied, his tone confident.

"When did you arrive?"

"Around eight."

"Was Adeline expecting you?"

"No."

OUT OF the corner of her eye, Julia watched Harry McDonald return Craig Whitmore to his cage, then announce that he was leaving to scare up some lunch. Neither he nor Bert Griffith would return until Steve Liebman's defenses had been thoroughly probed. Whitmore's lunch would be served by a uniformed officer.

Julia turned back to the Liebman interrogation just in time to hear Betty ask, "Tell us why you decided to visit your stepmother unannounced."

"I was in a jam," Liebman admitted. If he noticed his attorney's sharp wince, he paid it no mind. "I was behind in the mortgage payments on my co-op and the bank was crawling up my ass. Adeline, she was her usual consistent self. I had a trust fund and I was to exist on the income it provided and that was all she wrote."

"And how did you respond?"

"I left."

"Without another word?"

"Pretty much."

Julia watched Betty nod once, then change the subject, leaving the essential lie uncorrected. In fact, according to Flora Esquival, Steve and Adeline had argued. Julia wondered if Liebman knew that any lie told to the police, if material, could be presented to a jury as evidence of a guilty mind. Or if he realized those lies could neither be refuted or explained unless he testified. Whereupon his violent past would be up for grabs.

"You're sixty-three years old," Betty said, "and you don't have access to the principal in your own trust fund. How does that make you feel?"

Seamus Fowler objected to the question before Liebman could answer. But that was all right. It was apparent, even on the little monitor, that Betty's jibe had pierced the core of Steve Liebman's macho heart. His face tightened into a ball, his eyes squeezing down into slits.

"Okay," Betty said, "let's move on. Mr. Liebman, you told me that you hadn't spoken to Adeline's attorney, Craig Whitmore, in six months. You wanna stay with that?"

"I think I said *around* six months."

"Ah, that's slick, but the truth is that you had dinner with Craig Whitmore and your sister at a restaurant called Anselmo's just last week."

Liebman chuckled. "I'm gettin' older," he said, "my sense of time, it's not what it used to be."

"Great," Betty replied, "now you can plead not guilty by reason of senility." She paused briefly, then continued when Liebman failed to reply. "Tell me when the dinner took place? What time did it begin? Did you have reservations or did you just show up unannounced?"

As Betty led Steve Liebman through the details, she made no mention of Adeline's will, though she knew it had been discussed. Betty wanted this lie to also remain uncorrected, at least for the moment. Nevertheless, she milked the subject, demanding that the general conversation be rendered specific. Giving Steve Liebman every chance to come clean.

BETTY WAS still at it thirty minutes later when Julia heard someone come up behind her. She turned to find Lily Han.

"Anything important?" Han asked.

"Liebman admitted that he met with Adeline last Thursday. According to him, their conversation was brief and civil. He also admitted to having dinner with his sister and Craig Whitmore on Friday but failed to mention any discussion of Adeline's will."

"What about Whitmore? Griffith have any luck with him?"

Julia shook her head. "We're still softening him up."

"Well, I just looked in on Mr. Whitmore a moment ago." Lily Han smiled. "If he was any softer, the bastard would melt."

"NOW, YOU told us," Betty continued, "that it's been five years since you discussed Adeline's will with Craig Whitmore. You wanna stick with that?"

Bit by bit, Liebman began to retreat. That he tried, at the same time, to draw lines in the sand, was as foolish as anything he'd done thus far. His best course would have been to freely admit he'd originally lied, perhaps because, having been arrested in the past, he simply didn't like cops. But when he backed up, claiming he might have discussed the will in the last six months but wasn't exactly sure when, he only made things worse for himself.

Liebman repeated this error when asked about his knowledge of the abortive break-in at Adeline's townhouse and her antiquated alarm system. He may have heard something about the break-in, something about the system, he told Betty and Serrano, but he couldn't recall any details. So sorry.

"No problem," Betty replied. "Now you told us, Mr. Liebman, that you didn't speak to anybody on the night Adeline was killed. You said you were home alone. Was that how it really was?"

"Not exactly."

"What does that mean?"

"I did make a few calls. And I got a call from Hannah, too."

"That's right," Betty agreed. "Hannah told us about the call."

"Somehow, I'm not surprised."

"Hannah talks a lot, does she?"

"With Hannah, it's not how much, it's when."

"I see. Now I should tell you at this point that we subpoenaed your phone records and we know you made other calls. Those calls, they came pretty close together, even if they were short and sweet. But there's a gap that needs explaining."

"And when would that be?"

"Well, according to your phone records, you received a call exactly at midnight which lasted two minutes. That was the call from Hannah. Then, at twelve forty-eight, you dialed the number of Mr. Humberto Echeveria, who lives on the Lower East Side of Manhattan. We want you to account for the time in between."

"Forty-six minutes? You think I ran uptown, killed my stepmother, then got back to make a call forty-six minutes later? That's impossible."

Carlos Serrano spoke for the first time. "I have to disagree with you, Mr. Liebman." In his mid-forties, Serrano's face was dominated by an aquiline nose, a dimpled chin and a thick mustache that appeared to be as soft as silk. His basic expression was quizzical and mild, and that was the way he played it with Liebman, despite the fact that he was going to lie through his teeth, a tactic granted to the police by the United States Supreme Court some years before. "I know it can be done," he added, "because I did it."

"See," Liebman said to Betty, "all the time you thought I killed Adeline and now you've got a confession from somebody else."

"This is not a joke." Serrano's voice carried just a hint of a Spanish accent. "I re-created the entire sequence, starting and ending outside your apartment. It took me thirty-seven minutes and I was never in either building before. With a little practice, I could probably get it down to a half-hour."

"Bully for you, Detective . . . what was your name? Gonzalez? Ramirez?"

"Serrano," Serrano corrected.

"Then bully for you, Detective Serrano, but I'm afraid you wasted your time, because while my dear departed stepmother was being killed, I was otherwise occupied." Liebman looked from Serrano to his lawyer before settling his gaze on Betty Cohen. "Specifically, I spent the four hours between ten and two o'clock on the night and morning in question with a whore. Mai Ling was her name and she was sent over by an escort service, Peony Asian Escorts. That name, by the way, it really describes Oriental merchandise. You can pee on 'em all night long and they never complain." He winked at Betty. "My kind of woman."

Seated to Liebman's right, his attorney, Seamus Fowler, broke into peals of unrestrained laughter.

23

THEY BROKE for lunch after Liebman's revelation, ostensibly to prepare for a final assault on Craig Whitmore. But they didn't come together right away. Instead, sandwiches in hand, they wandered around SCU's squad room without really communicating. They did, though, share a common frame of reference. First there was anger. Steve Liebman had spit directly in their faces, not only with his final statement but two days earlier when he'd first lied to Betty and Julia. The team had wasted many hours tracking Liebman's movements on the night Adeline was killed, hours they might have spent on Craig Whitmore.

Their collective anger aside, Julia and her detectives fully understood that Liebman's alibi had a very positive aspect. If Steve Liebman did not kill Adeline Rose, Craig Whitmore did. It was as simple as that and they could always hope that Craig would incriminate Steve Liebman, that they were co-conspirators. What the team feared, though, was that Whitmore, having been left so long to his own devices, would demand a lawyer. About his guilt, they had no doubt. Barring the very slim possibility that Mai Ling and Peony Asian Escorts were created from whole cloth, Whitmore had murdered Adeline Rose. Only his motive remained obscure.

Julia folded the last few bites of her tuna melt into its wrapper and tossed the bundle at a wastebasket. When it fell inside without grazing the rim, Betty said, "At least somebody's on her game."

Though she felt called upon to console her detective, Julia maintained her silence. The bits and pieces, all those little chunks of evidence she'd listed the night before, had begun to coalesce around a definite strategy. Maybe the evidence gathered at the crime scene, her reasoning went, had yet to be processed, but if Whitmore was guilty, traces of his presence would eventually show up. No matter how well prepared, he could not have killed Adeline, not in that way, then cleaned up without leaving pieces of himself behind.

Focused now, Julia walked over to Bert Griffith and Harry McDonald who sat on either side of Griffith's desk, snatching a mug of coffee on the way.

"Captain," Griffith said. "What's the word?"

"I was going to ask you the same thing."

McDonald took the opportunity to make his case. He gestured to the room that held Whitmore, then said, "I look at this jerk with his face in his hands and I don't see the point to waltzing him around. He's ready to go right this minute."

"I gotta agree." Griffith shifted in his chair to face Julia. "But if you want, I'll run him in circles until he falls over."

Julia shook her head. "I don't want him to fall over, Bert. I want you to knock him down and keep on the floor until he confesses. Tell him about Liebman's alibi and say we know he murdered his client because there isn't anybody else who could have murdered her. He can tell us about it now, or we can prove his guilt at a later date. In the end, it's not gonna matter."

That said, Julia sat on the edge of Bert Griffith's desk to discuss the details.

Harry McDonald broke the silence. "Bad news, Craig," he said, "the worst. Your buddy, Steve Liebman, he's got a one hundred percent unbreakable alibi. That leaves you. That means you killed Adeline Rose."

Whitmore reacted sharply to the bad news. He'd taken off his glasses and laid them on the table before Griffith and McDonald walked into the room. Now when he looked up, his eyes were dull and muddy. "I had no reason to kill her," he said.

"Reason?" McDonald sank back into his chair. "Face it, Craig, we don't need no stinkin' reason. And we don't need a stinkin motive to convict you, either. But if we did need a motive, I'd put theft at the head of the list."

"Theft?"

"From that safe deposit box Adeline filled with the treasures of an entire lifetime. Now, if there was an inventory, written and signed by her, that'd be one thing. But Adeline hasn't visited her box in three years and it's your name that appears on the sign-in card, over and over again. You might've snatched anything outta that box and nobody the wiser. Jewelry, coin collections, uncut gems—in case you haven't heard, rich people buy stuff like that all the time as a hedge against inflation. Then they stick what they bought in a safe deposit box until it's needed."

"You can't prove any of that."

"You're right. We can't even bring it up." McDonald inched still closer, his smile actually joyful now. "Unless your lawyers ask a jury to acquit you because you don't have a motive. If you do that, the prosecution is allowed to speculate." He tapped the edge of the table. "That safe deposit box? What it does, really, is close off an avenue of your defense."

Lily Han turned to Julia. "Does he have any idea what he's talking about?"

"Harry's stripping away Craig's hope," Julia replied. "Like tearing bark off the side of a tree. Like he was pulling off Whitmore's skin."

Lily Han flinched, struck by the casually violent metaphors, but Julia barely noticed. Her attention was riveted to Craig Whitmore whose smile, though tiny, held a full measure of triumph. It was a sure indicator that he was about to tell the truth.

"Last year," he declared, "Adeline Rose paid me five hundred thousand dollars to manage her affairs. In addition, my own portfolio, acquired as a direct result of Adeline's generosity, now runs to the mid-seven figures, not including my unmortgaged home in Port Washington which is worth another two million. There is nothing in Adeline's safe deposit box so valuable as to tempt even a psychotic to risk all that. And you will never convince a jury there was."

"So you killed her because you hated her. What's wrong with that?"

Bert Griffith interrupted before Whitmore could reply. "Hold that thought, Craig, because there's something I need to ask you. When I was at your place, I noticed that you owned a couple of vehicles. Which one were you driving on the day you worked late at the office? I could find out myself, naturally, by checking with your parking garage where they write down the plate numbers. But I got me the kind of workload could break a mule's back and I like to save time whenever I can."

"I was driving the Mercedes."

"The 600 SEL I saw parked outside your house?"

"Yes."

"Good. We'll put it right on the search warrant. Now, let's talk for a minute about the blood. After you killed Adeline—"

"I didn't kill Adeline. I had no reason to kill Adeline."

Griffith's face turned grave as he shook his head. "I know you murdered your benefactor," he insisted, "and I'm not gonna pretend I don't. So like I was saying before you interrupted me, after you slashed Adeline to pieces, you went into the bathroom to clean up. You took off your bloodiest clothes and most likely stuffed them into a plastic bag, trying your absolute best not to get blood on the outside of the bag. Then you washed off in the sink, cleaned up the bathroom and got out of there. Any questions so far?"

"Am I under arrest?"

"Not yet. Now, you finished cleaning up and went out the front door, not the back. We know this because we found a smear of blood on the wrought-iron fencing at the top of the stoop, which means you didn't clean up as well as you thought. It's the kinda thing gives a cop hope." Bert glanced at his partner who nodded agreement. "Anyway, goin' out the front door was a big mistake. It let us rule out the burglar gambit.

"Your second mistake was not dumping the bloody clothes before you got in your car. And we know you didn't because we searched every Dumpster, garbage can, and storm drain within two blocks of Adeline's townhouse. You know how it is with blood now. They've got this chemical, Luminol. It reacts even to microscopic traces of blood so the blood shows up under ultra-violet light. Doesn't matter if you cleaned up with bleach, doesn't matter what you did, if any blood came in contact with any part of your Mercedes, we're gonna know."

* * *

JULIA WATCHED Craig Whitmore as he faded under Griffith's relentless attack. His very skin appeared to sag and his fish-white hands were motionless on the table. Though Julia wanted a confession, she now realized a confession was no longer necessary. Craig Whitmore knew it too. The truth was apparent in his slumping shoulders, in his shallow breathing. Bert was driving the nails deep and Craig Whitmore's coffin was closing around him.

"So where," Griffith continued, "did you go? That's what I asked myself. Where did you finally dump your bloody clothes?" Griffith's smile was not unkindly. "Kind of a no-brainer, Craig. I mean, you got the Atlantic Ocean in your backyard and a boathouse feeds right onto the water. Not only that, there's a little shower room attached to the boathouse where you had a final cleanup before you took your puppy for his late-night romp."

Griffith stopped suddenly, then tapped his head as if something very important had just occurred to him. "Know what, Craig? You say you wanna prove your innocence? So how about you voluntarily give us permission to search your home, your boathouse, that shower room and your car? Save us the trouble of getting a warrant?"

When Craig Whitmore simply maintained his silence, Harry McDonald jumped in. "Can we go back to the motive thing?" he asked. "The part about you hating your client?"

"Everybody hated Adeline," Whitmore said. "And they'll be more than happy to admit it when the time comes."

"That's fine, Craig, that's accurate, only with you it was special. The others, Craig and Hannah, they had their own lives and they kept away from her. You on the other hand. . . . Hey, Craig, you know what she used to call you? The name she used when she spoke about you to friends like Dorothy Farber?"

"Yes, I do. Adeline made sure to tell me."

"Why don't you tell us what that was?"

"Her little bush baby."

McDonald roared with laughter. "I had to look that one up." he said after a moment, "in the library. You know what a bush baby turns out to be? A bush baby is a tiny primate with great big eyes and great big ears that comes out at night to eat insects." McDonald hitched up his belt and shifted forward in his chair. "Even the bush part makes sense. That's where she found you—right?—in the bush, in an orphanage for unwanted animals? I wonder what made her pick you. She had all these tiny orphans and she coulda picked any one of them, but she chose Craig Whitmore. It musta seemed like a miracle, at least at first. But then . . . then you became her bush baby, her tiny subhuman primate."

Again, McDonald laughed, a sardonic bark that ricocheted from wall to wall. "What a life. By night you're makin' the rounds of the S&M clubs: Master Craig, king of the hot wax torture. By day you're Adeline's bush baby, doing her bidding, coming when she calls, begging for table scraps."

Bert Griffith spoke up before McDonald's words died away. "Oh, yeah," he said, "there was something else I was supposed to tell you, but it somehow slipped my mind." He shrugged apologetically. "I don't know what's goin' on with me. I'm forgettin' everything these days. The other morning I left home without my gun. You believe that?"

Smart enough to know a punch line was coming and he was the one about to be punched, Whitmore continued to stare down at his glasses on the table. Nevertheless, when Bert Griffith finally got to the point, Craig Whitmore responded with an audible groan.

"What we're gonna need," Griffith said, "before you leave here tonight, is a DNA sample, a hair sample and a set of your fingerprints. I'm not holdin' out hope on the fingerprints, but if you so much as breathed on the mirror, or spit in the sink, or left a few hairs on the floor, we're gonna put you in that bathroom. Maybe it'd be alright if you went up to Adeline's sitting room on a regular basis, but you told us you always conducted business in the parlor. You told us you never went above the first floor."

"And thereby," McDonald added, "sealed your fate."

24

CRAIG WHITMORE held out for another two hours. By that time, the team had abandoned all trace of aggression. Harry McDonald had pushed his chair several feet away from the table and was out of Whitmore's line of sight. Bert Griffith was nearly whispering as he repeated a single message, over and over. This is your one chance to get your side of things on the record, to finally unburden yourself. The part about guilt and innocence is over. Not only are you certain to be convicted at trial, but given the evidence against you, most likely your attorney will plead you guilty in return for a lighter sentence. It's now or never.

Watching from outside, Julia could sense the moment coming, as she'd sensed it so many times in the past. The hours had broken Whitmore's spirit and sapped his will. With neither spirit nor will to call upon, he was sucked into every facet of Griffith's argument.

There was no longer a reason to hold back, to prolong the agony, when he was going to be convicted anyway. And, yes, he did want to tell someone. He wanted to confess, to relieve himself of pressures from within and without. After all, his actions were not those of a common criminal intent on material gain. They were justified by the circumstances and ultimately moral. They were based on principle.

The end came suddenly, as it usually did. Whitmore put on his glasses, carefully settling them on the bridge of his nose before looking directly at Bert Griffith whose gaze he had been studiously avoiding. "I couldn't," he announced, "allow the monster to die in her bed. That's what we called Adeline Rose. Hannah, Steve and myself: the monster."

Shielded by his glasses, Whitmore's eyes were swollen and very wet. Nevertheless, his rage was apparent. He would use that rage, Julia knew, to recover some measure of self-worth. That his rage could also be used against him no longer mattered.

Behind her, Julia felt the crowd stir. One by one, her detectives had come back from their assignments, then gathered to watch the last act of the drama unfold. Julia could sense their excitement and their satisfaction as Craig Whitmore continued.

"Adeline was sinking and everybody knew it. She had no life-threatening illness the doctors could name or that they could treat; she was just shutting down. As I watched the process I kept thinking of all the monsters who died in bed. People like Joseph Stalin and Mao Zedong and a hundred more who spent their lives administering pain to others before slipping gently into the night. It haunted me, the injustice. I knew if Adeline went unpunished, I would carry the shame of it into my own grave."

To Julia's right, Lily Han bristled. "You believe this? The jerk's comparing Adeline Rose to Joe Stalin." She shook her head. "Maybe he's preparing an insanity defense."

"Craig's just trying to make himself bigger. The poor little bush baby who wanted to be a gorilla."

The words came easily, though Julia's focus remained on Craig Whitmore as she waited for him to wind down so that Bert or Harry could get to the point. But Whitmore was in no hurry. He piled on the grievances, zigzagging back and forth through his life, stacking evidence of Adeline's perfidy like pancakes on a plate. Curiously, as he plodded forward, his anger faded. Except for his lips as they moved over the words, his features gradually approached a state resembling paralysis.

Ever the patient interrogator, Bert Griffith did not interrupt. He did, however, ask the essential question fifteen minutes later when Craig ceased to speak. "Craig," he said in his most cajoling voice, "did you tell anybody else what you were going to do? Did anybody help you?"

Whitmore sniffed, the hiss loud enough to be heard by Julia in the squad room. "The others," he declared, his tone dismissive, "may have hated Adeline Rose, but they would never have risked their inheritances. They were cowards, both of them."

"Does that mean no?"

"It does."

THAT WAS enough for Julia who exchanged somewhat restrained congratulations with Betty Cohen and Carlos Serrano. They'd busted the Wild Jewish Rose murder case in under a week. There'd be glory enough to go round, along with a war story they would retell at a hundred rackets before they put in their papers.

Inside the interrogation room, Craig Whitmore explained that he'd originally planned to strangle Adeline, not stab her, which seemed more in keeping with his burglary-gone-bad-scenario. But then he'd come into the room, seen the contempt in her eyes and lost control of himself. It was only after he'd finished that he considered the ramifications. His trench coat was soaked with blood. There was blood on his face, in his hair, on his shoes.

"I lost control," he told Bert Griffith. "I couldn't help myself."

Betty Cohen laughed out loud. "The song of the eternal loser," she declared.

Serrano raised his coffee mug. "I'll drink to that," he announced.

"Why," Betty wanted to know, "do they think they can get away with murder? I'm talking about the amateurs. Do they read too many books? Is it maybe some kind of mass delusion?"

"More like a genetic defect," Carlos observed.

As the banter continued, it became apparent, to Julia, that the subject of Steve Liebman was not to be broached. The last thing they needed was a rainy cloud hanging over their celebration. Not when the time for celebration was so inevitably short. Tomorrow morning, there would be other bad guys to chase, other victims to avenge. Despite the massive drop in the crime rate, from their point of view it was just one mutt after another, *ad infinitum*, all the days of their lives.

Julia remained in the squad room until she heard the phone ring in her office. By that time, she was glad to slip away, to get back to the work, to the routine. She had no inkling of how long that process would take, not until she picked up the phone to find Chief Linus Flannery, Manhattan North Borough Commander, on the other end. Flannery came directly to the point.

"For the last ten minutes," he announced, "I've been on the phone with the U.S. Attorney for the southern district of New York. The way the feebs tell it, your boyfriend came within an inch of strangling one of their witnesses." Flannery paused long enough to clear his throat and light a cigarette. "Nobody said you were involved, Julia, but I've been told to relay the sad facts of life. For your own good, stay clear. According to a special agent named Raymond Lear, Foley's gone off the deep end. You jump in after him, you're gonna drown too."

Julia took a moment to absorb the words, only to find that they bounced off the outer walls of her consciousness like tennis balls thrown against a trampoline. Still, she came up swinging. "We just put away the Adeline Rose case," she announced. "A full confession."

But Flannery was having none of her bluff. "You know I like you, Julia," he said, "and I like Peter Foley too. If not, I wouldn't be making this call personally. But Foley's trapped inside himself and he can't move on and that's all there is to it." Flannery paused briefly, then added, "You have everything it takes to move up in the job. We've known that for a long time. But you have to commit yourself. You can't play both sides of the fence forever. You can't be a hotdog and a team player. If you make the wrong choice here, there's no coming back, not this time. Remember, your present rank of captain is provisional and you can be returned to your former rank of lieutenant any time your performance is deemed unsatisfactory."

LILY HAN'S face appeared in the doorway a moment after Julia hung up. "You okay?" Han asked.

Julia looked down at the paperwork on the desk, then up to her boss. "Sure," she said, though that was far from the truth.

"Well, you put the case down, Julia. Congratulations are in order."

"It wasn't all that much of a case. Whitmore's just another dork who wanted to be Superman. Easy meat."

Han sat down in front of Lily's desk. "I won't argue with that," she declared, "even though it's not true. Now, we're too late for the six o'clock news, so why don't we do the press conference around nine-thirty?"

"Lily, do you think, just this one time, Bert and Betty could sit in for me? I've got a problem I have to deal with."

"Family trouble?"

"With a vengeance."

In fact, it was an offer Lily Han was very unlikely to refuse. A celebrity murder? A quick arrest? A chance to reserve the spotlight for herself? There was nothing not to like.

"That'd be fine," Lily replied. "You do what you have to do. But there's one more thing I need to mention. We got another case this morning, a homicide from the seven-two in Brooklyn. Some mutt named Habib al Rif'at, who took one to the head in his video store."

"What?"

Though Julia's question was meant to convey total confusion, Lily Han extracted a more obvious meaning. "Why did it come to us?" she asked. "It was routine. A trunk loaded with child pornography was found in the store. By the way, you might want to speak to Peter, get his insights."

Julia nodded thoughtfully. Lily didn't yet know of Foley's problems, or of Julia Brennan's for that matter. She would, though, and soon. What Ms. Han would do next was anybody's guess.

"I'll set up a meet with the locals before I leave," Julia promised, "and put a team on it tomorrow morning."

"Great." Han ran her fingers through her hair. "Well, it was all wonderfully accomplished," she said before delivering the ultimate compliment. "I couldn't have done it better myself."

Satisfied with her exit line, Han departed, leaving Julia to stew in her own juices. Those juices were simmering nicely when the phone rang again a few minutes later. She stared down at it through several rings, asking herself, What now? The answer was Peter Foley requesting they meet as soon as possible.

For reasons Julia couldn't begin to fathom, Foley's voice returned her to her rational self, the transition as physical as it was psychological. She glanced at her watch. It was now six o'clock.

"Why don't we make it about eight," she said. "I've got a few things to do before I can get away."

To her credit, Julia's voice was so close to unguarded, Foley picked up neither her fear nor her anger. "Eight o'clock," he responded. "I've rented a car, so I'll be circling the block. Look for me on Centre Street."

25

PETER FOLEY was on Worth Street about to make the left onto Centre when he first caught sight of Julia Brennan. She was walking up Centre Street toward the Criminal Courts building, a cool blonde in a white trench coat and white boots holding a five-dollar throwaway umbrella above her head. As always, Foley was impressed by her firm self-possessed stride, the confidence so apparent in her squared shoulders. If she was aware of the men who surveyed her body with calculated over-the-shoulder glances, she gave not the slightest indication.

When the light finally changed, Foley made the left and a moment later came up beside Julia. He tapped the horn, stopped just long enough for her to get in next to him, then moved off. Parking in lower Manhattan was made impossible after September 11. Not only were there cops on constant patrol, but National

Guard soldiers and New York State troopers as well. This was the municipal heart of New York and virtually every building was fronted by concrete barriers.

Instead of offering a kiss, Julia tugged the seat belt across her lap and chest. "So," she said, "how was your day?"

"Unproductive."

Though Foley didn't elaborate, the single word described his morning and afternoon well enough. He'd run down the names of the president and treasurer of Proximate Services, Inc.: Lorenzo and Emily Contorno. A trip to Sunset Park confirmed that they were out of business, though Foley couldn't be sure exactly when.

He might have gotten the information from the building's management or the security guard stationed at the front entrance, but was afraid that he would be remembered if something happened to the Contornos at a later date. By that time, he already knew they were married with two children, knew their home address in the Astoria section of Queens, knew they had no criminal record.

He knew a good deal about Proximate Services as well. Dun & Bradstreet had provided the business with a triple-A credit rating and estimated a yearly gross of eight million dollars derived from the company's freight-forwarding operation. Under contract to various foreign exporters, Proximate cleared merchandise through customs, then reshipped to various retailers throughout the country.

All the information had been obtained legally and Foley sincerely hoped it would be enough when he parked his car a few doors away from the Contornos' single-family home on 82nd Street off Northern Boulevard at noon. But it was not to be. Though he held the stakeout until after six o'clock, nobody entered or left, no shade was raised or lowered, no light turned on or off, not even when the shadows lengthened as the short March afternoon faded into evening. Again, he might have gotten more direct information from the neighbors. Again, he spoke to no one.

"And your day?" he said. "How did it go?"

"We put away a big case just a few minutes before you called. We were celebrating."

"Adeline Rose?"

"Yeah. The press conference is due to start an hour from now."

"Will you be going back for it?"

"No."

Julia swiveled against the lap belt, until she was looking directly into Foley's eyes. The force of her gaze nearly broke his resolve. He wanted to take her in his arms, to take refuge in her embrace. Meanwhile, her strange indigo eyes were pulling him apart while giving absolutely nothing away. When she said, "You've found Patti," he was caught completely off guard.

"I've found a trace of her," Foley admitted after a moment. "On a video tape." He watched Julia's look gradually soften as she calculated the emotional ramifications of his last statement, then added, "I only watched a few frames. To be sure."

"And are you?"

"I'm as sure as it's possible to be, given the years since I last saw my daughter."

Foley made a left turn onto White Street, then a second left onto Lafayette, finally slowed to a halt in front of the Family Court building when the light turned red on Leonard. Faced entirely in black stone, the courthouse was featureless except for an overhang above the main entrance that seemed to Foley as menacing as the carapace of a foraging beetle. It was beneath this overhang, he knew, and between angled columns that might have been teeth, that many thousands of children had been led to have their futures determined.

On other days, when he was less preoccupied, Foley had mused on the designers, the architects, and city planners, who'd created and approved the monstrosity, then dedicated its use to the interests of children. He'd wondered if the city fathers had set out to frighten them, if the inspiration of fear was their original intention. Now he saw family court as a very real possibility for his daughter.

THEY'D ALMOST reached Worth Street before Julia broke the silence. "I got a call this afternoon," she announced, "from Manhattan Borough Commander Linus Flannery. He says you nearly strangled a federal witness. That's when I knew you'd found Patti. Strangulation is a bit on the excessive side, even for you." When Foley started to reply, she waved him off. "Chief Flannery also instructed me to stay away from you if I value my career. He says you've gone off the deep end. So what do you think, Pete? Should I write you off as a liability? Cut my losses in a down market?"

Foley paused long enough to consider what he'd already done, what he might yet do. He was steeling himself because at that moment he wanted Julia Brennan almost as much as he wanted Patti. And what he wondered, as he searched for the right words, was if the woman on the seat next to him had been sent by his good or his bad angel.

"It's the other way round, Julia. Where I'm going, you can't come."

Julia Brennan's smile held more than a hint of defiance. "Does that," she asked, "mean you're dumping me?"

Foley turned the rented Dodge onto Centre Street and began to retrace the same slow circle. They were a block north of the Criminal Court building before he admitted that Julia was a step ahead, that his argument was no more than ritual. Nevertheless, he stated that argument as succinctly as possible. "A year ago," he said, "before you made me a part of your family, I would have lured you into helping me. I would have set a trap and let you walk into it just to see what you'd do. Now there's Corry to think about. And her fate if you're not around to raise her."

But Julia wasn't interested. "What do men do?" she asked. "Do they make a ledger sheet, write down a woman's good and bad points, then tabulate the credits and debits? Because I'm telling you, Peter Foley, that a woman doesn't love that way. It's too fucking rational."

Foley replied without hesitation, his voice huskier than he would have liked. "There's nothing rational about what I feel for you. Nothing." Then he repeated, "Where I'm going, you can't come."

"Well, I guess that's that."

"No, it's not. I want you to do something for me."

"Something that won't ruin my entire life for which you have suddenly become ultimately responsible?"

"If I should find my daughter," he said, "but not be able to care for her, I want you to become her legal guardian. I want you to watch over Patti."

Julia drew a sharp whistling breath, forcing the air between compressed lips. In an instant, her eyes filled with tears. Foley knew if they spilled over, if he made her cry, she'd never forgive him. Instinctively, though he didn't believe it mattered, not in the long run, he lowered the tension. "Why don't you talk to Corry and Robert Reid, Julia. Call one of your family meetings and hash it out."

"I've already done that," she replied. "I was hoping you'd be there."

Foley answered by pulling the car to the curb. Outside, the rain was no more than a heavy mist that sparkled on the street lamps. Julia looked at him for a moment longer, her gaze now speculative, before throwing off her seat belt, then gathering her purse and umbrella. Without a backward glance, she threw the door open and slid her legs out onto the pavement. As she straightened, she slipped, dropping to one knee for a moment. Then she was up and striding away, a tall cool blonde in a white trench coat, shoulders squared, head erect.

26

I N   H I S   early forties, Joseph Grande's computer investigator
and partner, Alonzo Johnson, was a tall black man with a penchant
for cashmere turtlenecks, pleated pants and Italian shoes of
extremely supple leather. His prematurely gray hair and mustache
made him seem older than his years, a look he cultivated and
which was reinforced by an emerging double chin faintly visible
below a firm jaw. Invariably, his dark eyes were friendly and warm,
as was an engaging smile which he flashed at the least provocation.

It was with this smile that Johnson greeted Pete Foley when he
walked into the offices of Joseph Grande Investigations at ten
o'clock that same night.

"Didn't think you were gonna make it," Johnson said.

Foley shrugged off his coat. "Thanks for staying, Lonzo. I just
couldn't get away earlier."

"Nothin' to it." Seated before an enormous desk, Johnson was virtually surrounded by computers and peripherals. "Now, my couch is empty, so tell me your problems."

"I need to run some credit card numbers, pronto."

"What are they?"

"That's what I want you to find out. All I have is a two names and an address."

Pete hung his coat in the closet before rendering the details concisely. He was fully aware of the risk he was taking. He'd not spoken to the Contornos' neighbors or to the security guard at their place of business, for fear of attracting attention. Now he was putting himself on record. Now there was another human being who could tie him to Lorenzo and Emily Contorno. It couldn't be helped, though. It was either run the cards, assuming there were any cards to run, or give up on the Contornos.

Alonzo Johnson listened carefully, nodding from time to time as if the implications were only too clear. After Pete finished, he flashed a thin smile, then began his magic act with a theatrical flip of a bloated Rolodex, a decidedly low-tech investigative tool that was, nonetheless, the key to his success.

"This," he bragged, "is not a problem."

When confined to the parameters of a legal search, Alonzo Johnson was a good, though not great, investigator. It was on the darker, the flip side, that he excelled. Alonzo belonged to civic organizations in all five boroughs and was active in every one of them.

Gregarious by nature, Lonzo had met hundreds of people at a multitude of functions and courted many, especially the young men and women who worked for giant corporations and government agencies. They were, these men and women, personal assistants to mean-spirited executives, or underpaid and overabused customer service reps, or sullen civil servants, or junior programmers who toiled at web sites like AOL, MSN, Earthlink and Yahoo. Though they did not know one another, they shared, these men and women, a single attribute in that each had access to confidential information, a commodity every bit as precious as gold.

Though Alonzo approached only a selected few with the suggestion that they pad their meager wages by trading in this precious commodity, not everyone jumped at his offer, not even a majority. But Alonzo was a persistent man, a man with a plan first implemented fifteen years before when he'd grasped the primary significance of the computer revolution. Now he was a full partner. Now he was knocking down a hundred large per annum. And that didn't count the skim.

"I'm gonna use Eva Paleaz," he announced as he picked up his phone. "Her baby's been sick and I heard she could use some change. Eva's a supervisor at TRW. She works strictly four to midnight and never misses a day." Johnson dialed the woman's pager number, left his own number, and smiled. When the phone rang five minutes later, he picked it up and said, "I'm calling on business, Eva, and I don't wanna talk about yesterday's news." He listened for a minute, then sighed, "I know I left you hanging and I know I'm a needle-dick asshole. I know it because you already told me ten thousand times. Now I'm in a big hurry, Eva, so if you don't want the job, I'll just move my black ass down the line, see what's behind door number two."

Apparently Eva wanted the job because Alonzo reeled off the Contorno name and address without further debate, then hung up. "Eva Paleaz," he told Foley, "she's Filipino. In my experience, Filipino women are very emotional. The slightest thing, they don't forget. You can't even admit your guilt and beg for mercy, which I don't understand because they're mostly Catholics and the Catholic religion is based on forgiveness. But there it is."

Alonzo was still going at it ten minutes later when Eva
Paleaz called back, demanding that her commission be paid before
she handed over the requested information. Again, Johnson alternately begged and threatened until Eva finally capitulated. Then
he scrawled a few lines on a piece of paper which he handed to
Foley after hanging up.

"That good enough?" he asked.

Foley scanned the page and nodded. "Perfect," he said.

"Then I'll be on my way."

Pete showed Alonzo to the door but remained behind. He was,
in fact, at home, or as close to home as he would get until he somehow patched things up with Raymond Lear. He walked over to the
couch on the other side of the room, his bed for the night, and sat
down to consider his options. The facts were very simple. Using an
American Express card, Emily and Lorenzo Contorno had registered, along with two unnamed children, at the Park East Hotel
on the prior Tuesday, twenty-four hours before Pete's confrontation with Matsunaga. Thus, the disappearances were unrelated.

This decided, Foley moved on to the location of the Park East
Hotel at 75th Street and Madison Avenue which had struck him as
odd when he first read it. He tried to imagine Charlie Terranova,
or his top gun, Joey Cadillac, registering at an upscale hotel on
Manhattan's Gold Coast if they were on the run, but couldn't do
it. No, their first option would be to leave the country altogether.
If that option was foreclosed, they would seek refuge at the home
of a relative in a distant city. All the while hoping *America's Most
Wanted* passed them over.

Then there was the matter of the whole Contorno family going
along. When you ran, you ran because you were desperate and you
ran fast. You didn't bring the wife, much less the kids. Not unless

you were so unprepared that you had no place to put them or you feared for their safety as well as your own.

His mind racing forward, Pete began to pace the room as he put the pieces together. Neither of the Contornos had a criminal record which was significant all by itself. Also significant was Proximate's triple-A credit rating. The company was no front organization. With a yearly volume of eight million dollars, it certainly provided the Contornos with a comfortable living. So why would Lorenzo, a man who donated liberally to Catholic charities, risk everything by handling kiddie porn, even assuming he was a pedophile? Buy it, sure. Trade it, sure. But sell it?

Foley left the question unanswered as he turned to the manner of the Contornos' flight. They'd closed down Proximate Services and abandoned their home right after Charlie Terranova's arrest. Their subsequent journey, as short as it was sudden, had taken them all of ten miles to a hotel in Manhattan. True, the Upper East Side was the last place Charlie Banana would look for them. But it was also the worst place to be if Lorenzo feared arrest. If the feds who'd busted Terranova set their sights on Lorenzo Contorno they would simply do legally what Pete had done illegally. And that would be that.

Still on the move, Pete walked over to Grande's small refrigerator and removed a beer which he promptly opened. Though he instinctively resisted the idea that Contorno was a victim, he knew there were a number of ways it might have come about. The various scenarios were common enough. A small businessman gets in deep with the shys or the bookies or both, then trades a piece of his business for the privilege of remaining alive. The same result could also be produced by simple extortion with no debt involved, especially where immigrants were concerned.

Either way, any self-respecting gangster, once inside, would use the business for nefarious purposes. The kind of nefarious purposes that can put you in a maximum-security prison for the rest of your miserable life.

A simple decision, Foley told himself. Pick one: Contorno the hardened criminal on the run or Contorno the victim in fear of his life.

Though Pete knew he not only had to choose, he had to prepare an approach based on his choice, it took him another two hours and another two beers to do so. But he was more than satisfied with the end result. So satisfied, in fact, that when he lay down on Joe Grande's couch and closed his eyes, he was not haunted by visions of his wife and daughter, either before or after he fell asleep.

27

O N T H E following morning, precisely at nine o'clock, Peter
Foley knocked on the door of room 5E at the Park East Hotel on
Madison Avenue. He was wearing a light wool coat over a navy
Brooks Brothers suit, a fitted blue shirt and a silk tie. Ordinarily
reserved for the odd wedding or funeral, the outfit was now worn
in an attempt to reassure. Reassurance was the key here, reassurance and rapport. Establishing both was so important that Pete
had snuck back into his apartment, risking a further confrontation
with Raymond Lear, in order to retrieve the clothing.

"Who is it?" The tentative voice behind the door was male and
had a faint Italian accent.

"Peter Foley," Pete replied.

"Whatta you want?"

"To speak with Lorenzo Contorno." Though Foley was already standing to one side of the door, he backed off another half step. He'd decided not to carry a weapon into the hotel, so if he was wrong about everything, if the bullets began to fly, his only option was flight.

"About what?"

"Are you him?"

After a brief hesitation, Lorenzo Contorno made the first of what Foley hoped would be many admissions. "Yes," he said.

"Would you mind opening the door?"

"Whatta you want?"

"You think I should just scream it from here in the hallway? About what Proximate Services did for Charlie Terranova? About those videos?"

A heated, though low-pitched, discussion began on the other side of the door. It went on for a moment, then Contorno said, "I can't let you in. I got my family here."

"Then why don't you come out?" In fact, separating Lorenzo from his family was a necessary step in the progression Foley had worked out the night before. "Look, I'm here to help you, Lorenzo. If I was here to hurt you, I wouldn't have knocked on your door and introduced myself. Think about it."

Contorno did, briefly, then asked, "You a cop?"

"I was once, but no longer. Now enough with the bullshit. I'm already attracting attention out here in the hall. Next thing you know, somebody's gonna call security and it'll be over for the both of us."

In an attempt to emphasize his point, Foley placed himself directly in front of the door, then banged it three times with the heel of his hand. By that time, he no longer feared attack.

"Hey, hey, hey. Stop that."

"You gotta show some courage here, Lorenzo. You've got to be a man and not take your family down with you. You've got to accept the fact that you've been caught, put on your coat, come outta there. We'll take a stroll in Central Park and talk things over *mano a mano*. Believe me when I say I'm here to help you. Believe me when I tell you I'm your only hope."

FOLEY WAS never to know which element of his appeal swayed Lorenzo Contorno, the challenge to his masculinity or the offer of aid, but the door opened a moment later and Contorno stepped into the hall, closing the door behind him. Short and chubby, Lorenzo's broad face was all white skin. Skin dominated his small eyes, which were some indeterminate shade between olive and brown, and his short nose. Above a wide fleshy jaw, his mouth was little more than an irregular line with a mournful downturn at either end.

Baby face was the description that sprang to Pete's mind as he led Contorno out of the hotel, down 75th Street and into Central Park. It was a beautiful day, the sky rapidly clearing, the sun bright through the limbs of the budding trees lining the paths. Here and there, the green shoots of daffodils on the move broke through dry winter lawns.

"It's good," Foley declared as he drew a deep and very theatrical breath, "to be out in the sunlight in winter. The streets are so dark, if you're not careful you get depressed." He smiled. "And who needs old Mr. Gloom?"

Contorno said nothing, though his growing anxiety was more than apparent as Foley led him beneath one of the park's many pedestrian bridges to an underpass that must have seemed as dark as the far side of the moon. Still, he came, following along, prepared to meet his fate.

"Something you need to think about," Foley said as he offered Contorno a seat on a sunny bench at the far side of the underpass, "I found you pretty easy and I don't even know you. So you can imagine how easy it'd be for the cops or Charlie Banana."

"I—"

"You don't have to say anything, Lorenzo. I know how it is. In the movies, on the tube, it looks so easy. The bad guy jumps on a plane, the next minute he's in Rio with a Brazilian beach bunny on either arm. Everything's different in real life. In real life you don't even have passports for the whole family. In real life you don't know how to book a flight without revealing your identity. In real life, you can't take a piss without leaving a trail."

Contorno was studying Pete's eyes as though trying to read a foreign language written in an unfamiliar alphabet. He said nothing for a long time, then squared his shoulders and demanded, "Tell me what you want from me."

Foley was unsurprised by the firmer tone, the erect posture. It had suddenly dawned on Contorno that he was not in imminent danger of being arrested or summarily dispatched, that Foley wasn't a cop and wasn't going to kill him either. But Foley could—and did—pop Contorno's half-inflated balloon with practiced ease.

"Listen to me carefully, Lorenzo. I know Proximate Services routinely shipped child pornography for Charlie Terranova. I have Terranova's ledger and Proximate Services is all over the debit side. Now maybe you participated because your life was at stake and you were frightened. I can't say and I'm not here to judge you in any event. All I want is a little bit of information for which I'm willing to exchange my considerable expertise, not to mention my contacts at the Federal Bureau of Investigation."

"I can't go to jail," Contorno said. "I'll never survive. I'm not like Joey and Charlie."

Music to Foley's ears. "Then you need all the advice you can get before you surrender."

Contorno's eyes narrowed and his voice, when he responded, was sly. "Like, from a lawyer?"

"Ordinarily, an attorney would be a good idea, but not in this case."

"Why?"

"Because you have to get off the streets before Joey hunts you down. Accept it, Lorenzo, with Charlie facing life without parole, you're a weak link. But you know that, right? Fear was why you ran in the first place."

"What's that got to do with a lawyer?"

"A lawyer has to listen to your story, then approach somebody in the Justice Department, then make a proffer, then negotiate terms. In the meantime, you're still on the street where Joey might find you. The way I'm gonna work it, you and your family go into protective custody this afternoon, plus you get a lawyer from jump street which allows you to negotiate from a place of safety. If your story holds up, if you were really a victim, it's just a short step to the witness protection program and a new life. Plus, you have to consider a third possibility which is that I hand Charlie's ledger to the FBI and they take you right off the street. If that should happen, not only will your bargaining power be greatly diminished, you'll be incarcerated at the federal lockup on West Street instead of a hotel. Somehow, I don't think that's a positive outcome for you."

"You'd do that?" Contorno asked.

"Not right away, Lorenzo. First, I'll break every bone in your body to get that little bit of information I'm after. Then I'll hand over what's left of you." Foley winked as he gave Contorno's arm a squeeze. "I'm highly motivated here," he declared. "You should really take that into consideration."

28

WHEN CONTORNO finally broke, the words bubbled out of his mouth like water from an opened tap. Exoneration was what he was after, as though Foley was his confessor and not his interrogator. Foley listened patiently, as priests often do, while Contorno related his tale of woe.

Proximate Services, or so Lorenzo claimed, was a freight forwarder, clearing merchandise through customs, than re-shipping via common carrier to retailers and warehouses throughout the country. It was all on the square and might have remained that way if Contorno hadn't had the misfortune to be seated alongside Joey 'Cadillac' Novarro, his nephew, at a wedding in 1997. Lorenzo had gotten tipsy enough to brag about his business success to Joey Cadillac who'd been absolutely fascinated by Proximate's day-to-day operations, asking one question after another.

Two months later, accompanied by his boss, Charlie Terranova, Joey Cadillac visited Proximate's offices to request a favor. Just this one time, help us out please. When Lorenzo demurred, citing the potential threat to his family and his livelihood if he should involve himself in some illegal activity, Terranova had made it clear that the favor they asked could not be refused.

"My life was on the line," Contorno explained. "It was do what they said or have my brains blown out."

Predictably, Contorno had chosen the first option. After all, the only thing Charlie and Joey asked was that a crate delivered to Proximate's warehouse be relabeled and reshipped to an address they would provide.

"What you're lookin' at here," Joey had explained. "Is pirated software. *Windows* and all like that. There's no fuckin' risk."

Contorno had been less than satisfied with this rationale. Nevertheless, he'd put the cash Charlie insisted that he take in his pocket and gone along with the program for six months, until Joey Cadillac upped the ante. From now on, the crates were to be opened and the contents reboxed and shipped to several different addresses.

Only then, Contorno claimed, did he become aware of what he was handling.

"It was filth," he declared to Peter Foley, "It was evil. *Malvagio*. It damns my soul forever."

Somehow, neither Charlie nor Joey saw it that way. From their point of view, kiddie porn was just another way to make money.

"They tell me," Lorenzo told Foley, "that I got a beautiful daughter. She's comin' up on her first Holy Communion. What a shame it would be if she never got to wear her pretty white dress."

"You know," Foley said after a moment, "the FBI—they're gonna put you on a polygraph. If you're lying, they'll bury you in some federal pen for the rest of your life."

Contorno's protest was so quick, his tone so indignant that Foley waved him off. Having established the man's truthfulness to his own satisfaction, it was time to ask the big question. Foley's heart gave a distinct flutter as he crossed his fingers before speaking. "These shipments you received," he said, "you mind telling me where they came from?"

Lorenzo shook his head. "The crates were delivered by a van. There was no return address on the crates."

"But you do know where the merchandise went after you repacked it?"

"I kept a list."

"Just in case you were arrested?"

Contorno smiled that little sly smile again. "Just in case," he admitted.

Foley took a small notebook and a pen from his pocket. "Alright, time to go to work," he declared. "First, do you remember handling a tape called *Patti's Dance* sometime around last Christmas?"

Contorno took a few seconds to search his memory, then said, "Yes, I remember they had pink labels and that nobody wanted them. I had to throw two cartons of tapes into the bay. Charlie was very pissed off."

SPECIAL AGENT Raymond Lear, when Foley called three hours later, jumped at Foley's peace offering. Lear had known Foley too long to doubt his judgment. The agent was annoyed only because Foley had promised Contorno access to a lawyer before questioning. But that, Foley knew, was a minor quibble for Raymond Lear who was not motivated by ambition, like most of his colleagues, but by a sharply drawn distinction between good and evil. Raised on a farm in Kansas, Lear was a Pentecostal by birth and by inclination.

Nevertheless, the transfer was tedious. Lorenzo's wife, Emily, had come near to hysteria over the thought of losing contact with her sister. Said hysteria was then visited on the adolescent children, whose every hope for happiness depended upon remaining at St. Angela's Academy until they graduated.

Foley responded with the necessary reassurances. Charlie Terranova and his crew were not made men, he explained, but ordinary gangsters. Once put away, they would be promptly forgotten. Thus any separation would only be temporary. Besides, if their lawyer worked it right, the Contornos would be allowed to retain their assets and the new life they started would be no less comfortable than the one they left behind.

Through it all, Foley made a continuing effort to suppress the dark thoughts flicking across his consciousness like tracer rounds across a moonless sky. His best hope for discovering the origin of the *Patti's Dance* tape had crapped out and he was no closer to finding his daughter than on the day he showed her photograph to Matsunaga. Those were the facts, ma'am. Matsunaga was gone, Contorno didn't know, Charlie Terranova was incarcerated.

Which left Joey Cadillac who maybe knew, who maybe wasn't gone, who would kill Peter Foley as soon as look at him.

29

JULIA BRENNAN was standing on 78th Street, a hundred yards from York Avenue, when she first caught sight of Peter Foley. He was walking toward her, a tall handsome man in a wool coat and suit that seemed wrong for his quick athletic stride. To his credit—or so Julia thought—that stride did not shrink by so much as a millimeter when he finally saw her leaning against the fender of his car. Instead, his reaction was limited to the beginnings of a quizzical smile. Julia could almost see his mind working the possibilities when his eyes jumped to Bert Griffith and Betty Cohen seated in a department Ford parked down the block.

By the time Foley stopped a few feet away from Julia, his smile had widened slightly. "I take it," he said, "you had that family meeting with Reid and Corry."

"I did," Julia replied. "I took the position that you were an unrepentant scumbag who should be left to boil in his self-created cauldron."

"But you were outvoted?"

"Something like that."

Foley walked around the car and knelt by the passenger door. He reached beneath the rear quarter panel, fumbled around for a moment, finally came up holding a small metal box. "Yesterday," he said, "you fell to one knee when you left the car. Nice move."

Julia stretched out her hand. "Better let me get that back where it belongs. It's an expensive model, sends a signal up to a satellite." Julia pointed to the sky. "Funny, that satellite is just a tiny little speck up there, but it knows exactly where you are at all times. Never falls asleep on a stakeout, never needs a bathroom break."

"It doesn't know where *you* are," Foley pointed out as he handed the transmitter to Julia. "It only knows where the box is."

"And just think how many boxes I could have planted on this car in the four hours I've been waiting for you." When Foley didn't reply, Julia went on. "SCU's been assigned the Habib al Rif'at homicide. Me and Bert and Betty, we're heading up the team."

Though they continued to stare into each other's eyes, a silence stretched out between them. Julia was anxious not to give anything away, especially the part of her that wanted to jump his bones right then and there, or the part of her that selfishly wished he'd never shown Patti's photo to the man who identified her, or the part of her that dreaded the prospect of losing him forever.

"We're in sync on this." She gestured to Griffith and Cohen, remembering Betty's reply to her request for aid: *If it was my kid, I'd be stockpiling weapons of mass destruction.* "We're ready to help you find Patti and we've got badges. If that's what you want."

"Why," Foley asked, his smile gradually expanding, "do I think something very bad will happen if that's what I *don't* want?"

"Because you and I, Peter Foley, are of the same flesh. What I know, you know. What you know, I know."

Foley's cool melted away like an ice cube in a pizza oven. Looking into his eyes, Julia saw a gray trail of regret and sorrow retreating back into a region of the human brain that does not think, that can only feel. She closed her eyes for a moment, selfishly, in the vain hope that Foley's sorrow would remain where it was. Then she was in his arms, her face pressed against his shoulder, eyes filling again.

It was pure luxury, his hands against her back, the strength of his arms, and Julia would have liked to remain where she was, to put off all the rest, but that was impossible. They would have to thrash it out later that night. Corry had been sent to stay with her uncle for the duration, a price she'd reluctantly accepted as the cost of her demand that Peter Foley be rescued from himself. Hence, Foley and Julia would have Julia's Woodside home to themselves.

As she broke free, Julia glanced at Betty Cohen and Bert Griffith. Betty was wiping a tear from her eye with a tissue. Bert, on the other hand, merely wet the tip of his finger before making a note on the little pad he carried everywhere.

"Somehow," Julia told Foley, "I think I'm gonna have trouble reestablishing my command presence."

As THEY walked toward First Avenue in search of a midafternoon lunch, Julia related the particulars of her remedy if Foley had refused her offer. The purpose of the lunch was to bring everybody up to speed and to formulate a strategy. Bert and Betty trailed behind on the narrow sidewalk, their conversation focused on Steve Liebman. Now that the thrill of victory had worn off, it was clear to both that Stevie had committed that most heinous of crimes, Contempt of Cop, and that he was going to skate. The very heavens, according to Bert, cried out for justice.

Oblivious, Julia took Foley's arm. "What I was planning to do," she told him, "if you crapped out on me, is throw you into the system, bounce you from precinct to precinct. The way I figured, if I called in every marker and signed enough IOUs to keep me in hock for the rest of my career, I could send you spinning for the next four days while I fumbled around looking for Patti."

"Fumbled?"

"Without your help, that's what it would be."

"Were you at all worried that I might lose her in the process?"

Instead of answering, Julia began to the describe the current status of the Habib al Rif'at murder investigation. She'd been in touch, she told him, with a sergeant over at the Crime Scene Unit and with the Assistant Medical Examiner who performed the autopsy. Neither had produced a shred of relevant evidence. According the AME, the shooter was standing at least three feet away when the fatal shot was fired, but might have been on the other side of the room. Worse, the bullet was useless for forensic analysis because it had broken into many small fragments.

The crime scene was no more promising. There were tons of fingerprints, of course, but certain key areas, like the trunk containing the illegal tapes, had clearly been wiped. Thus it was unlikely that the killer's prints would be found among the hundreds collected. Neither was the blood evidence expected to be of use, mainly because there wasn't much of it.

"Habib was shot once in the forehead," Julia explained. "He died instantly and external bleeding was minimal, so the killer wasn't contaminated. Not if he was standing at least three feet away and we know he was."

But the lack of physical evidence wasn't the only problem. OCCB, the Organized Crime Control Bureau, had linked Habib to a gangster named Charlie Terranova who was currently in a federal lockup awaiting a bail hearing. As Charlie was a notoriously violent sociopath, the local dicks could hardly be blamed for believing Habib to be a permanently severed link in the chain that bound Terranova.

Julia went on for a bit, describing the local detectives' futile efforts to uncover witnesses among the prostitutes working beneath the Gowanus Expressway before she finally lapsed into silence. The silence extended briefly, until Peter Foley took her hand in his, then without so much as glancing in her direction, said, "If I loved you any more, Julia Brennan, I'd explode."

30

THEY ATE a hearty lunch, the four of them, at Jimmy's Joint on First Avenue. Though excellently prepared, the ribs and fries Julia consumed with guilty pleasure were greasy enough (she was sure) to sink directly below her waist, somehow bypassing her digestive system altogether. The illusion was so strong that she could, as she continued to fill her mouth, sense her buttocks expand, her thighs coagulate, her very ankles swell. Nevertheless, she paid close attention to the story Peter Foley related, and to the fact that he related it without undue prompting and in precise detail.

Foley first described his meeting with Toshi Matsunaga at the behest of Special Agent Raymond Lear, sparing no element of the methods he'd used to persuade Matsunaga to reveal the source of the *Patti's Dance* tape: Charlie Terranova. From there, he skipped to Proximate Services and Lorenzo Contorno, concentrating on the most important facts uncovered before the man was turned over to the FBI. At no time did he mention Habib al Rif'at.

"Contorno told me that he's been getting monthly deliveries of kiddie porn through a common truck bay on the first floor of his building. These deliveries arrived without warning and Contorno didn't learn about them until he was notified by security just before the merchandise was unloaded." Foley paused long enough to empty the lost drops of his coffee. "Now, Lorenzo might have gone to the loading dock and personally supervised the delivery, but not being the boldest of fellows, he had no desire to look into the eyes of anyone associated with those tapes. So what he did was watch the operation from his office window on the third floor, too far away to get a plate number. But Lorenzo did notice something strange about the van that made the drops. The van was a green Ford Econoline, a commercial model with no windows or lettering on the sides. What was unusual was that it had a white spoiler over the back doors. Spoilers are for kids and hot rods, not delivery vans. At least according to Lorenzo."

"A green van with a white spoiler?" Griffith observed after a moment. "Ya know, Pete, you tell a good story, but somehow I can't see how that helps us."

Foley dipped a french fry into a little vat of brown gravy and ate it with evident relish. "I'm only telling you what I know," he said.

"Which isn't much."

"What could I say, Bert? I know where I have to go, but I can't seem to get there." Foley dipped another fry, then held it between his thumb and forefinger. "Right now, Terranova's lieutenant, Joey 'Cadillac' Navarro, is my only hope."

A waiter approached the table and Julia ordered a pot of coffee. She was trying to manufacture some strategy by which Joey Cadillac might be separated from his crew, at least briefly. But no matter how she spun it, the same message rose to the top of her crystal ball: False arrest. Of course, they could always snatch Joey off the street, torture him until he talked, then kill him and dump his body in the river. But that wasn't a place she was willing to go, not even for Peter Foley, not even for his daughter. She would go there for her own daughter, though, and she knew it. She would go there for Corry in a heartbeat.

"We're getting nowhere," Betty Cohen declared after a few minutes of discussion. "With his boss in the slammer, Joey's gotta be lawyered up. We grab him without probable cause, the ACLU will have us for breakfast."

"There is one thing," Foley said after a moment. "Contorno gave me a list of the addresses he reshipped to. The FBI will have these addresses whenever Contorno's debriefed, but they won't act on them right away because they never act on anything right away. Slow is their game and we should be able to take advantage. If we move fast."

Julia's smile was rueful. Foley had begun devising his strategy the minute he laid eyes on her. More than likely, he'd been devising it still when he declared his near-to-bursting love. Whether or not that love was genuine was irrelevant; in fact, Julia was certain that Foley had been absolutely sincere. But Foley was not prepared to put Julia Brennan, or anybody else, ahead of Patti.

"Spell it out, Pete," she said. "Tell us what you have in mind."

Foley nodded once, then looked directly at Julia. "One of the addresses Contorno gave me is a porno bookstore, KRS Books and Videos in Queens Plaza where I made a buy six months ago. While I was in the store, Joey Cadillac arrived with two of his boys. They went into a back office without asking permission. That means Joey and Charlie have a piece of the action, at least."

Bert Griffith interrupted. "The FBI," he asked, "do they know about this?"

"They've had it for months, Bert. That's what I mean by slow."

"Tell me," Betty Cohen said, "about this store. Could you make another buy there?"

"The man I dealt with—his name's Maurice Wilson—still works at KRS. I know because I called from Contorno's hotel room and he answered the phone."

"You tell him who you were?"

"Yeah."

"And what did he say?"

"Come on over." Again, Foley looked at Julia. "What I planned to do before I found you in possession of my car," he told her, "was convince Maurice that his life depended on getting Joey Cadillac into that store."

"But now you have a better idea."

Foley leaned forward. "Register me as a confidential informant. That way, if I make a buy at KRS, you can use my affidavit to get an arrest warrant for Wilson and a search warrant for the store. Then all we have to do is lure Joey Cadillac into KRS before you hit the place. I'll take care of that myself."

A question, apparent to Julia, hung over the table when Foley stopped speaking: What happens next? It was a question she'd hoped to avoid, a question Peter Foley would not let her avoid. He wanted to know where the lines were being drawn and Julia, for her part, would have been more than happy to tell him—if she, herself, had known.

"Why don't we register you and make the buy," she said, "then call it a night. What I heard on the news this morning, tomorrow's gonna be a sunny day."

* * *

THREE HOURS later, the paperwork completed, Julia watched Peter Foley walk into KRS Books and Videos. She was sitting in the backseat of the department Ford. Betty Cohen was behind the wheel, Bert Griffith alongside her. Bert was talking about his second son, Kenneth, who'd won honorable mention at a Townsend High School science fair. That was all to the good, especially because Townsend High was one New York City's best schools. But Kenneth wasn't satisfied. He felt that he should have won, that his failure to do so was the result of racist policies fostered by the school's administration. All his friends agreed with him.

"I told him, 'Kenny, you've got to stop findin' sheets under every bed.' You know what he said to me?"

"What?" Betty asked.

"He said, 'They don't keep the sheets under the bed anymore. They wave 'em in your face.'" Bert slapped the steering wheel with the palm of his hand. "Swear, Betty, I wanted to put a phone book on the boy's head."

Bert's *phone book* was a reference to the bad old days in the NYPD when confessions were routinely coerced. One especially beloved method was to place a phone book on a suspect's head, then slam it with a nightstick. Though incredibly painful, the technique left no marks—on the outside.

When Bert began to list the pernicious effects of rap music on the young and vulnerable, Julia tuned out. Bert was a lifelong jazz fan and he'd been over this ground before. For a short time, Julia's mind drifted as she stared through the window at the hookers working her side of the street, at the cars pulling up, the quick negotiations.

Broad enough to accommodate sixteen lanes of traffic, Queens Plaza might have been a truly impressive space. This was especially true at its western end where the plaza swept up onto the 59th Street Bridge with its elaborately braced towers, towers that were mere foreground to the skyline of midtown Manhattan. That possibility had been precluded, however, when the city fathers divided the plaza with a pair of elevated subway lines, stacked one atop the other. These lines stood thirty feet above the plaza, supported by perpetually rusting girders. Morning and night, at the height of the rush hour, a train passed over their tracks every three minutes.

No surprise, then, that Queens Plaza had been a working stroll for as long as Julia could remember.

A s B E R T continued to vent, Julia's thoughts settled on Corry Brennan. Twenty-four hours before, Julia had explained Pete's situation to her daughter and uncle as concisely as possible. She'd expected a strong reaction from Corry, but not a bone-white blanch. And what she wondered now, as she watched the night unfold, was if her daughter was still under the spell of 9-11, if it was possible to be as close to the flame as Corry and not be burned. These days, it seemed as if Corry feared all loss. Her closets were jammed with outgrown clothing.

"Captain?"

At the sound of Betty's voice, Julia returned to the present. "Yes?"

"I was wondering what you thought."

"About what?"

Far too respectful of the chain of command to directly accuse her boss of being a space cadet, Betty merely smiled her chipmunk smile. "We were talking about Pete."

"And?"

"We decided that Pete's not playing in our ball park. We're playing in his."

"That's what he thinks." Julia shook her hair out of her face. "He won't betray us, though. He'll use us when it's to his advantage and desert us whenever it's convenient, but he won't set us up to take a fall."

"Does he know that?"

"Yeah, he does."

"What makes you so sure?"

"Because Peter Foley is in love with me." She hesitated briefly, a smile playing on her lips. "And because Peter Foley, in his heart of hearts, is just another priest-haunted Irishman."

"Ah," Betty declared, "the ace in the hole."

31

WHEN FOLEY emerged from the bathroom into the upper hallway of Julia Brennan's Woodside home, he stepped directly onto a hard metal object. Looking down as he yanked his foot away, he saw the buckle of the belt he'd been wearing only an hour before. The belt, he noted, was at the very end of a trail of clothing that ran the length of the hall to the stairs.

Under other circumstances, Foley might have ignored the mess in his eagerness to return to the bedroom and Julia, but he knew he was going to don these clothes on the following morning because they were the only clothes he had. Thus he gathered them, his and Julia's, following the trail all the way to the front door.

It was mistake and Foley knew it when he reentered Julia's bedroom to find her wrapped in a chaste white robe that fell to her ankles. She was perched on the edge of the bed, her eyes somber and determined, while he was standing buck naked, his dignity shielded only by the clothing piled in his arms.

"You have me at a disadvantage, madam," he declared.

"Yesterday," she said, ignoring both his comment and his predicament, "I didn't think of you once. I should have known something was wrong when you didn't return my calls because we never play those kinds of games with each other. But I didn't. I never thought of you at all. I wanted Adeline Rose's killer and there wasn't room for anything else."

Julia somehow crossed her legs without exposing a square inch of her flesh. Foley watched in amazement. What she was saying, though, came as no surprise.

"The worst part," Julia continued, "was that the victim was such an ugly human being that I really didn't think about her either. It was the scalp I wanted, the trophy, another triumph for Julia Brennan."

Foley was about to offer the truth as an excuse. He was about to tell her that she was just a cop, with a cop's instincts for the kill, but Julia's *mea culpa* was not yet complete.

"I can't stop thinking about the case even now." She pulled the robe tight across her chest. "Tell me, have you ever known a homicide suspect to conceal an unbreakable alibi?"

"Yeah, to cover up an infidelity."

"Liebman's not married and Mai Ling from Peony Escorts wouldn't qualify as a lover anyway. No, this asshole wanted us to think he had opportunity, even though he knew he'd be the focus of the investigation." Julia was silent for a moment; then she smiled, her shoulders relaxing slightly. "What am I gonna do," she asked, "when they finally put me behind a desk?"

There was no way Foley could answer that question and he didn't try. There had always been tension between Julia's pleasure in the hunt and her ambition. In the past, she'd been able to keep both balls in the air while she moved up the ranks, and she was juggling still. As a captain, the only reason she wasn't already behind a desk was the significance of the Sex Crimes Unit to various women's groups in New York. Putting a captain in charge was the mayor's way of acknowledging that significance and the votes it represented.

But Julia could not remain at SCU forever. The job didn't allow for permanent posts. Within a year, and probably sooner, she would be transferred to some administrative duty where she would push that pencil until the day she retired.

Julia finally broke the silence. "What are you doing with those clothes?" she asked.

"I was going to put yours in the hamper and hang mine up."

"So, why don't you?"

Out of options, Foley complied, prancing from the hamper to the closet, acutely aware of Julia's evaluating gaze. He was standing in front of the closet, gathering hangers, when she declared, "Ya know something, Peter Foley, you have a nice ass. And your shoulders aren't hairy, either."

"Two for two," Foley observed.

"But you haven't had a haircut in a while and you're getting a bit shaggy in the back. And your toenails could use a little work."

"Is that it?" Foley slid his pants and jacket onto a hanger.

"No, turn around."

"If I turn around, Ms. Brennan, I'm gonna tear that robe off your body."

Julia's reply was immediately forthcoming. "What robe?" she asked.

* * *

I T W A S characteristic of his and Julia's relationship, Foley mused later on, that their betrayals brought them closer together. He was lying on his side, his body spooned into hers, his fingers idly drifting through her hair. It was very late and they had to be up and moving at a reasonable hour. Foley thought Julia already asleep, or at the very least beyond questions of guilt and innocence, but she surprised him again.

"Did you kill Habib al Rif'at?" she asked.

"I did," Foley replied without hesitation, having hours before considered the near impossibility of lying to Julia without getting caught.

"Was he reaching for a gun?"

"Julia, I entered his place of business and threatened his life. If anybody has a claim to self-defense, it's Habib."

"Answer the question, Pete."

"I'll answer both questions, the one you asked and the one you didn't. Habib al Rif'at was reaching for a weapon when I shot him, but I don't know what I would have done if he hadn't resisted. Without doubt, killing him was among the leading possibilities."

He felt Julia move away from him, rolling forward a mere fraction of an inch. That was the cop part of her, drawing those straight lines between right and wrong.

"I think about Corry," Julia said. "If it was Corry out there, I know I'd do anything to get to her."

Hours earlier, when Foley had emerged from KRS Books and Videos bearing, among other items of evidence, a copy of *Patti's Dance*, the detectives who received it had finally understood exactly what was at stake. Nobody had spoken, not for a long time; nobody looked at anybody else as they collectively imagined their own children starring in a similar production. Foley had watched

from the backseat, half amused. Detectives Cohen, Griffith, and
Brennan were staring out through his eyes and they didn't like
what they saw. They didn't like it one bit.

AT TEN o'clock on the following morning, Foley made a single
phone call, after which he surrendered control of the search for
Patti on the promise of ten minutes alone with Joey Navarro.
What he told himself, as he dialed, was that acting alone he could
not take Navarro off the street, even if he lured him to some
lonely rendezvous. He could not even guarantee the man would
come to that rendezvous unarmed or alone.

So he was resigned when he punched Navarro's home number
(supplied by a friendly lieutenant at OCCB) into the phone and
closed the door of the booth. A young girl answered, her voice
uncertain as she said, then repeated, "Huh-woe, huh-woe."

In the background, Pete heard a man say, "Angelina, give Daddy
the phone."

"Ho-kay."

A moment later, a man's voice declared, "Yeah?"

"Joey?"

"Who wants to know?"

"The man who has Habib al Rif'at's ledger."

"What?"

"The man who knows all about Proximate Services and Lorenzo
Contorno. Who knows about KRS Books and Videos. Who knows
enough to put you in prison for the rest of your life."

For a time, long enough to be suspenseful, Pete listened to
Navarro pant into the phone. Pete imagined the man's anger, the
unreasoning rage of the frustrated psychopath. He knew there was

nothing for it except to wait patiently. Sooner or later, Navarro would realize there was only one path open to him. At least for the moment.

Navarro took that path when he finally asked the appropriate question. "What do you want?"

"Are you Joey Navarro?"

"I'm not gonna say who I am on the fuckin' telephone."

"That's probably a good idea," Foley said. "Why don't I give you a number. You can call me back from somewhere safe. Like in thirty minutes or less."

"Look—"

"I should warn you, though. If my call isn't returned, I'm gonna run over to the FBI, see if maybe there's a reward out for your ass."

"That's it?"

"No, one thing more. I know where to find Lorenzo Contorno. Just in case you're interested."

THE WAIT was shorter than Foley expected, a mere eighteen minutes until the phone rang in the booth. By that time, Novarro had calmed considerably. "Yeah," he announced, "I'm Joey Navarro. What the fuck do you want?"

"I want to do a little job for you."

"What?"

Foley repeated his request. "I want to do a little job for you."

"Listen, you got a name?"

"Goober."

"Bullshit."

"Listen to me, Joey. I know where your Uncle Lorenzo is hiding and you don't. I can kill him and you can't." Pete gave it a couple of beats. "You hear what I'm saying? I can solve your problem or I can be your problem. It's up to you."

Navarro didn't hesitate, which led Pete to conclude that the man was about to lie.

"Okay, I'll bite. Whatta you want?"

"Twenty grand for Contorno, payment in advance."

"In advance? You gotta be kiddin' me."

"Tonight, Joey, at nine o'clock. I'm not gonna wait for you."

"Hey, you know who you're fuckin' with here?" Navarro finally lost control. "Are you crazy?"

"KRS Books and Videos. Nine o'clock. Don't be late."

32

JULIA BRENNAN was a woman given to details. Details and her attention to them had played a significant part in her rise within a New York Police Department that ran on paperwork like any other bureaucracy. Ever the obsessive, Julia's paperwork, from the beginning, was near perfect, as were her handwriting, spelling and grammar. That alone would have garnered favorable mention on the yearly evaluations prepared by her immediate supervisors, but Julia's attention to the little things was also reflected in the way she handled evidence and processed the hapless felons she and her partner arrested, in her always being within her sector when jobs were dispatched or the street sergeant came calling, in her ready acceptance of overtime assignments despite the pressing necessities of single motherhood.

In the early stages of her career, before the ambitious side of her
personality revealed itself, Julia had been motivated by a general
unwillingness to endure the criticism of her male superiors. Later,
she'd come to understand that reliability was an advantage she
could trade upon. You might not like Julia Brennan (or women
cops in general), but when you gave her a job it got done on time,
every *t* crossed, every *i* dotted.

On the day of the KRS raid, Julia applied both her instincts and
her experience to the forthcoming assault. Like any other cop,
Julia knew (even as soldiers and politicians and gangbangers know)
that the most prudent course in any potentially violent confrontation is to present your enemy with a show of overwhelming
force. Hence, Julia wanted cops stationed inside KRS when Joey
Cadillac made his appearance. She could have chosen these officers
from within SCU's team of investigators, but she preferred cops
with experience working undercover. Posing as ordinary customers, they would have to drift into KRS before Navarro's arrival
and remain there, inconspicuous, until the main force charged
through the door.

Julia had a second reason for using undercovers, one that cap-
tured her attention. Like most pornography outlets, the windows
of KRS Books and Videos were covered by thick plastic shades,
thus affording privacy to the browsers inside. That was to Julia's
advantage because her team could approach KRS without being
observed. Unless Navarro, fearing a trap, stationed a guard outside.

A guard, Julia believed, or even a pair of guards, would easily
be overcome by the show of force she intended to present. Julia's
main fear was that once she and her team made their appearance,
the guard would duck inside to warn his boss. Given the probability of there being a legitimate customer or two inside KRS, that
warning might lead to a hostage situation.

Hostage situations caused by clumsy assaults on retail businesses were a definite no-no down at One Police Plaza. Especially when Julia might have prevented that hostage situation merely by taking Maurice Wilson down as he opened the store on the following day. Bottom line, lives were being put at risk in order to trap Joey Cadillac and those lives had to be protected. Assuming there were customers in KRS when Joey Cadillac arrived, the first job of the undercovers would be to ensure their safety.

What they called it, in the legal world, was due diligence.

JULIA MIGHT have reached out to Narcotics or the Street Crimes Unit, but chose Vice instead because she owed Inspector John Hammond, Manhattan Vice commander, a favor. The work of Vice representing perhaps the grimiest aspect of New York policing, the division rarely drew the attention of the media. Now they would have a chance to shine.

When Julia finally got through to him, Hammond acknowledged his appreciation, then reminded Julia that it was Sunday, that most of his people were enjoying a peaceful morning with their families, that she wasn't giving him a lot of notice.

"I see your point, John," Julia replied, "but the window of opportunity is too small here. It's gotta be tonight at nine o'clock or we lose Joey Navarro. If you can't do it, I'll have to look elsewhere."

As John Hammond's definition of "elsewhere" was confined to rival commanding officers like Inspector Mark Price at Narcotics who already got too much undeserved publicity, he capitulated without further dissent. By five o'clock, at the latest, Julia would have four Vice cops in SCU's squad room ready for briefing.

"You want a woman?" Hammond finally asked.

Julia thought it over. "Would you mind rephrasing that?"

Hammond laughed. "On the team," he explained.

"I don't want to be disrespectful, John, but wouldn't a woman be somewhat out of place in a porno bookstore?"

"Not necessarily. Hookers sometimes take their johns into the stores to rent videos. The johns, I'm told, find the tapes stimulating."

Julia nodded to herself. This was why she'd sought outside help. Having never worked undercover or supervised an undercover unit, she was woefully lacking in practical experience and not too proud to admit it.

"A female will be just fine," she said, "and don't spare the latex."

WITH HAMMOND out of the way, Julia postponed a decision she would eventually have to make, concentrating instead on the search warrant for KRS, the arrest warrant for Maurice Wilson, and an ADA named Alice Merkerson.

Everything, Merkerson complained while her fingers worked furiously at a computer keyboard, was complicated by its being a Sunday. As the rookie on Lily Han's prosecutorial team, Alice had been drafted for the duration. Lily Han herself did not expect to show up until after the arrests had been made, and only if Joey Cadillac was among the arrested. Otherwise, Julia had been instructed to dump whomever she busted into the system and let Alice handle the resulting paperwork.

"It'll take me a couple of hours," Alice explained, "to hunt up a judge, get these signed."

"I'm not worried about it, Alice. If Lily didn't have faith in you, she wouldn't have given you the assignment."

Alice got the message and was gone a moment later, followed by Julia who entered the squad room to find Betty, Pete and Bert gathered before a laptop computer. Betty was frantically working a joystick while the machine gave off a series of improbable grunts, groans and whistles before finally erupting in a hailstorm of explosions.

"Damn," Betty said as she handed the console to Bert. "Damn, damn, damn. Those mutants are too quick."

Pete looked up and caught sight of Julia standing just outside her office. "You've stepped into a very competitive environment," he explained. "They're playing for lunch."

"Speaking of lunch, why don't we order in? I have to make a decision and I want to talk it over."

THE QUESTION she put to her team, over two pizzas and several quarts of soda, was quite simple: Did they need more help? The answer, however, was not so simple. Julia could, if she chose, call in a full-out Emergency Services Unit SWAT team. She could procure the whole nine yards, from the flak jackets to the visored helmets to the street-sweeper shotguns. If Joey Cadillac showed up, if he brought along company, the end would justify the means. But what if it was just Maurice Wilson and an army of cops? In that case, they would look ridiculous.

Then there was the fact that Joey Cadillac saw himself as an Italian gangster and Italian gangsters preferred to fight their legal battles with lawyers, not bullets. Surprised by undercovers who would draw their weapons and expose their badges while a second team burst through the door, how likely were they to fight?

Not very. That was the consensus which Bert Griffith was reenforced with an observation guaranteed to start the testosterone flowing: "You call in a SWAT team, we're gonna have to cool our heels outside until they decide it's safe enough for us to enter. Somehow, that's not my idea of being a cop."

Julia might have pointed out that SWAT teams were trained to
secure dangerous scenes and SCU detectives were not. Just as SCU
detectives were trained to investigate sex-related crimes and SWAT
teams were not. She didn't. Instead, she nodded final agreement,
then announced, "But I'm going to borrow some uniforms from
the local precinct. When we come through the door, I don't want
anybody inside misunderstanding our motives."

Already compiling a list of which SCU detectives she would call
in, Julia looked from Bert to Peter Foley. Foley hadn't opened his
mouth except to put food into it. That meant, or so Julia hoped,
that he'd accepted his role which was to remain in the backseat of
an unmarked Crown Victoria parked blocks from KRS Books and
Videos. Eventually, if all went well, Navarro would be placed in
that backseat alongside Peter Foley. Eventually. If all went well.

33

WHEN THE undercovers from Vice presented themselves exactly at five o'clock, there was no woman among them. Instead, Hammond had sent an enormous black cop named Rashid Lamb in full-out drag. Rashid wore enough metallic green eye shadow to blind a peacock. His lips were cherry red and his impossibly blond wig hung to the center of his back. Trimmed in sequins, a latex miniskirt barely concealed his gender.

Julia's team, already assembled, was awestruck, especially by Rashid's artificial bosom which projected from his chest as if he'd stuffed his bra with a pair of footballs. Carlos Serrano, who'd been drafted for the operation along with Harry McDonald, was especially impressed. He stared hard at Rashid for a moment, until Rashid bent over to kiss the bald head of the luckless Vice cop chosen to be his john, then whistled appreciatively. The john was named Gilbert Morrisey and he wiped the lipstick off the top of his hairless skull with a white handkerchief.

"Life is tough," he announced, patting Rashid's butt, "and you gotta take what you can get. Anybody got a stepladder?"

The other two undercovers, Nick Puzo and Arnold Espinoza, nodded thoughtfully, as if the subject had already come up too many times to mention.

After a quick briefing, Julia led her entourage, including Peter Foley, to the 108th Precinct in Long Island City where she found three uniformed cops, all volunteers, ready and waiting. They introduced themselves as officers Larry Minh, Sharon Carr, and Dexter Montgomery. Though Bert Griffith was handling the arrangements with the locals, Julia evaluated the recruits carefully.

Young and well scrubbed, their eagerness was apparent in their attentive eyes, in their straight backs and pressed lips, in their snappy uniforms and polished brogans. They reminded Julia of her first days on patrol. In order to rise, you needed an appointment to one of the squads that were favored by the brass. In order to secure that appointment, you needed to attract the attention of someone higher up the ladder, someone who had the power to make your dreams come true. You needed to find your first rabbi.

"Alright," Julia said. They were gathered in a small room on the third floor of the precinct. The room was bare except for a few scattered chairs and a blackboard. "I'm gonna brief you in depth a half hour from now. What I want you to do in the meantime is get to know each other's faces. If worse comes to worse, we don't want to be shooting each other."

That said, Julia headed off to find and thank Lieutenant Frank Flynn who'd authorized her use of his patrol officers. For Julia, this detail, this glad-handing, was second nature. You made friends whenever possible. You chose your enemies carefully.

Flynn's eyes widened in surprise when Julia walked into his office on the second floor. Small and wiry, he rose to his feet, his lips expanding into a lopsided smile, then reached across a desk piled with manila folders to take her hand.

"Hey, no big deal," he said. "Just bring 'em back alive."

As Julia returned to the third floor, she ran the details back and forth. She paused only once, at the top of the stairs, to consider Peter Foley. Not only had she offered no explanation for his presence, either to the undercovers or to Flynn's uniformed officers, she had yet to mention that he wasn't a cop. Foley had introduced himself by name without mentioning his rank. Or lack thereof.

Julia walked to the front of the room, picked up a piece of chalk and began to sketch the interior of KRS Books on the blackboard. She drew a basic rectangle with the rear two-thirds divided by a row of shelving stacked with video tapes. The front of the store, devoted to various marital aids, was left open. At the rear, a poorly drawn door indicated the entrance to a back office and not to the street. In fact, the only way in or out of KRS Books and Videos was through the front.

"Listen up," Julia said. "First thing, let's deal with the office in the back. It's possible, maybe even likely, that Joey Navarro will go into that office before the assault team arrives. But even if he doesn't, we have to assume that somebody's in there. Rashid, once the assault begins, the door becomes your personal responsibility. It's your job to control anyone who opens it. Understood?"

Rashid nodded once and Julia pointed at another of the Vice undercovers, Gil Morrisey, Rashid's john. "Gil, you're gonna go in wired. If Joey shows up alone, tap the transmitter three times. If he has company, tap four times. If it gets to be nine-fifteen and he hasn't arrived, look for us at the front door. I won't leave you in there for more than a half hour."

"Praise the Lord," Rashid answered. "It's well known that I can't hold out for more than thirty minutes."

Julia ignored the banter and continued, piling up the details. The undercover team would wear light body armor while the assault team would don flak jackets with the letters NYPD stenciled on the front and back. The undercover team would be ferried the eight blocks between the precinct and KRS in unmarked cars while the assault team would use ordinary patrol cars. The undercover team would be dropped three blocks from KRS while the assault team would proceed directly to the store. The undercover team would separate innocent bystanders from bad guys. The assault team would divide upon entry—first cop to the right, second to the left, and so on—in order to cover the two aisles.

By the time she finished, Julia was acutely aware of a thick layer of glaze dulling the eyes of her borrowed officers. Her own detectives, by contrast, were paying careful attention. They knew her too well to fall into the boredom trap.

"Nick," Julia said to Nick Puzo after a brief silence, "what's the first thing you're gonna do when the assault team comes through the door?"

Nick Puzo answered without hesitation. "Protect the civilians."

"Wrong. Do you want another chance or should I ask someone else?"

When Puzo didn't reply, she turned to the hulking undercover in the aquamarine fake-fur jacket. "How 'bout you, Rashid? You know the answer?" Julia noted the anger in Nick Puzo's gaze with some satisfaction. As she would, in all probability, never work with him again, his morale was of no concern to her. What was important was that he get it right this one time.

"Yell *Police, freeze!* and display our badges," Rashid promptly answered.

"Thank you." Julia paused for a moment, then added a final note. "It's Sunday and it's raining so there's not gonna be a lot of pedestrians on the sidewalks. But there will be vehicles running to and from the Fifty-ninth Street Bridge and we're going to take the position that any shot fired might cause the death of any occupant of any vehicle. Therefore we *must* assert our authority as police officers right from jump street. Keep in mind, Joey Navarro is a suspect in a dozen homicides and the rest of his crew are equally prone to violence. Keep in mind, we have good reason to believe there's enough child pornography in that store to send Joey to prison for the rest of his life. Keep in mind, Joey was lured to KRS Books and might be smelling that proverbial trap even as we speak. Keep in mind, the most vicious criminals will surrender when faced with a hopeless situation. It's our job, yours and mine, to present that situation with enough force to make its nature abundantly clear."

34

THE SIGNAL came at 9:01 P.M., four sharp clacks loud enough to echo in the first-floor office where the assault team had gathered. Joey Navarro had not only risen to the bait, he'd brought company. Julia looked from one member of her team to the other. She was about to say something really dumb, like, "Are we all set?" But she caught the words at the last second, before she made a fool of herself, limiting her final advice to a single observation: "To the victors," she told them, "belong the spoils."

She led them, then, five detectives and three uniformed officers, past the sergeant at the front desk, past two uniformed cops half-carrying a disheveled suspect into the house. Obviously drunk, the suspect was bellowing a Stephen Foster tune, "Old Black Joe," at the top of his lungs. He stopped abruptly when Julia and her entourage marched past.

"Man, man, man," he declared, "that is one snooty bitch."

Ignoring the epithet, Julia proceeded to a line of three patrol cars double-parked in front of the precinct and climbed into the front seat of the first of these.

She did not have to tell her officers which vehicles to enter. After the undercovers left at eight-forty, she'd addressed the subject of who would be first through the door at KRS, who second, who third . . . all the way to the pair of unfortunates assigned to control pedestrian traffic outside the store. Her tone had made her intentions clear as she rattled off their names. Here's how it's gonna be. Live with it.

Everybody wanted to go first, of course, and some would inevitably feel slighted. But that couldn't be helped. As commanding officer, she had to decide and the old saw held true: Better a bad decision than no decision at all.

Or so Julia had thought as she nominated herself to make the initial entry, then quickly established the pecking order. By putting herself first, she was making herself the target of their resentment. But that was better than the alternative. Singling out Bert or Betty or Harry or Carlos for the honor might easily lead to resentments that festered for months.

THE CARAVAN, once under way, moved swiftly. It ran without lights or sirens, along Vernon Boulevard to the massive footings of the 59th Street Bridge, then turned right onto Queens Plaza South. It was raining hard now, an icy March rain that pounded on the elevated subway lines dividing the broad plaza, loud enough to obscure the rattle of the 7 train as it pulled into the station. As Julia had hoped, there was no one outside KRS Books and Videos when they pulled up a moment later, no pedestrians, no hookers, no gangsters.

For just a moment, as the rain popped on her stiff body armor like spit on a griddle, Julia felt a twinge of pity for Detective Carlos Serrano and Patrol Officer Larry Minh who would remain outside. Then she was striding toward the entrance to KRS Books, Minh walking just ahead of her. He would hold the door open while his brothers and sisters charged through, then try to dance between the drops until somebody came out to fetch him.

Once he had his hands on the handle of the door, Minh looked back at Julia. At her nod, he yanked with both hands and she charged inside, her weapon extended, eyes sweeping the interior as she swung around to cover the man behind the cash register at the front. "Police! Police! Raise your hands!"

A chorus of overlapping commands followed as the rest of the team burst through the door.

"Police! Down on the floor!"

"Police! Put your hands on top of your head!"

"Police! Police! Police! Freeze! Freeze! Freeze!"

"I said, Get on on your goddamned face!"

The commands were conflicting by design, their purpose to produce the effect of a stun grenade, to temporarily forestall *any* response.

The man Julia held at bay apparently got the message. A balding African American, he was standing on a raised platform behind a counter devoted to the sale of dildos and condoms. At the sound of Julia's voice and the sight of her 9-millimeter Glock, he simply froze.

"Put your hands on top of your head!" she bellowed. "Do it now! Do it now. Put your hands on top of your head!"

When he didn't respond, she encouraged him with a simple hand-signal, jerking the barrel of her weapon from his chest to his face. Then his hands moved slowly upward until they rested on his head and he drew his first breath of the encounter, a ragged phlegmy gasp that could not possibly have satisfied.

"Maurice Wilson?" Julia hesitated long enough to receive a confirming nod. "I want you to come down from there. I want you to do it right now. I want to step off the platform and lie face down on the floor. Let's—"

Julia's instructions were interrupted by a crash from the rear of the store. The crash was followed by the voice of Rashid Lamb. "Come out of there!" he shouted. "Right now. Come to mama."

The sounds of a scuffle followed, a cacophony of curses, grunts and shouts of pain. Instinctively, Julia glanced over her shoulder, her attention flagging for just a second. Maurice Wilson took advantage of that second to duck behind the counter.

Though Julia caught the movement in her peripheral vision and was already turning back when he came up with the shotgun in his hands, though she was certain both that she fired first and that her bullet struck him, the barrel of the shotgun twice exploded in flames. Then she was on her back, in a place beyond thought, watching the corrugations in the ceiling writhe in time to the gunfire surrounding her.

Suddenly, Bert Griffith was kneeling at her side, rooting in her abdomen like a faith healer in search of a tumor. When he finally raised his hand to display an object, Julia found that she couldn't see the object clearly. She couldn't know it was the slug fired by Maurice Wilson's shotgun or that it had been contained by her body armor. But she did note that Griffith's normally grave expression had been transformed, that he now looked as though he'd stuck his finger into an electrical socket.

And then she was gone.

35

I T   W A S   eight o'clock on the following morning when Peter Foley stepped from an elevator onto the fifth floor of Manhattan Medical Center on East Sixty-first Street. Though faced with a long corridor that extended in both directions, he did not have to ask for the location of room 559. The uniformed officer seated before a closed door at the end of the corridor to his right was a dead giveaway.

As Foley approached the officer, he withdrew a billfold from the inside pocket of his coat, opening it to reveal a lieutenant's badge and a police identification card. The badge was stolen, the ID forged by Foley himself.

The uniformed officer jumped to his feet and half saluted. At least forty pounds over his best weight, one tail of his blouse had slipped from his trousers to hang over the rolls of fat encircling his waist and hips.

Unfazed by the man's appearance, Foley stared directly at his name tag before addressing him. "Officer Rambeau," he said, "I'm gonna go inside, have a little talk with the prisoner. Anybody comes along, a doctor, a nurse, you knock three times on the door. Got that?"

After a moment, Rambeau smiled. "Sure thing, lieutenant," he declared. "Don't worry about me."

JOEY NAVARRO'S head turned ever so slowly when Pete walked into the small private room. The movement was so languid, so without apprehension, that Foley immediately knew the man was stoned out of his mind on what doctors euphemistically call painkillers. It was only fair, though, in light of his bad break.

Julia's team had acted with great restraint the night before, holding their fire as soon as Maurice Wilson dropped his weapon. Altogether, the four officers involved had discharged a mere eight rounds. Six of these found their mark and Maurice Wilson was dead before his body came to rest on the dingy blue carpeting. The two stray rounds passed harmlessly through the store's front window to fragment against a pillar of the el dividing the plaza where the Crime Scene Unit recovered bits and pieces several hours later.

The only bystander injured in the melee was Joey Navarro. Maurice Wilson's second shot had penetrated Joey's left thigh, shattering the long bones of his upper leg while tearing out a fist-sized chunk of his flesh. At the time, he was already cuffed.

Foley pulled a chair up to Joey's bed and sat down to assess the situation. Joey, he knew, had been taken to Manhattan Medical simply because it was the major trauma center closest to KRS Books. Within a few days, he would be moved to a secure facility, most likely the prison ward at Bellevue Hospital. As he'd been found in an office which also contained sixty-three video tapes and thirty-one DVDs, all depicting adults and children having sex, the charges against him were serious indeed. That was why, despite an elevated cast that ran from his left hip to the sole of his foot, his right wrist was handcuffed to the bed rail.

"I got a lawyer," Joey Navarro said. "I don't gotta to talk to no cop."

"I'm not a cop." Foley reached out to pull an earplug from Navarro's left ear, then used the remote to shut down a television bolted to the far wall. "I'm Goober."

Navarro's eyes grew just a bit more focused. "You set me up."

"I did," Foley admitted, "but that's neither here nor there. What's important is that we can be of mutual benefit to each other."

"I don't gotta talk to you, whether you're a cop or not." Navarro's full lips parted to reveal a coated tongue that snaked from one corner of his mouth to the other.

"You want some water, Joey?"

"Yeah."

Pete filled a plastic cup with ice water from a pitcher set on a table. The table was too far away, Foley noted, for the handcuffed prisoner to reach it.

"Here ya go." He handed the cup to Joey who quickly drained it.

"Do that again," Joey said.

Foley complied, then set pitcher and cup on the table. This was, he knew, his one chance and it was important that he play every card in the proper order. That meant he absolutely could not dwell on the rage Joey Navarro inspired.

"You're probably wondering why I'm here," Foley said.

"I don't gotta talk to you," Joey repeated for the third time. "I got a lawyer."

"True enough, but you're still probably wondering. Am I right? Do you wonder why I'm here?" Foley took Navarro's silence for assent and continued. "Well, I'm here about the girl on this video." He fumbled in his briefcase for a moment, then withdrew a tape and held it up for Joey's inspection. The tape had a pink label with the words PATTI'S DANCE printed in neat black letters.

"Now," Foley continued. "I'm not asking you to say anything. I don't have to because I already know you're familiar with this particular tape. This is the dog you couldn't sell. This is the video Habib al Rif'at was tossing in as a freebie because nobody wanted to pay good money for it. Not enough action."

Navarro's jaw tightened and his eyes jumped to Foley's. For the first time, he seemed fully alert. "You did Habib. You fuckin' killed him."

"Is that what you think?"

"Yeah, else how'd ya know he was givin' the tape away?"

Foley answered Joey's question with several of his own. "Then you admit you're familiar with the tape? The one I'm holding here? You've actually watched it?"

"You think I'm a fuckin' pervert?" Navarro was incredulous. "You think I get my jollies watchin' little kids? Gimme a fuckin' break. I got a family."

"But you sold the tape, isn't that right?"

"That don't mean nothin'."

It did, of course, mean something, especially to Peter Foley who felt utterly degraded by playing the role of supplicant to Joey Navarro. Nevertheless, Foley continued to implement the strategy he'd formulated in the course of a long and mostly sleepless night.

"Well," he said, "that's neither here nor there. What's on the tape is not why I came to see you. I'm here to find out where the tape came from. See, the little girl on that video, her name really is Patti. She's my daughter."

Navarro recoiled as if struck, but Foley remained calm. "Patti disappeared some years ago," he continued, "and I've been looking for her ever since. That's natural, of course, me being her father, but now I'm very close to finding her and that makes a big difference. In fact, the way I see it, all I have to do is locate the person who made this tape and I'm home free."

"Hey, man, I got a lotta sympathy here. Trust me on that. But what I'm gonna do is take my lawyer's advice and keep my mouth shut." Navarro's fleshy mouth curled into a near-infantile pout. "You can see," he declared, "what I'm up against."

Foley ignored the observation. "Now, Joey," he said, "I know you have a daughter, Angelina, and I could ask you to think about Angelina. I could ask you to imagine how you'd feel if Angelina was on the tape. But I realize this is not the way your mind works. So what I'll do is give you something in return for your help. I'll give you information you can use to make sensible decisions about your future. I'll make a trade."

Navarro lay back against the pillow and drew a breath. He tried to move his right hand toward his face, but the handcuff restrained him, clanking hard against the bed rail. He looked at the handcuff where it encircled his right wrist, then said, "Shit."

Foley nodded sympathetically. "How old are you, Joey? Thirty-four? Thirty-five?" In fact, as Foley knew, Joey Cadillac was forty-six years old and looked every day of it.

"Thirty-nine," Navarro answered. "Why?"

"I don't know. It's just like . . . like when you're sentenced to life without parole, the younger you are, the more years you actually get. I always found that strange."

Foley's commentary was interrupted by three sharp raps on the door. The raps were followed by the voice of Officer Rambeau: "Breakfast's on the way."

Though Foley contained his disappointment, he silently cursed himself for not forcing the issue sooner. Badge or no badge, he would be forbidden to reenter the room if Joey made a complaint.

Foley rose to feet, then exercised his only option. "I'm gonna step out into the hall for a minute," he said. "While I'm out there, think on this: I know where to find your Uncle Lorenzo. When I come back in, you'll know too."

36

FOLEY CAUGHT two bad breaks, neither fatal, as he waited in the hall for a turbaned Sikh to deliver Joey Navarro's breakfast. The first of these came in the form of a nurse in a starched blue uniform who swept past him bearing a loaded syringe in her right hand. Foley correctly assumed that the syringe contained a painkiller of some kind and that Joey, already too stoned for Pete's liking, would be even more stoned when Foley got back to him. If not actually unconscious.

Foley's second bad break was entirely of his own making. In an effort to appear inconspicuous, he asked Officer Rambeau, "So, how's life in the one-eight?"

The 18th Precinct was Rambeau's home base and had been for many years. Thus his passionately held opinions were fully formed and ripe for expression. The one-eight, he told Foley, was a sinkhole of incompetence. Naming names, he began with the duty sergeant and proceeded upward to the precinct commander, liberally sprinkling his monologue with descriptive epithets like dumb-ass, jerkoff, fuckup and shit-for-brains.

Foley endured it all, even nodding from time to time, until the nurse returned to her station at the other end of the hall. Then he stepped back into Navarro's room, realizing as he did so that he much preferred Navarro's company. Typically, Rambeau's assignment was given to the most incompetent officer in the house, the cop who simply could not be trusted with anything more complex.

NAVARRO'S EYES, closed when Foley resumed his seat, fluttered open at the sound of his voice. If Joey's movements before had been languid, they were now viscous.

"Joey, you with us?" Foley asked.

"Every way, every day." Navarro's lips parted slightly, then fell to their normal set.

"You remember what I told you before I left?"

"About my breakfast?"

Foley looked at the tray which was resting beside the water pitcher. Too far away for Joey to reach it.

"About the help I offered you in exchange for information about the tape."

Navarro nodded, his attention slightly more focused now.

"Well, there's two parts to this help I'm offering. The first part concerns your Uncle Lorenzo and his family who are now in the hands of the feds. Lorenzo's gonna testify against you."

Joey's eyes closed momentarily and he sighed. It was the worst, the absolute worst, the news he'd been hoping never to hear. But it was valuable news too, because it brought his options into sharp

focus. Before, he might have claimed to know nothing of the contraband recovered at KRS Books and Videos. After all, the con-
veniently dead Maurice Wilson was the day-to-day manager while
he, Joey Cadillac, only occasionally visited the store. Now, however,
with Contorno singing, Joey's options were reduced to a simple
choice. He could either rat on Charlie Banana or spend the remainder of his unnatural life in a federal prison. And that was only after
New York State was done with him.

"It was a good thing you had going, Joey. Real sweet. You never
touched the product, the profits were large, every transaction was in
cash." Foley leaned forward. "But it had a flaw, a little soft spot right
in the center named Lorenzo Contorno. Tell me, did you miss Uncle
Lorenzo by much? Was he just a little too smart? Did he get out just
a little too fast? Well, it doesn't matter now because a special agent
named Raymond Lear is debriefing Contorno even as we speak."

When Navarro didn't reply, Foley poured himself a glass of
water and drank it. Then he filled a second cup and handed it to
Joey who also drank. The only sound in the room was the inter-
mittent squeak of an infusion pump as it forced a mix of antibi-
otics and normal saline into a vein on Joey's free arm.

Finally, as Foley had hoped, Navarro broke the silence. Though
he still slurred his words, his tone was much steadier. "What's the
second thing?" he asked. "The second thing you're gonna tell me?"

Foley shook his head. "From here on out, you have to earn your
revelations."

"You wanna know where Charlie got that tape?"

"That's what I want to know."

Navarro's eyes turned up to the ceiling. "You'll pardon me if I
think it's strange that you're askin' me this question. You'll pardon me for wonderin' why you don't already have the answer. Bein'
as you're so fuckin' tight with the feds."

It took Foley a moment to admit he'd been a complete fool. Then he thanked his good angel for keeping Toshi Matsunaga alive. "You're talking about Matsunaga?"

"You didn't get that from me. That's just a shrewd guess on your part. But lemme say this here. It's awful strange when the feds use somebody who *makes* a product to get to somebody who *sells* a product. You see what I'm sayin'? All the feds wanna do is bust the guineas. They got Mafia on the fuckin' brain."

Foley leaned back to think it over, several items jumping out at him as he began to rearrange the pieces. Joey Navarro was wrong, that was the first thing. Toshi Matsunaga had sold Raymond Lear a bill of goods, then vanished, not from any fear of Peter Foley, but because he knew Lear would find out. That was why there was no FBI presence at Proximate Services in Sunset Park or at Lorenzo's home. Matsunaga couldn't reveal the role of either without also revealing his place at the top of the pyramid.

The second point, equally important, was that Matsunaga hadn't shot the *Patti's Dance* tape. Foley had examined Matsunaga's product and knew it to be highly professional, the kind of work that commands top dollar in the chicken-hawk marketplace. This was simply not the case with *Patti's Dance* which had obviously been shot by an amateur.

Foley stood up. "You know, there's something I've always wanted to ask a wise guy. For years I've been dying to ask this question."

"Don't bust my balls, man."

"Relax, it's not incriminating." Foley smiled. "But what's with those stupid names? Charlie Banana? Joey Cadillac? Don't you think it's a bit retro? You're like the Mustache Petes of the new millennium."

Far from offended, Navarro took a minute to consider the question. Then he turned to stare up at Foley through pupils reduced to infinitesimal black dots. "It's my heritage," he said. "It's who I am." As Foley turned to go, Navarro quickly added, "The second thing, I guess you're not gonna tell me what it is?"

"Not unless you have something to trade for it, something like the place where Matsunaga shot those DVDs or the names of his associates?"

Navarro shook his head. "I got no idea where his merchandise came from. As for his partners, if he had any, I never met 'em."

"Then the only thing I have for you is a suggestion. If you're gonna rat on Charlie Terranova, do it right away. And tell Agent Lear that Goober sent you."

37

TWO FLOORS above room 559 at Manhattan Medical Center, in room 731, Bert Griffith described the reaction of Joey Navarro to the sudden appearance of Rashid Lamb on the previous evening.

"First thing," Bert explained, "one of Rashid's boobs came loose in the excitement and it was pointing up at his head when he kicked in the door. Plus his wig had fallen off and his head underneath was shaved to the scalp. It made a nice contrast with the green eye shadow and the lipstick and those feather-duster eyelashes." Here Bert Griffith turned slightly to direct his remarks to Corry Brennan. "Corry, Joey's blood pressure musta been through the roof because his eyes were bulging out of his head. He goes, 'Wha', wha', wha' . . . .'"

Bert was playing to an audience of three, two of whom, Robert Reid and Corry Brennan, were not only paying close attention but laughing in all the right places. Not so Julia Brennan who was fully dressed and impatiently awaiting discharge. She was sitting on the edge of the bed, her attention drifting this way and that as she contemplated the unpleasant truths surrounding her night at Manhattan Medical Center.

Though sorely tempted, Julia refused to blame anybody else for her plight. She wasn't suffering from amnesia; she remembered the moment before the shooting began with absolute clarity. There'd been a commotion behind her, the sounds of a scuffle, cops shouting, somebody screaming in pain. For just a second, she'd turned away from Maurice Wilson to see what was happening. Wilson had taken advantage of that second by trying to kill her. Those were the facts, ma'am, the unalterable facts.

She should never have done it. That was the top line, the middle line, the bottom line. Wilson was her responsibility, her sole responsibility. If she hadn't looked away, he might never have grabbed that shotgun. And even if he had, he would not have lived long enough to use it.

From there, by Julia's reckoning, it only got worse. Wilson's first round had impacted her body armor just below her breastbone, the force of the slug more or less paralyzing her diaphragm. It was no surprise to the ER doctor who treated her that she'd passed out from lack of oxygen. Or that she'd begun to breathe on her own a few seconds later.

"You were very lucky," Dr. Krantz had observed. "A foot higher and they would've had to bury you in a closed casket."

These same sentiments had been offered by Manhattan North Borough Commander Linus Flannery when he paid an obligatory visit to his wounded warrior. "You've got the luck of the Irish," he'd declared.

Meanwhile, Julia was certain that Linus Flannery, along with all of her detectives, not to mention Lily Han, was enjoying the image of Julia Brennan knocked on her ass. It was the kind of story that could (and *would*) follow you throughout your career.

Julia looked at her daughter. Corry was laughing now, but the night before, when she'd burst into the emergency room, the fear in her eyes had cut directly into Julia's heart. Corry's terror, it had seemed to Julia, embodied the wild and hopeless desperation of a rabbit trying to outrun a forest fire.

As she'd wrapped her daughter in a tight embrace, ignoring a sharp protest from her bruised abdomen, Julia had fully realized that she'd put many lives at risk when she turned away from Maurice Wilson. There were her own detectives and the undercovers from Vice and the borrowed uniforms, any one of whom might have been killed or wounded. Then there was her daughter, and Robert Reid, and Peter Foley.

Julia was still awaiting discharge, some twenty minutes later, when Lily Han called on Julia's cell phone. Bert Griffith had left by then, and Robert Reid was asleep in a chair. Corry was standing with her back to the room's single window, pondering her mother's response to a simple question. Why, Corry had wanted to know, did Maurice Wilson decide to shoot it out with the cops when he had to know he couldn't win?

Julia had given the question brief consideration, then announced, "Suicide by cop. Wilson was fifty years old and he'd been in and out of prison all his life. He chose what he believed to be the better of his two options."

Lily Han was exuberant. "You did everything right, Julia. Really. It was absolutely perfect: a righteous shooting, great restraint, no cops seriously injured, tons of contraband. You're a superstar, Julia Brennan. You oughta write a book."

"Well, Lily," Julia replied, one eye on Corry, "as I've got a week off due to my injury, maybe I'll write the first chapter. I'll call it, The Night I Got Knocked on My Ass."

Han laughed appreciatively. "All part of the legend. Look, I gotta run, but there was one thing I wanted to tell you. I received a call from Craig Whitmore's wife this morning. She told me her husband has pancreatic cancer and his doctors are giving him between six months and a year to live. I don't see what that has to do with us, but I'm passing it along for what it's worth. *Ciao.*"

Julia hung up, and lay back on the bed. Be a good bureaucrat, she advised herself. You had a homicide. You made an arrest. *Finito.* Remember, it's not solved crimes that make problems for the job. It's unsolved crimes—of which there are many assigned right now to detectives under your command. Remember. . . .

"Mom?"

Julia opened her eyes to find her daughter standing over the bed. "What?"

"You went to Never-Never Land again."

"I have a constitutional right to go to Never-Never Land. I thought we already agreed on that."

"Not this morning. This morning it could mean there's more damage than we thought."

The *we* referred to Dr. Krantz who'd insisted that Julia remain overnight for observation. Just in case the bruise on her upper abdomen was merely the outward manifestation of a pulverized liver.

"Okay," Julia said as she sat up on the bed, "I'm paying attention."

"Tell me what you were thinking about."

"I was thinking about the Whitmore case. According to his wife, Craig Whitmore has terminal cancer and he knew it when he killed Adeline."

Corry sat down next to her mother. Though Corry seemed all arms and legs, they were nearly the same height now. Their eyes were the same color as well, a dark disconcerting blue that faded to indigo when the light was poor. "What has that got to do with anything?" she asked.

"On one level, the cancer adds to his basic motive. Whitmore knows he's gonna die and this is his last chance to even up for all the pain Adeline caused him. Plus, if he's gonna die anyway, how hard can he be punished?"

"What's the second level?"

"There is no second level. And you, Corry Brennan, are too smart for your own good." Julia smiled. "But there *is* something bothering me about the case. You want to take a guess? Being as you know as much about it as I do?"

"You don't understand why Liebman didn't establish his alibi right away."

"We already discussed that. Try again."

Corry's tongue emerged to probe the center of her upper lip and she raised her eyes to the ceiling. Both gestures were characteristic of Corry Brennan in deep thought and Julia relished their appearance. For a moment, the simple fact that she might have lost this daughter of hers threatened to overwhelm her. But then Corry's eyes came down and her tongue went back into her mouth as she turned to her mother with a triumphant smile.

"The question," she announced, "is why Steve Liebman talked to you at all. I mean, he already had a lawyer, right? And his lawyer must have told him to keep his mouth shut, right?"

"Now you're thinking like a cop."

Encouraged, Corry plunged on. "But . . . but maybe Liebman just likes to get in people's faces. I mean, he knew he had an alibi, so, like, what could you really do to him?"

38

CORRY BRENNAN'S question was left dangling when Peter Foley walked into the room a moment later. Emitting a purely adolescent squeal that might have expressed anything from delight to outrage, she flew into his arms.

The squeal woke Robert Reid who rubbed his eyes for a moment, then glanced up in time to catch the look that passed between Julia and Peter Foley. Both were smiling identical half smiles that seemed, to Reid, nearly triumphant. Peter Foley, the night before, had been seated in the back of an unmarked car two blocks away from KRS. In theory, he should have still been there when Harry McDonald went in search of him after the shooting stopped. Instead, the vehicle was empty.

"One less element for me to justify," Julia had casually explained to her daughter and her uncle. "And Pete knew it. He'll be back."

W HEN CORRY finally decided to release Foley, she stepped back and punched him in the stomach. The blow was soft enough to qualify as playful. Barely.

"You're a rat," she accused.

Foley confirmed her judgment without hesitation, adding just a single qualifier. "A trapped rat," he said.

"You didn't even come to see how Mom was."

"I didn't have to. I was on the El in the Queens Plaza station when she walked out of KRS under her own steam. If I remember correctly, she was chewing out a paramedic who tried to take her arm."

Julia smiled. She'd yet to take her eyes off her lover. "I was under some stress at the time," she admitted, "and I may have acted impulsively."

Reid pushed himself out the chair and headed for the visitor's bathroom. He was at the door when Foley said, "I spoke to Joey Cadillac. As it happens, he's recovering from his injuries in this very hospital. Joey was reasonably forthcoming, given the circumstances."

"Which were?"

"That he was stoned out of his mind and facing life in prison."

"But he did name a name, right?"

"Right. Toshi Matsunaga."

Julia didn't ask Peter Foley how he'd gotten past the uniformed officer assigned to guard Navarro's person, though she was certain the duty had been routinely assigned to someone in the 18th Precinct. She didn't want to know. Knowing couldn't help either one of them.

"You feel alright?" Foley asked.

"Never better."

"Then it's time we went to work."

Corry thrust herself between Peter Foley and her mother. "Mom's not going anywhere," she declared, "but home to bed."

Robert Reid entered the room in time to hear Corry's final remark. Though he agreed with his niece, he looked into Julia's eyes and knew that Corry Brennan's cause was hopeless. Still, he thought it a low blow when Julia turned Corry's own words against her.

"We had this conversation," she told her daughter, "a few days ago. If I recall, you instructed me to do what I had to do."

"You're hurt, Mom. Why can't you face it?" She whirled to confront Peter Foley. "And you!" she said, "you were supposed to protect her."

If Corry realized she was completely reversing the vigorous stand she'd previously taken, she gave no sign of it. Nor did she seem to realize that the charge laid against Foley was without foundation. Foley had offered complete protection for Corry and her mother when he walked away from the Brennan family. That the Brennan family had decided, after careful consultation, to refuse the offer was not his fault.

"I think," Robert Reid told Corry, "that's it's time for us to leave."

"You're taking their side?"

Julia finally reached out to seize her daughter's hand. "Why don't we go have some breakfast. I promise, if I pass out, you can take me straight home."

The door opened as Julia finished speaking and a nurse stuck her head into the room. Before she could so much as open her mouth, Julia said, "I want those discharge papers in this room five minutes from now. They don't arrive, I'm walking through the door without your consent. As if I needed it in the first place."

The nurse promptly withdrew and Julia looked from one member of her family to another. "I think," she said, "it's gonna be one of those days."

A S S H E dug into her bacon and eggs, Julia was keenly aware of
Peter Foley's impatience. She knew he had every reason to be anxious. All along, he'd been afraid that whoever held his daughter
would get wind of his search and disappear into the pedophile hin-
terlands. The encounter with Toshi Matsunaga had occurred five
days ago. Hence, there was every reason to believe that Toshi was
long gone.

Corry had calmed down by the time her meal, a stack of silver-
dollar pancakes, was served. She slathered the pancakes with
pats of butter and maple syrup before she finally spoke. "Last
night," she said, "I was really scared. I've never been so scared in
my life. Not even on September eleventh. Please don't scare me
like that again."

Julia started to reassure her daughter, then hesitated. All I have
to do, she told herself, is transfer out of SCU. That would make
everybody happy, from Corry Brennan to Lily Han. And Bea Sheperd would be eager to arrange a move that would take me from the
front lines at SCU to the bowels of 1 Police Plaza. I'd never have
to visit a crime scene or talk to a victim again. A year ago, it was
exactly what I wanted.

"That's okay, Mom," Corry said, driving the guilt straight down
through the top of Julia's skull. "I know you're a cop. I know you
can't promise."

Robert Reid watched the exchange. Like Corry, on the night
before he'd entered a state bordering on abject terror. And why
not? He'd been notified of the "incident" by an inspector who
claimed to know only that a wounded Julia Brennan had been
taken to Manhattan Medical Center.

But Robert Reid, unlike Corry, had been studying the NYPD
for decades. As knowledgeable about its shifting alliances as Julia,
he was fully aware of her options. He was aware of her love for

Peter Foley as well, aware and envious, and of her natural aptitude for the craft of policing.

Which way she'd finally go was anybody's guess, but if he had to bet, he'd bet on her remaining a cop for as long as she could. As for the other part of it, the wild card, Peter Foley, of that Reid had no doubt at all. Their commitment was absolute. He'd known it the minute Foley walked through the door of Room 731.

"Well," Reid finally said to his grand-niece, "it's time for us to go."

To his surprise, Corry meekly folded her napkin, then kissed her mother on the cheek. "I know," she said to Peter Foley, "that you won't let anything happen to Mom and I'm sorry for what I said before."

39

PETE AND Julia headed, first, to Julia's house and a .38 caliber revolver, a Colt, presently snugged into a box stacked on a closet shelf. The revolver was a relic associated with the days when cops were forbidden to carry anything more powerful than a Chief's Special, but it was all she had. Her regular weapon, a 9-millimeter Glock, like every other weapon discharged at KRS, had been confiscated by the shooting board pending a forensic examination.

They drove in Foley's rented Subaru with Foley doing most of the talking. He put the facts, both of them, on the table before they reached the Manhattan Bridge. First, Navarro's claim that the tapes and DVDs delivered to Proximate Services came from Toshi Matsunaga. That part of it, both agreed, was true. The second revelation, that Matsunaga produced the tapes and DVDs, was a bit more iffy because it depended on Matsunaga's word. They would go with it, however, because they had no choice.

"Here's the question I've been asking myself all day," Foley declared as they followed a line of cars onto the Brooklyn-Queens Expressway at Tillary Street. "Why did Matsunaga meet with me? Almost to a man, the chicken hawks I've set up over the years were motivated by lust. But Toshi . . . ? Let me give you an example of pedophile lust, so you can gauge just how deep it runs. Maybe a year ago, the feds busted a small pedophile network in the Midwest. This network had a unique feature. The members used some kind of Napster-like software that allowed them to browse and download the chicken porn stored in one another's computers. But the technology wasn't the reason why the network was small. No, it was small because in order to become a member, you had to have at least ten thousand photos in your database."

"Ten *thousand*? You've gotta be kidding."

"I tell ya, Julia, these guys are as driven by lust as serial killers."

"But not Matsunaga?"

"The material I traded him was relatively collectible, but it was-n't near the quality of the DVDs Matsunaga was hawking to Char-lie Terranova. If Toshi was actually filming those kids . . . well, I can't believe what I had to offer was much of a turn-on. Or not enough turn-on for a man under federal indictment to risk a cozy deal he'd cut with the FBI."

As they rose to the top of the Kosciusko Bridge, Julia glanced past Foley at the Manhattan skyline three miles away. Last night's storm was breaking up into raggedy dark clouds that streamed past the spires of the Chrysler and Empire State buildings. Automat-ically, she glanced to the south, toward lower Manhattan where the towers of the World Trade Center once stood. Her uncle, Robert Reid, had always hated those buildings, had referred to them, con-

temptuously, as upended salt and pepper shakers. But when she'd
spoken to him on September 11, after hours of trying to get
through, he'd been devastated. "They were ugly," he told her,
"but they were mine."

"So," Julia asked Foley, "why did Matsunaga meet with you? If
he wasn't interested in the goodies you had to offer?"

"Back it up a bit. I had no idea who Matsunaga was at the time Lear
asked me to make contact. And if Lear hadn't given me the name
Toshi used in the chat rooms, I wouldn't have had any way to get to
him. In this business, you can't just call up and introduce yourself."

"What was the name?"

"ZenMaster," he said. "That was the name Matsunaga used. And
he used it often. Toshi was all over the net before I started looking
for him. That's the point. Matsunaga was taking risks before I
crossed his trail. Keep in mind, Toshi never met with Peter Foley.
He met with a pedophile celebrity named Goober. Goober who's
been working the chat rooms for years. Goober who had his own
web site. Goober who never got arrested. Goober the legend."

Julia shifted as close to Peter Foley as her bucket seat would allow
and laid her left hand on his thigh. Her touch was familiar and pos-
sessive. "A thrill seeker. Toshi thinks he's too smart to get caught."

"He not only ran a scam on Raymond Lear and lied to me when
his life was the line, he fooled both of us. If I'd thought, even for
one second, that Matsunaga was telling me anything but the truth,
he'd be dead right now. Toshi knew it, too. He had to know it
because I came with an inch of killing him even when I thought
he was being straight with me."

THE POINT, as Foley went to explain, was that it was just possible that Matsunaga, motivated by a profound narcissism that

shielded him from any point of view not his own, was still out there making videos and DVDs. And it was also just possible that the maker of *Patti's Dance* had not yet been warned.

Though Foley had yet to closely examine the DVDs he'd gotten from Matsunaga, he was certain, even at a cursory glance, that the crude video of his dancing daughter was produced by somebody else. How had Matsunaga gotten his hands on it? Pedophiles commonly photographed and videotaped the children they molested, their motivation, of course, being lust. Almost as commonly, pedophiles exchanged photos and videos with their molester buddies or sold them outright to distributors like Toshi Matsunaga. From Matsunaga's point of view, child pornography was like heroin. There was never enough product to meet a demand that expanded in direct proportion to every increase in supply.

"So why should Matsunaga warn this guy who happened to sell him a couple of tapes? What's in it for Toshi?" Foley halted for the light at Woodhaven Boulevard and the Long Island Expressway. "On the other hand, if I do catch up to Matsunaga, the guy's name could be the bargaining chip that saves Toshi Matsunaga's life, a potential that would not escape his attention."

EXCEPT TO ask an encouraging question from time to time, Julia did not interrupt Foley's monologue. Foley need to talk. She understood that. He needed to uncover whatever glimmer of hope remained to him, to weigh and measure it, to give his fading hopes weight and density. Hence she did not object, either, when he pulled down the bed covers, then virtually ordered her to go to sleep.

"You've been up all night," he declared, "and you need some rest if you're gonna be any good to me."

"And what will you do in the meantime?" she asked.

"I brought the DVDs Matsunaga gave me. While you're asleep, I'll take a close look at them."

"I thought you gave that material to the FBI."

"Not before I copied it. Anyway, it's possible there's some clue to where the DVDs were made on the DVDs themselves. Of course, you could always come downstairs and watch them with me. If that's what you want."

Julia wasn't remotely tempted. She sat on the edge of the bed and pulled off her shoes, then began to unbutton her blouse. "Wake me when it's over," she said. "Right now, I need my beauty rest."

40

I T W A S four o'clock in the afternoon when Julia climbed out of bed, pulled on a terry-cloth robe and headed for the shower. Curiously, as she lathered her legs, then picked up her razor, her thoughts were not on Peter Foley or his daughter, or even on the close call of the night before. Instead, she focused, quite involuntarily, on Stephen Liebman.

The questions Julia initially asked herself were the same questions she'd discussed earlier with Corry and Robert Reid and whoever else would listen. What was new was her acceptance of the fact that she would not stop asking the questions until she found the answers. And there was something else bothering her, some small element of the Liebman and Whitmore interrogations that flitted from shadow to shadow like an elf protecting a pot of gold. That rock would also have to be turned over before she was satisfied.

Julia was out of the shower and applying her makeup when she set brush and lipstick aside to call Bert Griffith on his cell phone. Before the technological revolution, she might have spent hours trying to reach him if he happened to be in the field. Now, at least in theory, he was available on a 24/7 basis.

Not that the NYPD contract signed by the Detectives Benevolent Association required detectives to carry cell phones. It was just that, on elite squads like SCU, the commander's wishes had a certain do-it-or-else quality. Julia had expressed a wish that detectives under her supervision carry cell phones on the day she'd taken command of the unit. The ones who complied were still on the team.

"Griffith," Bert Griffith said.

"Bert. "

"Hey, captain, how ya feelin'?"

"Great." Now that she'd made what she believed to be an appropriate decision, Julia wanted only to be downstairs with Peter Brennan. The urge was nearly physical. "I assume you've heard about Craig Whitmore by now."

"The cancer?"

"Yeah."

"The word came down from Han's office this afternoon. Whitmore's doctors confirmed his disease and Lily's gonna press for a quick trial. You think it means something?"

"My brain is telling me it doesn't, that his illness reinforces his motive. But . . . look, what I want you to do is compare Whitmore's and Liebman's phone records. Let's see how often they were in contact before the murder."

"Cellulars and land lines? You want both? From his home and from his office?"

"It's what we would have done if we weren't under pressure to make a quick arrest."

"What about Whitmore's wife? If she has a cell phone registered in her name, her husband might have used it to make contact. I mean, why not go the whole nine yards?"

Though Julia registered a hint of sarcasm in Griffith's tone, along with a certain disinclination to resurrect a cold case, she answered without hesitation. "By all means," she said. "And if you think you can justify a subpoena for Hannah's phones, let's get those too."

JULIA CAME downstairs fifteen minutes later. Lured by the odor of freshly brewed coffee, she walked straight into the kitchen, filled a mug, added a dollop of milk and a package of artificial sweetener before returning to the living room.

"Any luck?" she asked as she dropped onto the couch next to Foley.

"A place to start, anyway. Check it out."

The television screen displayed a static image: two adult males and a child, a girl, in a kitchen. All were fully dressed, a blessing for which Julia was thankful.

"So, what am I looking for?"

"You see the two windows behind the sink?"

"Sure."

"Now look in the right-hand corner of the room, where the wall and the ceiling meet. Do you see that stain?"

"Looks like a water stain."

"It does, but that's not important. What matters is that the windows and the stain reappear in every scene. Living rooms, bedrooms, playrooms, kitchens. And not only in every scene, but in every DVD."

Julia sipped at her coffee, then took a deeper swallow. "What does that mean?"

"That we're looking at a sound stage, a professional setup. The quality of the audio and video tell the same story. Nobody shot this in a basement with his brother-in-law's camcorder. The action was blocked out in advance with the various camera angles in mind."

Foley shifted a bit closer to Julia. He was considerably more hopeful now, and with that hope came a familiar restlessness. He needed to be out there, on the streets, right this minute. Waiting for Julia to come downstairs had exhausted whatever tiny reservoir of patience he possessed.

"You're not saying the DVDs were made at . . . NBC, for example?"

"They're not that good."

Julia put her hand on Foley's shoulder, as if trying to hold him in place. "Tell you what, Pete, I won't ask any more dumb questions if you'll just present me with the facts as you understand them. All the facts."

"No problem," Foley replied. "As long as we're in the car and driving before I start, I have no objection whatever."

41

THOUGH FULLY aware of Pete's restless mood, Julia simply followed him out to the Subaru. She made no effort to slow him down because his mood so exactly matched her own. The nerves beneath her skin tingled with anticipation. As they approached Woodhaven Boulevard, she found her eyes sweeping the road and the sidewalks with the eager intensity of a schoolyard bully in search of a victim *du jour.*

The fuel for all this, she knew, flowed from the shooting at KRS, and it struck her as strange indeed that so close a brush with death could evoke a desire for confrontation. Julia had not remained inside KRS for thirty minutes because she needed immediate medical attention. Her problem was a good deal less complex. Her legs simply refused to support her.

She was that scared.

"WHEN MOST people think of commercials," Foley explained, "they think of the Pepsi ad on the Super Bowl halftime show. But there's a lower tier out there. I'm talking about one-eight hundred spot commercials made on the cheap for privately minted coins, abdominal machines, fortunetellers, stain removers. I'm talking about the ethnic cable stations with shows in Spanish, Korean, Greek, and Chinese. An agency serving clients like these would be a perfect cover for Matsunaga's operation."

"You forgot infomercials," Julia said. "Somebody's gotta make them too."

Foley brought the car to a halt before the full-service pumps of a gas station on Yellowstone Boulevard. "Believe it or not, infomercials are a step up." He rolled down the window, instructed the attendant to fill the tank, then turned back to Julia. "What I'm thinking here is a small studio that works free lance for second-tier ad agencies when ad work is available. When it's not, they do still photography, wedding and bar mitzvah videos, whatever comes to hand."

"Including chicken porn."

"Well, that's the thing. Once Matsunaga has a legit operation up and running, he can sneak the kids in at night, maybe three or four times a year. Keep in mind, the profit margin here would make a heroin smuggler jealous. Videos and DVDs can be duplicated for next to nothing."

Foley reached into his trouser pocket and extracted a small roll of bills. Behind him, the attendant was arguing with another man in Arabic. Or at least Foley took the rolling r's and percussive syllables for Arabic. He was far more concerned with the pump jockey's failure to insert the nozzle of the hose into the Subaru's gas tank.

"I was on the phone for three hours this afternoon," he continued, "calling ad agencies and photography studios in the city, claiming I just bought ten thousand sets of carving knives I needed to unload in a hurry. Unfortunately, there's no on-line database for tier-two ad agencies. I had to print out addresses and phone numbers for every agency and photo studio in the five boroughs."

"You're talking hundreds, right?"

"I'm talking four hundred and seventeen."

Julia stared out through the windshield at a floodlight mounted on a pole overhanging the very edge of the gas station. Despite temperatures hovering just above 50 degrees, a few tiny insects darted and dodged through the glare. "We need help, Pete."

"I was going to bring that up," Foley said, "tomorrow morning. For tonight, we can visit the possibles, take a look around. How can it hurt?"

IN TYPICAL cop fashion, Foley drove as though his was the only vehicle on the road. Both he and Julia had passed many thousands of hours on patrol; the interior of the sedan felt as comfortable and familiar to them as Julia's cozy living room. The only missing element was the cross talk of cop and dispatcher.

Initially, Foley confined his search to Queens, staying away from the heaviest of the rush-hour traffic, visiting several small studios clustered around Silvercup Studios in Long Island City. Once the site of the largest bakery in New York, Silvercup now stood at the very pinnacle of the East Coast film industry. Its success had lured a number of smaller studios to the neighborhood, including a few bottom feeders who subsisted on carrion filtering down from the surface. Only one of these bottom feeders was open when Pete and Julia drove by. Pete bluffed his way inside, employing the same pitch he'd used when he called them some hours before, introducing Julia as his partner. But its windowless sound stage proved to be far smaller than the one in Matsunaga's videos, and they were back in the car ten minutes later.

The night was closing around them as they cruised the low-rise industrial neighborhoods of western Queens: southern Astoria, Long Island City, Sunnyside and Maspeth. Most of the buildings they passed were one or two stories high and all were constructed with an eye toward unalloyed utility. This was also true of the small apartment houses they passed. Whether sided with brick or asbestos shingles, they were devoid of ornamentation, presenting rectangle-dominated facades, as anonymous as dried gum on a subway platform.

From Maspeth, Pete worked his way along Metropolitan Avenue into Greenpoint. He stopped only once, at a deli to pick up sandwiches, before proceeding along Metropolitan all the way to the Brooklyn waterfront where he found an open parking lot behind a brick building owned by the Hoskins Envelope Company. A hundred feet away, three men huddled in the shadows of the building. Initially, Julia made these men for burglars, but then she realized that, far from actively seeking a way into the building, they were sitting with their backs to the wall. Even more to the point, one of the men clutched a long plastic tube and a propane burner.

When Pete and Julia stepped from the car, the men rose to their feet and lumbered away as fast as their druggie legs would carry them. They did not look back.

"They made us for cops," Julia said.

"What else could we be?"

"Criminals?"

"Not a prayer."

"Then tourists. They could have made us for tourists, tried to take us off. It would've been fun."

Foley rolled his eyes before walking to the edge of a rotting pier. A full moon had risen behind them, lending the calm slack-tide waters a pale blue sheen that swirled around a barge moving north toward the Bronx. Across the river, the soft belly of Manhattan was penned between giant office towers to the north and south. For reasons unknown to Foley, the bedrock that rises almost to the surface in the rest of Manhattan, the bedrock necessary to support the great skyscrapers, dips between Canal Street and Midtown. The buildings here are much smaller, so much so that Pete, as he looked across the river, entertained a clear impression of opposing armies marching on an undefended valley.

"I KEEP thinking," Foley said after Julia divided the sandwiches and the coffee, "that I should have known Matsunaga was lying. I should have seen the lies in his reactions. Nobody—"

"That's it!" Julia froze with her tuna-on-roll poised an inch from her mouth, so intent she failed to notice the gob of mayonnaise threatening to drop onto her coat. "His reaction. I should have seen it right away." She slapped her forehead with her free hand. "I'm an idiot."

Foley calmly bit into his sandwich. "Can I assume we're no longer talking about Toshi Matsunaga?" he asked.

"Yeah." Julia took a step toward the water, gathering her thoughts before explaining. "We lured Craig Whitmore into the house early, figuring he was the weak link, and worked him over for three hours. We didn't bring him out until Liebman arrived because we wanted them to get a look at each other. That way, if they were co-conspirators, each would have to wonder if the other would decide to cop a deal. But it was as if they were expecting the move; and they hardly reacted. Later, though, when Harry McDonald told Whitmore that Liebman had a solid alibi, I thought Whitmore was gonna pass out."

"How does that matter?"

Julia's eyes widened in disbelief. "It was a classic double cross." When Foley didn't react, she continued with a shake of her head. Though she made an effort to avoid the tones she sometimes used to chastise her subordinates, her voice was sharp enough to bring a smile to Foley's lips. "If neither has an alibi, they're both protected. That's because, in a courtroom, whoever we accused could present the other to the jury as the real killer. Think about it. They each have a valid motive. They each have opportunity. They each have access to the means, which was waiting for them in Adeline's sitting room. It's the kind of smoke that leaves a jury completely befuddled."

"You're assuming they were co-conspirators."

"If they weren't, Craig wouldn't have reacted so strongly. He knew he was going down. Without meaning to, Harry yanked away his last hope."

"Then why didn't he implicate Liebman? For revenge, if for no other reason."

Julia finally bit into her sandwich, neatly lifting the gob of mayonnaise with her tongue. "That's exactly what I intend to find out." Then she smiled to herself. "And you know what, Pete? Now that Craig's had a taste of Rikers Island, I think, with just the tiniest bit of encouragement, he'll be more than happy to tell me."

42

THEY DIDN'T speak again until Foley turned the Subaru onto Kent Avenue and headed south. By that time, he could no longer contain his amusement.

"Something funny?" Julia asked.

"What makes you say that?"

"The smirk. To an experienced investigator, like myself, smirks are a dead giveaway."

"First thing, my so-called smirk is in fact a loving smile indicating tender affection as well as deep respect for the woman sitting beside me."

Though Julia folded her arms across her chest, she could not contain a quick grin. "Why don't we leave aside the question of what your smirk expresses until we discuss what motivated it in the first place?"

"Fair enough." Foley guided the Subaru to a halt at the intersection of Kent and Flushing avenues, then made an illegal right turn against the light. "Listening to you talk about Liebman and Whitmore back there, I got this feeling that you've reached a whole other level. Now you take *every* crime personally. Now you take *crime* personally."

"You can't believe that."

"No? Julia, I see the way you look at jaywalkers and I know you wanna drag them down into a precinct basement and kick the crap out of them. And God help the aggressive panhandlers and the squeegee men. You'd most likely hang them on the spot. Face it, Brennan, you've become a puritan. Next thing, you'll be hanging the Ten Commandments over the bed."

They both began to laugh, Foley for the first time in many days. Beside him, Julia wondered if he was taking those initial steps toward accepting the outcome of his search, whatever it was. She was fully aware of the pain that would engulf him should Patti again slip away. A year before, Julia had briefly entertained the possibility that her own daughter had been kidnapped by a monster in human form. Then again, on September 11, with Corry's school a few short blocks from the World Trade Center, Julia had been nearly overcome with fear.

Both alarms, as it turned out, were false; Corry had never been seriously threatened. Hence Julia had only gotten close enough to look down into the abyss. Foley, on the other hand, had fallen to its very depths, had been wandering those depths for many years. The same depths that had killed his wife.

Ten minutes later, they were in an industrial neighborhood given the name DUMBO by real estate developers in search of the next residential boom. The acronym stood for Down Under the Manhattan Bridge Overpass and the sharks hoped to transform the area into another Soho. Their ambitions were not without reason. Far from the catch-as-catch-can neighborhoods Pete and Julia had so far worked, the well-maintained buildings along Jay and Gold streets, like those in Soho, were ten and fifteen stories high. And like Soho, the enormous lofts they enclosed could easily be converted to elegant apartments that sold for millions of dollars.

There was one little difference, however. DUMBO was bisected by an elevated highway called the Brooklyn-Queens Expressway. As the Subaru paused for a light beneath that highway, Julia listened to the eighteen-wheelers above as they passed over what must have been a deep pothole, even by New York standards.

Bam, Bam, Bam, Bam, Bam!

"THIS IS the last one for tonight," Foley promised as he made a right onto Gold Street. "Tomorrow's another day."

"You wanna keep going, I'm okay."

"The chances of finding anybody still open are too remote to—"

Foley's arm came forward to shield Julia as he slammed on the brakes and jerked the car into reverse, finally coming to a stop fifty yards back. For a moment, Julia simply stared at him. Then she followed his eyes to a green van parked at the curb. The van bore no markings and no windows on the side facing her. Except for a single feature, a white spoiler mounted on the roof just in front of the rear doors, it was as anonymous as a New York pigeon.

"What am I looking at?" she said.

Foley took a minute, then began, "You remember what I told you about Lorenzo Contorno, the man who owns Proximate Services? About the van?"

"Refresh my memory."

"Lorenzo told me that he never found the courage to go down to the loading platform when the goodies were delivered. But he did watch from upstairs. According to him, all the deliveries over the last six months were made by a green van with a white spoiler mounted on the back. You think there are two like that in the city? And what's the chances one of them would happen to be parked next to a studio where the phone was picked up by an answering machine in the middle of the afternoon?"

THEY WENT the rest of the way to the twelve-story building that housed Cropper Studio Systems on foot, up to the only door not blocked by a steel shutter. Foley leaned hard on a buzzer. Above the buzzer, a plastic strip read: NIGHT BELL.

"Don't catch an attitude," Julia said. "If some square badge should make an appearance and be uncooperative."

Foley displayed his altar-boy smile. "I don't know how you can even think like that. I haven't killed anybody in almost a week."

The door opened abruptly, catching Julia poised at the edge a retort meant for Peter Foley. Instantly, she put the words aside as she arranged her mouth into a smile and displayed her shield.

"Hi, I was wondering if you could help us? What's your name?"

The man who stood before her was at least five inches shorter than Julia and skinny enough to fit through a keyhole. He wore an olive-green uniform that hung in a dead-straight line, from his armpits to his hips, without ever touching his body. In his right hand, he held a woven black leash. The other end of the leash was attached to the collar of an obese Rottweiler, a female, who wagged her tail and snuffled when Julia and Pete came into view.

"Walter Finkle," he said.

Julia reached out to shake his hand, allowing herself just those few seconds to read the man. He was looking up at her through watery green eyes, his mouth slightly open, his breathing shallow, as anxious to please as his dog.

"Walter," she finally said, careful to use his first name, "would you mind stepping outside for a minute? I want to ask you a few questions about one of your tenants."

"Sure."

When Finkle stepped through the doorway, his Rottweiler lumbered over to Foley who casually scratched the dog's ears. Finkle looked hurt. "You're not supposed to pet the dog when she's working," he said.

Foley stopped abruptly whereupon the dog rolled onto its back and stared up at him with beseeching eyes.

"Crown used to be a good security dog," Finkle said. "But she's an old lady now." He continued to stare up at Julia. "So what could I do ya for?"

"I'm interested in one of your tenants: Cropper Studios. What can you tell me about them?"

Finkle raised a finger to his mouth as he considered the question. "Not much," he finally replied. "I don't come on duty until eight and usually they're gone by then. They don't make no problems for the landlord as far as I know."

"Is that who you work for? The landlord and not a security agency?" Julia asked, though she knew the answer. Only the landlord, hoping to save a few bucks over the cost of hiring private security, would employ Walter Finkle.

"Yeah."

"Okay, what can you tell us about the owner of Cropper Studios?"

"I'm not a hundred percent sure who that is. These artsy types, they all act like they're boss. But I think the guy who runs the show is an Oriental."

"Describe him."

"Well, he's. . . ." Finkle looked down for the first time. "He's a short guy, maybe thirty-five. Wears his hair down over his eyes. Wants everybody to notice his fifty-dollar haircut."

"I got ya, Walter." Julia smiled as the use of his name brought Finkle's eyes back to hers. "Is this man's name Toshi Matsunaga?"

"No. His last name sounded like Sheehan, except it doesn't start with *s*, it starts with *j*, sort of."

"I get the point. Now, Walter, we're gonna have to go up there and knock on the door, see if maybe someone's inside."

"I don't know. . . ."

Julia waved off his feeble protest. "The man we're looking for, whatever his real name, is a fugitive from justice. There's a federal warrant out for his arrest and we have reason to believe he may be inside Cropper Studios. Now I'm not asking you to kick down the door, Walter. I'm asking you to accompany us along public hallways. As the landlord's representative, you have every right to allow us access."

Finkle drew himself to his full height which left him face-to-face with Julia's chest. " 'Course I got the right," he declared."

"Then what's the problem?"

When Walter responded by turning to lead the way, Julia's and Pete's eyes dropped simultaneously to the enormous ring of keys attached to his belt. Neither smiled.

43

THE DOUBLE doors separating the interior of Cropper Studios from the wide corridor where Julia stood presented themselves as two sheets of steel joined by four pick-resistant dead-bolt locks. There was no light visible behind the doors, either at the top or the bottom.

Faced with this obstacle, Julia looked at Pete for a moment, checking his volatility index. Without doubt, he wanted nothing more than to rip the keys from Walter Finkle's belt. But Foley appeared unperturbed and his eyes betrayed no emotion stronger than confidence. He knew—or so it seemed to Julia—that she would do whatever it took to get the door open, even though neither believed Matsunaga to be inside.

"You better stay back," Julia said to Walter Finkle as she made a show of withdrawing her weapon before pounding the side of her fist into the door. "Police!" she screamed at the top of her lungs. "Open this door!"

Julia listened to her voice echo back and forth across the hallway. Just as the echoes died away, she said, "Did you hear that, Walter?"

"What?" Finkle asked.

Though Foley had to turn away to hide his amusement, Julia maintained a straight face. "Police!" she again shouted. "Open up right now!" This time, she put her ear directly against the steel door and listened intently.

"Right there," she said. "How could you not hear that? It sounds like somebody moaning."

"I don't—"

Julia pulled back and assumed a solemnity she believed appropriate to an officer of the law in the performance of her duty. "I've got to get in there, Walter."

"But—"

"Walter, once I come to believe. . . . Whoa, did you hear it that time?"

"I—"

Julia shook her head. "Walter, I have reason to believe that a man or a woman may be lying injured behind these doors. My oath as an officer of the law requires me to investigate. Now, are you gonna open the door or do I have to take it down? And by the way, I naturally assume full responsibility."

THE ODOR that rushed over Julia when she pulled the doors open was so strong she could not understand why she hadn't smelled it right through those doors, why she hadn't smelled it while still outside the building. There was nobody lying injured within Cropper Studios. There was somebody lying dead.

Julia found a series of light switches mounted on the wall a bit to the right of the doors. She snapped them open and the interior jumped into sharp relief as a dozen fluorescent fixtures came on ten feet above her head. She was looking at a basically open space divided into a number of functions. The office was in the front, close to the door. Except for a Dell computer resting on a desk, everything appeared to be in place. The Dell's tower had been eviscerated, its transistors and resistors scattered, its various drives crushed and broken.

Behind the office, a tiny kitchen against the far wall had a two-burner stove, a mini-fridge and a tiny sink. Open shelves above the sink held a mismatched collection of plates, glasses and cups. Several of those cups sat unwashed in the sink.

The remainder of the open space was divided into mini-studios reserved for still photography. An unscrolled backdrop, six feet from a Hasselblad camera mounted on a sturdy tripod, depicted a crowned princess who bore a striking resemblance to the young Grace Kelly.

By this time, Julia was standing with her weapon raised, sweeping the room, aware that Foley had already drawn his own weapon. Walter Finkle, on the other hand, looked as though he was about to pass out. Older and wiser, his faithful companion was pulling as hard as she could in the other direction.

Finally satisfied that no enemy lurked nearby, Julia allowed herself to focus on the rear of the loft and a makeshift wall of plywood that spanned the room. The wall was entirely blank except for a wooden door near the center. As she approached the door, Julia angled to the right, placing her body outside the direct line of fire. To her left, Foley trailed slightly behind.

The stench of death grew stronger as they approached, until there was no longer any doubting its origins. Not only was somebody—or *some bodies*, Julia reminded herself—lying dead behind that door, the somebody or some bodies had been dead for several days at the very least. Hence, they were extremely unlikely to find a living human being on the other side of the wall. Nevertheless, she played it by the book.

"Police!" she shouted, as she had just a moment before. "Come out of there!" She repeated the command once again, then twisted the knob and pushed the door open, fully aware of Foley covering her. He was maintaining a shooter's stance, right leg back, hands extended, leaning slightly forward to cushion potential recoil.

The opening door revealed only a wedge of the darkened inner room, just enough for Julia to see a window mounted on the rear wall. A backdrop behind the window displayed sunny blue skies and the upper branches of a scarlet maple at the height of its autumnal display.

Without stepping inside, Julia ran her fingers over the inner wall until she found a light switch. The odor of death was now strong enough to coat her flesh and she was not surprised by what the lights revealed, not by the pair of windows, by the water-stain on the ceiling, by the bloated corpse, or the glimmer of writhing insects, or the skull crushed by the traditional blunt object.

As she turned away, having seen more than enough, Julia told herself that she had no good reason to examine the crime scene more closely. The corpse was male and fully dressed; the case would not go to Sex Crimes. Better to leave the scene undisturbed, let the locals do their thing.

It was a decent rationale, as rationales go, but it simply evaporated, revealing a somewhat more primitive motivation, when Foley lowered his weapon and said, his tone indignant, "What, you're not gonna take the poor guy's pulse?"

44

JULIA LOOKED over her shoulder, prepared to fire off a quick response, but Foley was already past her, his eyes focused on the office space at the other side of the loft.

"Slow down a minute, Pete," she said before turning her attention to Walter Finkle. "Walter, there's a dead body in that back room which I am now going to report to the Eighty-eighth Precinct. I was wondering if you'd go down to the front door and direct traffic when the locals arrive?"

More than eager, Finkle responded with a nod and a gulp, then headed off to the elevator. Crown was eager as well. Julia listened to the dog moan as she pulled her master along the corridor.

"Is that Matsunaga back there?" she asked Foley who was opening desk drawers and filing cabinets.

"Yeah."

"Do you think Charlie Terranova got to him?"

"No. Terranova wouldn't have destroyed the computer." Foley riffled through a stack of files. "I think Matsunaga became too hot for his partners and they cut their losses."

Julia collected her shoulder bag from the floor of the hall, plucked out her cell phone and reported Matsunaga's demise to a lieutenant named Girardi at the eight-eight. When she hung up after securing his promise to respond forthwith, Foley was standing ten feet away, holding a plastic box filled with floppy discs, each in its own little slot.

"You think there's anything useful on those discs?" She gestured to the mutilated remains of the computer.

"The computer was ripped apart because Matsunaga's killers didn't know another way to destroy the data inside. Maybe they didn't know what was on the discs either. Maybe they were in a hurry." Foley took a breath. "I have to play out the string," he told Julia. "I can't let anything go unchecked. If I do, I know I'll be telling myself, somewhere down the line, that if I'd just made this one more effort, I would have found her."

Julia crossed the room and opened her bag. "Dump the discs in here," she told him. "Nobody's going to search me."

Foley complied without hesitation. "I have another favor to ask," he announced. "I want to call in the FBI and Raymond Lear. I want to do it now."

"That's a biggie," Julia admitted. In fact, as both knew, Julia would rather surrender her weapon to a crack addict than surrender a case to the FBI. Like every other New York City cop.

"If I don't notify him, Lear's gonna take it very hard. That wouldn't matter if I didn't need him, but the way things are shaking up, I may have to ask him for a favor."

"Like?"

"I know Matsunaga had a computer in his home because I was able to trace his e-mails to a physical address. Most likely, Lear has already seized that computer. If I want to get a look at it, I'm gonna have to beg."

Though Julia believed the odds against Lear's allowing a civilian access to seized evidence were large indeed, she simply nodded. She was not about to foreclose any of Foley's possibilities.

"If all else fails," Pete said as he waited for Lear to answer, "I might go public, now that I know Patti's alive and I have a recent photo. Maybe I'll try *America's Most Wanted*. Somebody would have to recognize her, some neighbor, a teacher, someone. I know there's a risk. I know whoever has her might decide to—"

Two uniformed cops burst into the room at that moment. Instantly, Julia assumed her professional demeanor, a demeanor she'd been long in perfecting. She raised her left hand, palm up, as she displayed her shield with her right.

"Let's everybody get outside in the corridor," she ordered. "We've messed up the crime scene enough already."

J ULIA MADE a slight change to the sequence of events when she gave an oral report to Detective Karl Marevic an hour later. She told him she'd first smelled the odor of decaying flesh while still in the corridor, before asking Walter Finkle to unlock the doors. She was at Cropper Studios in the first place, she hastened to add, because her confidential informant, Peter Foley, had convinced her that Cropper Studios was being used to produce child pornography and that a federal fugitive named Toshi Matsunaga might be found inside its professional offices. Which, in fact, he was.

If Detective Marevic found her statement unsatisfactory, he gave no sign of it until Special Agent Raymond Lear, accompanied by three subordinates, stepped out of the elevator. Then Marevic tossed Julia a look of such loathing that it required all her self-control to maintain a straight face.

TALL AND dignified in his sharply pressed uniform, Inspector Laurindo Escobar arrived twenty minutes later to represent the interests of the NYPD upper command. The body, the crime scene and every item contained within the crime scene, he told Raymond Lear, belonged to the NYPD. There was nothing more to discuss.

Lear didn't argue. Instead, he whipped out his cell phone and stalked off.

Another twenty minutes passed before Inspector Escobar's own cell phone rang. By that time, the Crime Scene Unit was working the back room. Escobar listened for a moment, then said, "Yes, sir," before hanging up.

The NYPD, Escobar now told a smug Raymond Lear, was prepared to accept the presence of a federal agent, acting as a liaison, for the duration of the Matsunaga investigation.

Julia watched the process with some amusement, until she realized that she was going to be kept at the scene until Escobar, lackey though he undoubtedly was, decided to release her. As the gods were clearly angry with Julia Brennan, that might not be for hours.

She looked over at Foley who was talking to Raymond Lear. Lear was nodding from time to time, though his expression remained serious. For cops, goodwill is a promissory note to be redeemed at a later date. Foley now held Raymond Lear's marker and he was making sure Lear knew it.

Well, she had chores to do and it was past time to get to them. Quickly, before she could change her mind, she dialed Lily Han's home number.

"Sorry to bother you, Lily," she said, before presenting a concise summary of the evening's events, emphasizing the role of Walter Finkle, the landlord's representative, at every stage. "We're completely covered on this," she confidently concluded. "We have nothing to worry about."

Though Julia felt her summary encompassed all the relevant information, Han went directly to its weakest point. "What were you doing there by yourself?" she asked. "If you thought Matsunaga was inside, why didn't you at least call in the locals as backup?"

Before Julia could reply, Lily continued. "This is about Peter Foley's daughter, isn't it?" Again, she rattled on without waiting for an answer. "Isn't it strange that the person I rely on most is conducting an investigation using SCU personnel without telling me? Isn't it a little weird that her boss is the last person at SCU to find out? Remember, Julia, you don't work for the New York Police Department. Technically, you're on loan to the District Attorney's Office and your salary comes out of our budget."

"I went by the book." If there was anything Julia had learned in her eighteen years on the job, it was stick to your story. "Habib al Rif'at led me to Joey Navarro. Navarro led me to Matsunaga. As for backup, there were no lights on at Cropper Studios when I arrived and it wasn't until I was standing in front of the door that I came to believe there was somebody inside. Up until that point, I was just burning shoe leather."

"Enough," Han declared. "Don't tell me anything else. Save the bullshit for Internal Affairs if your game blows up in your face. Now, good-bye—"

"Wait, don't hang up. There's something else." Julia again looked at Peter Foley who, having caught the general drift of the conversation, was grinning from ear to ear. As for her own ears, she knew full well they were decidedly reddened. That was because they felt like they were on fire.

"And what's that?"

"I want to reinterview Craig Whitmore. I think he lied to us when he said he acted alone."

"And why would he do that?"

"Lie?"

"Yes."

"Because that was the deal he made with his partner or partners. Everybody knew, from day one, that any of them might be accused. The point was to take it like a man. To Craig, master of the hot wax torture, the macho aspect had to have appeal. He would stand up to Adeline, finally, and he would stand up to a charge of murder as well."

"So what makes you think he'll talk now?"

"For the last two days, Craig's been on Rikers Island. That's plenty of time for the S&M fantasy to depart and the S&M reality to set in."

45

FATHER JEAN Lucienne began his sermon at Holy Savior's 8 A.M. mass with an ecumenically inspired story lifted from a little book called *Tales of the Zen Monks*. The story was about a supplicant named Basho, a pious and determined young man who visited one monastery after another in a fruitless search for satori. Years went by, with Basho passing from youth into middle age, until finally, in a remote corner of the empire, he met an elderly monk who explained that satori is not to be found in the hours of formal meditation. It's the journey, he further explained, that really matters, not the destination. The old monk gave this technique a name that instantly enlightened Basho: Every-minute Zen.

"We are Christians," Father Lucienne declared, his gaze drifting to Peter Foley, who sat in a pew at the rear of the church, "but this teaching also applies to us. Call it Every-minute Charity. Not charity inspired by a panhandler's outstretched cup. Or by a mail solicitation from Doctors Without Borders or Catholic Charities. Or by your brother-in-law suddenly being thrown out of work. I'm talking about the charity you hold, second by second, in your heart. Charity that includes not just the worthy, but the unworthy as well. I'm talking about unrelenting charity, ruthless charity, charity that forgives every trespass, no matter how awful."

Though Father Lucienne's words were inspired, he was wasting his breath trying to reach Peter Foley. Foley was beyond the entreaties of his good and bad angels. His prayers were only for success in the moment. The floppy discs he'd spent much of the night examining had, with a single exception, proved innocuous. He'd found backup discs for the software installed in Cropper's now-destroyed computer, Cropper's legitimate accounts formatted for a *Lotus* spreadsheet, and thousands of still photos, all perfectly appropriate.

Thus, as he formulated his prayers, Foley was concentrating on the single exception. That exception was an encryption key. Though Foley had no good reason to believe it relevant to any data stored on Matsunaga's home computer, he was a man without immediately available options. Later, if necessary, he would attempt to formulate a strategy, no matter how desperate, that would lead him to Matsunaga's partners a step ahead of the NYPD and the FBI. For now, he had an encryption key and an unexamined computer. Maybe.

So Peter Foley prayed for success, for that long shot to crank it out in the stretch, to get up in the final strides. His prayers—and he knew this—were in large part selfishly motivated. That was because a series of very unpleasant hypotheticals, driven to the rear of his consciousness by the hope of finding Toshi Matsunaga, were again commanding the major part of his attention. Each of these hypotheticals began with the words *what if*, then led, step by step, to a realm Peter Foley defined as hell.

After mass, Foley stayed long enough to shake hands with Father Lucienne. "An excellent sermon, Jean," he told the priest, "but you left something out."

"What's that?"

"Instructing us to love our enemies isn't really that useful unless you also tell us how to do it."

Father Jean Lucienne was up to the jibe. He tapped the side of his long bony nose with an equally bony finger, then said, "You're right, Pete. I can't tell you how. But I can get you off to a good start. The road to loving your enemies begins with the *desire* to love your enemies. Something like losing weight."

JULIA STARTED her day with a note left on her bureau. The note was from Peter Foley. He was on his way to mass, he explained, then off to Lear's office where he would claim his marker. At no time would his cell phone be turned off and he would call her if anything significant developed. In the meantime, she should enjoy the hunt for Steve Liebman which he had no doubt she would personally pursue. In fact, as he was likely to spend the better part of the day at FBI headquarters while she would be only a few blocks away at SCU, perhaps they could have lunch.

Though Julia recognized the note's breezy tone for the fraud it was, she believed Foley's assurances. He would remain available. He would call her before taking any rash action. The issue was settled.

That he was also right about her intentions didn't bear a moment's consideration. Julia was out the door by seven o'clock, striding SCU's squad room a bit after eight-thirty.

There were six detectives in the room when Julia entered. She looked from one to another, her gaze finally settling on Bert and Betty. Julia was searching for any hint of amusement, for any sign that either was still relishing the image of Julia Brennan knocked on her ass. Vulnerability was never her strong point.

But the only emotion Julia recognized was mild curiosity. Captain Brennan had the week off. Captain Brennan came to work. What's up with that?

"Bert, Betty," she said, as she crossed the room to her office, "I need to speak to you."

She stepped aside to let her detectives precede her into the room, closed the door behind her, then revealed the demise of Toshi Matsunaga. As both had volunteered their services to aid Peter Foley, she felt they had a right to the details, even though one or both had blabbed to some detective who'd blabbed to Lily Han. That Foley might need their services again in the future did not escape her, either.

"How's he handling it?" Betty asked.

"Pete?"

"Yeah."

"He's taking the next step."

Griffith nodded. "The guy has real—" He looked from Betty to Julia, noted the incipient frowns. "What? You thought I was gonna use the word balls?"

"It did occur to me," Julia admitted.

"Integrity, captain. That's what Foley has in abundance. Integrity."

"Great. Now tell me how far you've gotten with the phone records I asked you to subpoena. I need to know because it looks as if Lily Han's gonna take another shot at Craig Whitmore. Or I'm hoping she will. Right now, she's pissed off at me."

"All the parties—Hannah, Steve, Craig, and his wife Margaret— own cell phones. Between them, they use three different carriers." Griffith dug out his notebook, wet his finger and flicked through the pages. "Here it is. They use MCI, Sprint, and Verizon. I served the subpoenas yesterday between six and seven-thirty. We should get a reply by midafternoon at the latest. If you want me to make a few calls, see if I can speed it up—"

Julia shook her head. "Midafternoon will be fine. Most likely it will take days to set up a meeting with Craig because we'll have to go through his lawyer and lawyers are never in a hurry to do anything. Besides, it was just a hunch, anyway."

"Amen," Griffith declared, "to that."

JULIA BRENNAN was wrong on every count. Her first inkling of just how wrong came a few minutes later when the phone on her desk began to ring. It was Lily Han, calling from her office. As Lily was almost never in her office before nine-thirty, Julia prepared herself for the worst.

Wrong again. Lily Han, it seemed, had spent her night preoccupied, not with Julia's indiscretions, but with Steve Liebman's departing words on the afternoon of his abortive interrogation. Specifically, Lily had focused obsessively on two words uttered by Steve Liebman in reference to Asian prostitutes: *Oriental merchandise.* A third-generation Korean American, Lily Han had moved far from her roots in pursuit of a career that required her to spend the better part of her working days in the company of Europeans. Nevertheless, she retained a certain sensitivity, a line in the sand which Steve Liebman had most decidedly crossed.

"I'd do almost anything," she told Julia, "to get that scumbag. I mean, I wouldn't actually frame the man, but if Whitmore tells us Liebman was involved, I'm prepared to give him the benefit of the doubt, even if there's no direct evidence."

"Put Liebman on that murder hook," Julia shamelessly encouraged, "then watch him squirm?"

"Exactly."

46

S ECURITY WAS tight at the Federal Building when Peter
Foley joined a line of visitors strung out along Church Street. Foley
didn't mind the wait. The skies above were clear, the day warm, the
streets alive with pedestrians though on its Vesey Street side,
the Federal Building faced the site of a deep pit where the towers
of the World Trade Center once stood.

Foley passed the time casually observing the interaction
between a sidewalk vendor of coffee, bagels and doughnuts, and
his impatient customers. Despite Foley's cynical (not to mention
obnoxious) remark following mass, the service had produced the
ratcheting-down effect he'd sought. He was already considering his
next move should Raymond Lear turn down his request for access
to Matsunaga's computer. The floppy discs he'd passed the night
examining contained the names and addresses of Cropper Studios'

legitimate customers, including a series of Catholic schools in Brooklyn and Queens. Surely, these repeat customers would know the names of Matsunaga's active partners, or at least of the photographers employed by Cropper.

If Foley got to them ahead of the FBI. . . . If he convinced Raymond Lear to give him a head start. . . . If, if, if, if, if.

When his turn came, Foley deposited his 9-millimeter Glock, along with the contents of his pockets, including his carry permit, in a gray plastic bin, then passed through a metal detector that remained blessedly silent. The two Federal Police officers who examined the contents of the bin were not visibly upset by Foley's Glock, though they scrutinized his permit carefully. When they were satisfied, they tucked the weapon into a locked cabinet where it would remain until his business with Special Agent Raymond Lear was completed.

Upstairs, on the fourteenth floor, Foley entered Lear's office to find him standing by the window. Foley often found him in this posture and suspected it was Lear's way of drawing attention to the fact that he had a window while others, of equal rank, labored away in cubicles.

"Take a seat," Lear ordered as he slid into the leather chair behind his desk. The desk was solid maple, highly polished and empty except for a few pens in a clear plastic holder and the requisite photos of Lear's wife and two children. "What can I do for you?"

"I'm here to collect, Ray."

"For what?" Lear swiveled his chair so that he was facing a framed diploma on the wall to Foley's left. The diploma was from Columbia University and proclaimed Lear to be a doctor of laws.

"For putting you in this office."

"You think that was your doing?"

"How many cases have I made for you, Ray? Be honest."

"Dozens."

"Dozens I could have given to the NYPD. Remember, for most of the time you've been making your living off me, I was a cop."

Lear's wide mouth expanded into a lopsided grin. "I found Terranova on my own," he declared.

"And blew the investigation. If I hadn't turned up Contorno, Charlie Banana would be a free man. And so would Joey Cadillac and the rest of the crew."

Clearly outgunned, Lear rose from his desk and walked back to the window where he apparently felt more comfortable. "Okay," he said without turning around, "I acknowledge the debt. You're holding my marker. Now, tell me exactly what you want."

"Access to Matsunaga's personal computer."

"Matsunaga has a computer?"

"Don't bullshit me, Ray."

"I'm not."

"Are you telling me you haven't been inside Matsunaga's townhouse?"

"I was hoping Matsunaga would decide that we were his best bet and come back, so I placed his home under surveillance while I applied for a search warrant. Then, after you brought in Contorno, Matsunaga was dumped on the back burner. We had the warrant and we were gonna serve it eventually, but—"

"But you didn't get around to it."

"No." Lear returned to his desk, centering his gaze on Foley's. "Look, Pete, I know you're a guy who needs his enemies, but I'm getting real sick of being cast as the monster in your fantasies. You didn't have to come in here waving your marker in my face."

Having already formulated a second line of attack in the event that Lear refused to acknowledge his indebtedness, Foley's response was quick and to the point.

"Fine," he said, "then let me appeal directly to your conscience. I'm almost within sight of my daughter, Patti, who was kidnapped six years ago and has been held in bondage ever since. Matsunaga's computer might get me a little closer and you are therefore morally obliged to allow me access. Remember, the Man upstairs watches everything you do."

B Y T H E time Julia Brennan walked into Lily Han's office bearing a video of Craig Whitmore's interrogation, Lily had already been on the phone three times with Deputy Warden Soong Park who presided over the men's jail on Rikers Island. Han and Park were active members of a small network of Korean Americans, men and women who'd worked themselves up the civil service and corporate ladders. At Lily's urging, Soong Park had taken her request for an interview to Craig Whitmore, along with a broad hint that agreement could lead to a marked improvement in Craig's living conditions.

Whitmore was currently being held in an open housing area along with seventy-three other prisoners awaiting trial. As this unit was patrolled by a single corrections officer, there was plenty of room for mischief. According to Soong Park, Whitmore had already been persuaded to exchange his Gucci loafers for a pair of well-worn sneakers.

Though careful to remain attentive, Julia waited patiently for Lily Han to move the topic of conversation from Craig Whitmore to Peter Foley. Julia was certain that at least one more lecture was forthcoming. That it did not come left her all the more apprehensive. Lily Han, she told herself, has already made a decision about Julia Brennan's future and the news will not be good.

"Assuming Whitmore agrees to an interview," Lily finally concluded, "you and I will conduct it. Right now, I need to be briefed. Convince me that I'm not just out to get Steve Liebman."

Julia sat up straighter. Lily Han was barely visible behind the stacks of file folders covering her desk and Julia wanted to look her superior in the eye.

"On that first day," she began, "right after we discovered Adeline's body, why did Liebman talk to us? Remember, he'd already spoken to a lawyer who no doubt advised him to keep his big mouth shut. Second, once he decided to talk to us, why did he withhold his alibi?"

"Liebman spent the night with a prostitute. Maybe he was embarrassed."

Julia laughed. "I know you have to play devil's advocate, Lily, but that's pretty weak in light of Stevie's attitude when he finally told us the truth. The man was proud of himself."

"Okay," Lily conceded, "what else?"

"Third, during his initial interview, Liebman not only withheld his alibi, he lied when he told us he wasn't familiar with Adeline's will and hadn't seen Adeline or Craig Whitmore in months. He had to know we'd find out, so why bother? Unless he *wanted* to make himself a suspect."

Julia pulled her shoulder bag onto her lap. Now that she was sure Lily Han was along for the ride, she began to relax. The future would take care of itself. For now, she had Steve Liebman. "I've got the clincher right here," she told Lily, "on video tape. All you have to do is watch."

The section of tape Julia chose to run unfolded in less than five seconds. Harry McDonald said, "Bad news, Craig. The worst. Your buddy, Steve Liebman, has got a one-hundred-percent unbreakable alibi. That leaves you. That means you killed Adeline Rose."

Even before McDonald finished, Whitmore's head and shoulders jerked up and his eyes widened. Then he fumbled for his glasses, knocking them across the table before he finally raised his eyes to meet McDonald's.

"What we're seeing, right there," Julia declared after a fourth run-through, "is shock. The man's not disappointed, he's surprised."

As a trial lawyer, Lily Han's instincts had been finely honed by the arduous demands of cross-examination, an art at which she was generally accorded the rank of master. "I'm embarrassed," she told Julia Brennan, "that I didn't see it myself. It was right there in front of me."

Julia leaned back in her chair. "If it wasn't for Steve Liebman, I wouldn't have seen it either. If he'd offered his alibi right away, served it in a gentlemanly fashion, I would have put the case behind me the minute Craig Whitmore confessed."

"'Pride,'" Lily Han, a practicing Methodist, observed, "'goeth before a fall.'"

"Let's hope so. Because if the son of a bitch gets past us again, we're gonna be very depressed."

47

JULIA SPENT the remainder of the morning at her desk while Lily ironed out the wrinkles. The problem was not Craig Whitmore who readily agreed to be interviewed in exchange for a transfer to the hospital unit where he could lay his head to rest without having to fear it's being cut off while he slept. The problem was Craig's attorney, Leon Weissman, who'd initially refused to make an appointment. Perhaps he could free up a few hours toward the middle of the following week, he told Lily Han. He couldn't be sure, though. The trip out to Rikers, what with the traffic and all, would play havoc with his schedule.

It was only when Craig Whitmore, on his own initiative, threatened to dump Leon Weissman, then place himself at the tender mercies of a Legal Aid lawyer, that Weissman reconsidered. Perhaps, he now suggested, if his client could be brought into

Manhattan, say to SCU's office, he, Leon Weissman, would be able to appear briefly at one-thirty that same afternoon.

It was a quarter after twelve and Whitmore was expected at any minute when Julia called Betty Cohen and Bert Griffith into her office. Neither of them, Julia bluntly explained, was going to interview Craig Whitmore. A higher power named Lily Han had decided that she and Julia, representing the District Attorney's office and the New York Police Department, could accomplish the task unaided.

"But I want you to stick around, Harry and Carlos, too. If Whitmore comes across, we're going to take Liebman down together. All of us."

Betty Cohen clicked a fingernail against her upper incisors, then said, "Can I put on the cuffs?"

"You know, Betty," Griffith observed before Julia could reply, "you gotta stop aiming low if you want to get anywhere in life."

"What does that mean?"

"It means you should've asked if you could do the body search. Assuming you really wanna get under the guy's skin."

PETER FOLEY set out for Toshi Matsunaga's Greenwich Village home shortly after eleven o'clock. He was accompanied by two FBI agents, Alfred Prescott and William Henderson, the same agents who'd escorted him to Lear's safe house in Staten Island. Though Foley was not a prisoner, they stayed on either side of him as they walked him to his car, then searched the briefcase he removed from the trunk.

Twenty minutes later, when they reached Matsunaga's two-story townhouse on Charles Street, Henderson produced a set of master keys and went to work on the door. The trick here was to get

off the street in a hurry. Lear had notified RiteWay Alarm Systems
of the FBI's impending search of the premises, but he hadn't
informed the detectives actively investigating Matsunaga's death.
The hope was that Foley and company would get in and out without being observed.

Once they were inside and the door closed behind them, Foley
hesitated just long enough to don a pair of latex gloves before sys-
tematically exploring the house. In the process, he found a large
room on the first floor set aside for the storage of video tapes.
There were hundreds: stacked on shelves, crammed into boxes,
scattered across the floor, a warehouse of tapes awaiting a legion
of eager consumers.

Motivated by the very slight possibility that he would find a box
filled with *Patti's Dance* tapes, a box with a return address, Foley
searched the room carefully. He found neither tapes nor address
and gave up the job twenty minutes later.

Next to the storage room, Foley discovered Matsunaga's office.
Except for noting that the computer mounted on a corner work
station was a high-end Sony, he passed the room by as he continued his methodical search, peering into rooms, opening closets and
cabinet doors for a quick inspection. He found nothing out of
place until he reached a bedroom at the end of the second-floor
hallway. From the posters of Britney Spears and the Back Street
Boys, to the stuffed animals leaning against the pillows, to the
frilly pink bedspread, the room had clearly been designed for a girl
on the verge of adolescence.

"Jesus Christ," Agent Henderson declared as he grasped the
implications.

Amused by Henderson's blasphemy, Foley glanced at Prescott
who remained expressionless, perhaps because Henderson, notoriously surly, was by far the larger of the two.

"Well, gentlemen," Foley said when it became clear that Henderson's outburst was going to remain unchallenged, "shall we go to work?"

J ULIA B RENNAN would have given her eyeteeth to make a similar request, though she might have deleted the gentlemen part. As it was, Craig Whitmore, sporting a purple half-moon beneath his swollen right eye, did not arrive at twelve-thirty as promised. Handcuffed and shackled, he hobbled into the squad room at one-thirty, dwarfed by a trio of burly corrections officers.

"Whose idea was this?" Julia said, pointing to Whitmore's shackled ankles. She knew, of course, that shackles were routinely used by the Department of Corrections when transporting prisoners to nonsecure facilities. She also knew Craig might easily view his chains as just another humiliation courtesy of a heartless system that definitely included Lily and Julia. Now she would ride to his rescue.

"Standard procedure." The corrections officer who responded, a black man who wore the stripes of a sergeant on his sleeves, folded his arms across his chest.

"Well, do you think we can take them off now?" Julia gestured to the seven detectives seated at their desks. "In light of the fact that Mr. Whitmore is fast approaching seventy years of age and everybody in the room is armed?"

The sergeant looked at her for a moment, then signaled to one of his underlings who reluctantly produced a pair of keys on a small ring. Julia waited patiently until Whitmore was free before guiding him into the largest of SCU's interview rooms.

"You want some coffee, something to eat?" she asked.

Whitmore rubbed at his wrists for a moment, then said. "Yes, I would like some coffee. Cream, no sugar. And a turkey club, heavy on the mayonnaise, with crispy french fries. Do you think you can manage that?"

Julia nodded agreement, even as she measured Whitmore's attitude. The offer they'd made to lure him into an interview room, she knew, could easily backfire. The state had promised Craig a transfer to the hospital unit merely for agreeing to talk. Maybe he'd regard that as victory enough and cling to his side of the bargain. A deal's a deal. A manly man doesn't rat on his partner.

As Julia turned to leave, Whitmore spoke, confirming her worst fears. "What I told you the first time," he said, "was the truth. I don't see what else you could want to know."

"Mr. Whitmore," Julia replied, as she was bound to reply, "we can't discuss matters germane to the investigation outside the presence of your lawyer. Hopefully, he'll arrive any second."

But it wasn't Leon Weissman who chose that very second to open the door and poke his head into the room. It was a frustrated Lily Han. "Bad news," she announced. "I just got off the phone with Leon Weissman. He claims he has to argue a motion during the noon recess and won't arrive until three-thirty or four. We'll just have to wait it out."

48

WHEN THE Sony booted up without demanding a password, displaying a constellation of icons on its flat-screen monitor, Foley was not discouraged. True, Matsunaga had not seen fit to protect his files with a password, the safeguard most common to home computers. But the obvious explanation, that Toshi had nothing to hide, Foley was able to reject out of hand. The e-mails they'd exchanged had been very frank. At Lear's suggestion, Foley had made sure of that, going so far as to attach the sort of images that resulted in very long jail sentences should they be recovered by a government agency.

"Tell me," Foley said to agents Prescott and Henderson who were seated behind him, "what do you know about computers?"

"Nothing," Prescott said. Next to him, Henderson limited himself to a shrug. His eyes already half closed, he'd apparently decided to sleep his way through what was shaping up as an extremely boring assignment.

For his part, Foley was pleased. If his minders didn't know what he was doing, they would remain ignorant should he make that essential discovery. Then it would simply be a matter of getting rid of them before he took the next step.

As EXPECTED, Foley not only discovered hundreds of files on the Sony's hard drive but a dozen floppies, each containing additional files, in a desk drawer on the far side of the room. The task of examining these files would have been enough to discourage even well-motivated amateurs. But Foley had been down this road before and knew, given time, patience and a high tolerance for pure tedium, the job could be done. Nevertheless, because the first element—time—was not unlimited, he made a simple assumption before getting down to business.

If Matsunaga was hiding anything, Foley decided, he would hide those e-mails sent to him by dear old Goober.

Foley went so far as to retrieve Matsunaga's "permanently deleted" e-mails. The same e-mails consumers foolishly thought were gone for good when the computer asked *Do you want to permanently delete all messages in this folder*, and they clicked on the YES button. Far from gone forever, the e-mails remained exactly where they were. Only now they were invisible, not to the experienced investigator, but to the poor jerk who'd naively accepted the computer at its word.

There were any number of ways to remedy this little deception, to write over the files, altering them forever. But these remedies were time-consuming and required the purchase of additional software. Matsunaga had not taken this route and eventually Foley worked his way back to where the e-mails he'd sent Matsunaga should have been, but were not. He accomplished the job in an hour, using readily available commercial software that he'd brought with him exactly for this purpose.

It was almost one o'clock when Foley completed the task. Tired by this time, and hungry, he wandered into Matsunaga's kitchen and opened the refrigerator. He knew, now, that the big Sony held secrets. But he did not know where they were or how they'd been concealed. Suddenly, he turned on his heel and went back into the office, to the floppies in Matsunaga's desk. When he didn't find what he was looking for, he began a closer search of the room, circling Agent Henderson who was snoring lightly.

Foley knew there were many software products designed to hide data in very ingenious ways. Though each had flaws, each had different flaws, which again raised the question of when Raymond Lear would pull the plug. Foley needed a little guidance, and he found it in the second of three filing cabinets set beneath a window looking out onto Charles Street. In addition to several dozen bank statements, the folder he extracted contained a single floppy disc. The disc's label bore the handwritten name of one of the more popular encryption methods currently available: PGP. Just like the disc Foley had recovered at Cropper Studios.

Well, Foley mused, that was the great flaw in the game of encryption. In order to either encrypt or decrypt, one had to have a key. This key, in turn, had to be stored, say on a floppy disc, and kept handy enough for practical use. If encrypted data and key were discovered together, pursuant to a lawful search warrant, you were screwed. The hope, of course, was that you'd feel the search coming and dispose of the disc beforehand. Whereupon you would no longer (and never again) be able to access your encrypted data.

NEITHER TIRED nor hungry now, Foley settled down to sys-tematically review each of the files in Matsunaga's computer. The job was no longer daunting because he knew what he was looking for. The files he retrieved either would or would not be encrypted; he would only have to glance at them to know. And Matsunaga's Sony was a real horse. With its 512 MB of RAM, it displayed data as fast as he could click the mouse.

Foley was still at it two hours later, halfway through the files in the hard drive, when Agent Prescott took a call from his boss. He hung up without speaking, then said to Foley, "We have to wrap this up in the next hour."

"Why?" Foley asked. He continued to work as he spoke, mov-ing the cursor smoothly across the face of the monitor.

"I don't ask my superiors to explain their orders," Prescott declared. "I just follow them."

Agent Henderson chose that moment to awaken. "What time is it?" he asked. Then he looked at his watch and answered his own question. "Three-thirty. I'm gonna go out for coffee. Anybody want anything?"

"We're supposed to remain with the subject."

"The what?"

"The subject."

Henderson, who'd spent eight years with the Cincinnati police department before joining the FBI, shrugged into his coat. "What I have to put up with to make a goddamned living," he said as he walked through the front door. "Insult upon fucking injury."

FOLEY SWIVELED his chair so he was facing Prescott. He was tempted to immediately present the agent with the business end of the 9-millimeter handgun nestled just in front of his left hip.

All along, Foley had suspected that it might come down to this, that he might be left with no choice except to remove the Sony's hard drive and transport it to a place where he could study the drive at his leisure.

"What?" Prescott said.

"Huh?"

"You're staring at me. That's rude."

Prescott's right hand, Foley noted, was in his lap and his jacket was unbuttoned. "Sorry," he said. "I was just thinking about something."

Foley turned back to the work station and began to fumble through Matsunaga's floppies, now stacked beside the Sony's monitor. He was annoyed with himself for being so blatantly transparent. Impatiently, his eyes flicked from label to label, barely recording the handwritten words. It wasn't until he finished, until the discs were again neatly stacked, that he realized that some little anomaly had caught his after-the-fact attention.

When Foley ran down that anomaly, he found it so obvious that he was again annoyed. His judgment was clouded; he needed to slow down, but his adrenals simply refused to get with the program. He felt like his nerves were on fire. To be this close!

Foley looked down at the disc in his hand. The labels on Matsunaga's discs, with this single exception, bore multiple file names. Here there was written only a single word, and it wasn't the name of a file at all.

LINUX.

49

F OLEY SLID the disc into the Sony's floppy drive, then popped it out again. In fact, he had no idea what would happen if he booted up. Linux was not a file but an operating system, an alternative to Windows. Although rarely found on a home computer (Foley had never before encountered any operating system except Windows), Linux was commonly used to run the computers of internet service providers and had many industrial applications. Unlike Windows, it was also free.

Again, Foley traced a slow circle on his chair. This time he had no interest in Agent Prescott who was nonetheless alert and who said, "What do you want?"

"Help," Foley replied as he came around to again face the computer.

But there was no help available, not immediately. For now, there were only a few educated guesses and a potential leap of faith. If he had the nerve.

Still, Foley was certain of one thing, a gleaming needle in a haystack of uncertainty. Linux was not on the disc he held in his hand. It wasn't on the disc because no operating system would fit on a single floppy. Or two or three. At most, only a piece of Linux was on the disc, a central core able to do a few simple tasks.

Like access data files.

That was Pete's first guess. His second guess was based on a recollection. Perhaps a year before, he'd attended a panel discussion on the new science of computer forensics. Vaguely, he recalled one of the panelists describing a technique designed to partition sectors of a computer's hard drive so as to render them invisible to Windows for all practical purposes. Though the details were fuzzy, it seemed obvious to Pete, as he continued to stare down at the disc in his hand, that Windows could not be used to make sectors invisible to Windows. You would have to begin with another operating system. Like Linux.

Those were the good guesses. There was a bad guess out there as well and it was based upon what Peter Foley would be likely to do if Peter Foley had files he wished to go unread by strangers. Peter Foley might very well prepare a little trap: say a floppy designed to crash a hard drive, or a program that would rewrite compromising files. And Peter Foley would take the next step, as well. He would add a label sure to attract the attention of prying eyes. A label so intriguing that if the disc in question suddenly became able to speak, it would surely say, *Boot me up, Scotty*.

Foley could see Agent Prescott's reflection on the surface of the Sony's monitor. Prescott was sitting up in the chair, knees slightly apart, his hands in his lap, staring at the back of Foley's head.

In an instant, Foley was seized by an unreasoning anger. His best bet was to remove the hard drive and carry it to someone who didn't have to guess, who knew the answers, but Agent Prescott was foreclosing that possibility. Foley wanted to seize the man's throat, to drive his fists into Prescott's skull, to feel the small bones of Prescott's face crack beneath his knuckles. He was turning in his chair, intending to accomplish just those ends, when he heard a door close. Seconds later, Agent Henderson strode into the room. He looked at Foley for a moment, then asked, "Are you sick?"

"What?"

"You're sweating, Pete. And it's not exactly warm in here."

When Foley ran his fingers through his hair, they came back wet. "I'm not sick," he told Henderson. "I'm just scared."

"Of what?"

"Of everything and anything."

Foley pushed the Linux floppy into the Sony's disc drive. *One for the money*, he told himself as he rolled the mouse across its little pad. *Two for the show*, his bad angel replied.

FOR JULIA Brennan, Leon Weissman's tardiness was a stroke of good fortune. Just ten minutes before Weissman showed up at three-forty-five, Bert Griffith walked into her office bearing the cell-phone records of Hannah, Steve, Craig and Craig's wife, Margaret. The records demonstrated heavy traffic between the phones of Margaret Whitmore and Hannah Liebman, beginning thirteen days before Adeline's murder, on March 1st, ending abruptly on March 8th.

On the surface, that made Hannah Liebman (if not Margaret Whitmore) a prime suspect. But Griffith had been in the detecting business for a long time. The fact that the calls ended so abruptly seemed more important to him than who owned what piece of hardware. Thus, he'd called Hannah's local precinct, the one-seven, and spoken to the precinct commander's personal assistant, a lieutenant named O'Fain. According to Lieutenant O'Fain, on March 8th, Hannah Liebman had come into the station house to report her cell phone stolen.

Alone again, Julia put together a line of attack while Leon Weissman conferred privately with his client. Betrayal, she decided, would be her theme. Liebman's betrayal of Craig Whitmore, which justified a further act of betrayal, this time on Whitmore's part.

Steve Liebman, Julia's argument would go, had played on Whitmore's physical illness, on his myriad neurotic twitchings, on their shared hatred of Adeline Rose. He'd created a fictitious bond while prepared at every minute to sacrifice his partner. That was why Liebman had initially concealed his alibi. Steve was happy to go along with the deal, to keep up his end of the bargain, until faced with imminent arrest. Then he'd quickly revealed the alibi he wasn't supposed to have in the first place. The one he'd carefully established for just such an emergency.

It was now four o'clock and Julia was in her office, seated behind her desk when Lily Han entered. "We're up in five minutes," she said.

"I'm ready," Julia replied.

"Me too."

In fact, Lily's role in the games to come would be minor but crucial. She would make the offer, dangle the carrot, then leave Julia to do the convincing. That way, if Craig didn't produce, it would be through no fault of Lily Han's.

"I trust you," Lily had declared earlier. "Handle it any way you want."

50

LEON WEISSMAN, attorney-at-law, was short, pudgy, and middle-aged. Everything about him was ordinary, from his off-the-rack suit to the fringe of curly hair just above the tops of his ordinary ears. Ordinary was the game Weissman played, in life and in front of a jury. An ordinary man communicating with ordinary men and women. He was the Joan Rivers of the courtroom: *Can we talk?*

Weissman was smiling his ordinary smile when Lily and Julia entered the interview room. Weissman always smiled. He smiled at judges and prosecutors and clients and jurors. He especially smiled at hostile witnesses, just before he ripped them to shreds.

Introductions were made, hands were shaken. Finally, Weissman settled back in his chair. He folded his hands and let them drop to his lap. "So," he said, "what's up?"

Julia sat, but Lily Han remained standing long enough to deliver a carefully prepared statement. "We are certain," she told Weissman, "that your client's confession was not totally forthcoming. We want him to tell us the truth. We—"

"It's not bad enough," Weissman interrupted, "that he already put his head in the noose, you're now requesting that he tighten the knot?"

"Quite the opposite. In return for Mr. Whitmore's complete cooperation, verifiable by polygraph examination, the state will not oppose reasonable bail. Nor will the state push for a speedy trial. In fact, if Mr. Whitmore's prognosis is even close to accurate, it's unlikely that he'll ever come to trial."

It was a good offer. If he took it, Whitmore would die in his own bed instead of on a cot in a prison ward where the caregivers divide up your pain meds among themselves. Weissman looked over at his client who stared hard at Julia as he shook his head.

"I'll answer any questions you have, but there's nothing more to tell."

Though Craig's tone was defiant, Julia was not discouraged. She crossed her legs, leaned slightly forward, then began a deliberately gentle interrogation with a classic opening statement.

"Mr. Whitmore, we know that you and Steve Liebman were in it together. The only thing we're unsure about is Liebman's motive. And that's where you can help us."

"I told—"

"Please, Mr. Whitmore, don't insult my intelligence. I already said we know Liebman was your co-conspirator. We know you planned it together. But his motive . . . now I have to admit that's a little fuzzy. I mean, Adeline was in failing health. Everybody says so, from her housekeeper to her buddies in the Gold Coast Glitterati. How much longer could she have lasted? A year? Two? So why would

Liebman conspire to kill her? Why would he take that risk? Unless she was gonna do something rash—like change her will."

Julia was fully prepared to offer a second explanation if Whitmore failed to respond. In fact, he blushed, the color rising through a general pallor to claim his cheeks.

"That's pure speculation," he finally said.

Julia responded by pushing her advantage. "I'm thinking that's why Steve went to Adeline's a week before you killed her. When they had that argument? He was trying to get her to change her mind. But not Adeline. Talk about a fool's errand. What was she gonna do, Mr. Whitmore, leave the whole bundle to Hannah? That would've made little Steve very, very angry."

Craig was leaning forward in his chair, legs crossed at the knees, hands folded across his groin. He opened his mouth, revealing a coated tongue. "Do I hear a question in there?" he asked.

"A question? Okay." Though Julia's smile was agreeable, she didn't ask Whitmore a question. Instead, she told him, "We're fully aware of what you and Steve did with the phones. How you kept in touch. Why you stopped."

This time, Whitmore's reaction was less subdued. "What a bitch you are," he said. "You are the queen of the bitches."

Julia didn't even bother to smile. "So, like I've already said, we know you and Steve were co-conspirators. We're only asking you to help us out with the why of it. And that goes both ways. We have to know why you needed Steve Liebman. Did Liebman supply you with something? What did he bring to the table?"

"Why don't you tell me?"

"Well, it could have been anything, when you think about it, from lessons in how to strangle the elderly to a house key."

Whitmore looked at Julia through reptile-flat eyes. "I've got a funny kind of cancer," he announced. "It's eating me alive, but it doesn't hurt. Not yet. At the very end, my doctors tell me, it will hurt very much."

Julia might have noted that Craig would never see those doctors again unless he cooperated. Instead, she opted to introduce her main theme. Allowing him to change the subject was not a possibility. The master walks the dog. The dog does not walk the master.

"Steve Liebman," she said, "he's some piece of work. You know, of course, that he was prepared to abandon you at any moment? Myself, I only wish I could've been a fly on the wall when you and Steve drew up your battle plans. Whose idea was it that you do the killing part? Did you bravely volunteer? Did Steve argue that since your days on earth were numbered anyway, you might as well take all the risk? Sure, I know. If you hadn't flipped out and cut Adeline to pieces, there might not be enough evidence to convict you, even with Steve's alibi. But what I say to that, Mr. Whitmore, is Steve Liebman, your good buddy, was prepared to sacrifice your sorry ass any time it became necessary, whether you fucked up or not. He went into the deal ready to give you up. You don't owe him a goddamned thing."

Satisfied for the present, Julia leaned back in her chair. For the first time, she saw just how sick Craig Whitmore was. The whites of his flat eyes were yellow with jaundice and his collar bones seemed about to jump through his skin.

What he's determined to do, she told herself, is to exit life with some dignity, even if that means keeping up his end of a bad bargain. I have to convince him that dignity and revenge go hand in hand. I have to keep pounding. . . .

WHEN BERT Griffith knocked on the door of the interview room, Julia came straight out of her chair. Her right hand curled into a fist and her eyes narrowed in disbelief. She whirled, instinctively, to square off against her detective who merely shook his head.

"It's Pete. I think you better talk to him."

Julia was off across the squad room before she could gather her thoughts. Part of her remained facing Craig Whitmore, patiently awaiting his reply to her last salvo. Another part of her was still ready to tear Bert Griffith limb from limb. A third part had recorded Griffith's tone and was already worried.

"Pete?"

"I've found her, Julia. In Riverdale. Write down this address."

Foley rattled off the address, then immediately hung up. In the background, just before her phone went dead, Julia noted a chorus of blowing horns. Pete was already moving.

When Julia walked back into the squad room, carrying her coat, Lily Han was standing in the doorway of the interview room thirty feet away. Lily's eyes had narrowed to the merest of slits.

"Lily," Julia said, "I gotta go."

"You cannot leave." Han spaced the words out, putting equal emphasis on all three. Her expression seemed, to Julia, as cold and calculating as it was angry. And wasted, too. Julia Brennan's mind was no longer divided.

"I'm already gone, Lily," Julia declared as she slid into her coat. "Betty, you finish up with Craig Whitmore. Bert, let's roll."

The last was purely for show. If ordered to accompany Captain Brennan, Detective Griffith could not be held accountable for her little mutiny. Unfortunately, Griffith had exposed the ruse. He was already standing at the other end of the squad room, in his coat, holding the door open.

51

I N T H E immediate aftermath of Patti's disappearance, Peter Foley had vacillated between two basic modes of thought: rescue and revenge. The rescue mode had faded over time, a victim of Foley's profession; the odds against finding his daughter alive grew day by day, and he knew it. The revenge fantasy had a far longer run and though it had any number of motifs, the underlying theme remained constant. Peter Foley unmasks his daughter's killer, then extracts (often literally) the appropriate penalty.

Foley returned to this second mode as he made his way north through heavy traffic on the West Side Highway. Of all the various thoughts and emotions that rampaged through his mind and body when he'd finally recognized the name, when he'd become certain, only revenge served to calm him. Thoughts of rescue inspired a near-paralyzing fear. What would he say to her? Don't be afraid, honey? You're safe now, honey? Daddy's got you, honey?

And what if Patti didn't know him, if she would never know him? What if he lost her again and again and again? And what if the opposite happened? What if he discovered nothing of the girl he lost in the girl he found? What if the Patti he found remained for all time a stranger?

There were other things going on as well—subcurrents like panic and recklessness—that also needed to be contained. Cold Sicilian revenge would do nicely for these too, he decided. One demon to rule them all.

As HE waited behind a long line of cars and SUVs at the 57th Street traffic light, Foley's mind was not plagued by doubt. He was not, he knew, answering a false alarm. The Linux code on the disc, as he'd reasoned, was sufficient only to perform a pair of tasks. It moved files from their little hidey-hole into Windows, then returned them to the darkness after they'd been edited.

One of those files was an encrypted spreadsheet. Decrypted, it revealed a name on the debit side that Foley had immediately recognized: CARPENTER, ALFRED. Then the words *Patti's Dance*, then an address in the Bronx neighborhood of Riverdale.

Foley remembered Carpenter well. Carpenter owned a store, an upper-end children's boutique on Second Avenue right behind the Little Kitty Daycare Center. When Foley had backtracked, following the route taken by the local detectives immediately after Patti's disappearance, he'd stopped in at the Purple Panda. Carpenter, though he'd seen nothing out of the ordinary on the day Patti vanished, had been very solicitous.

"So sorry. It must be terrible. If there's anything I can do. Your poor wife. A tragedy, a tragedy."

As Foley pulled onto the ramp leading up to the elevated portion of the West Side Highway, he drew Alfred Carpenter's face from memory and planted it at the forefront of his consciousness. This was the man who'd taken his daughter. This overweight creep with his greasy black wig and his thin mustache, with his blue suit and his red ascot and his patent-leather shoes.

There is almost nothing, Foley reflected, that I can't do to Alfred Carpenter and still call it justice. It's a nice spot, really. Not the moral high ground. The moral summit.

Curiously, he did not stop to consider the effect on Patti Foley's immediate future should he act out any of the various fantasies that flitted through his mind, alluring and gay as cancan dancers. He couldn't.

WHEN TRAFFIC stopped dead a mile south of the George Washington Bridge, Foley fought an urge to get out and start running. He told himself to face the facts. Manhattan was an island; to leave it, you had to cross water. Hence, there was no way around rush-hour traffic that wouldn't carry you into more traffic, and you'd come back to the same spot, a bridge or a tunnel, anyway. What you had to do was wait it out. Never mind the fact that every nerve in your body was spitting current at every other nerve in your body. Never mind the fact that you were on goddamned fire. Get in the far left lane, stay off the horn, follow along behind the car in front of you. Be a good boy.

Thus Foley consoled himself with thoughts of what he would do when Alfred Carpenter was finally in his hands. He was on a high bluff, the spine of New York rising up along the island's western edge, running from Harlem deep into the Bronx. To his left, across the Hudson River, the cliffs of the New Jersey Palisades kept pace with his ascent. It was very warm for late March, with temperatures near 80 degrees, and Foley's front windows were both rolled down. To his right, a woman driving a black Mercedes began to edge into his lane. She glanced at him, then changed her mind, slowing to let the Subaru inch ahead.

Foley laughed. Seriousness of purpose, he decided. Somehow, when your course is set, people can just see it in your eyes.

The section of the Bronx called Riverdale stretches from the Harlem River on the south to the border of Westchester County on the north. Steep cliffs overlooking the Hudson River mark the neighborhood's western edge and there are magnificent views to be had for the asking.

Always a haven for the wealthy, the topography of Riverdale was changed forever in 1936 when Robert Moses pushed the Henry Hudson Parkway right through its heart. Development quickly followed, ten- and twelve-story apartment buildings where there had once been spacious homes and patches of woodland. At the time, residents had forecast Armageddon, Riverdale reduced to a slum. Instead, sixty-five years later, Riverdale remained essentially what it had always been, a mostly white neighborhood of upper-middle-class professionals.

This was especially true of Riverdale at its southern end. The skyline, as Foley left the parkway at 230th Street, was dominated by hi-rise apartments. Foley had no interest in these buildings. His attention was focused on a little enclave west of Independence Avenue where some dozen private homes survived. He had an address now, and an open map on the seat next to him.

As it turned out, he needed neither. Though he checked the address on the mailbox, he recognized his destination the minute he caught sight of the stockade fence. The fence was easily seven feet high, high enough to keep out prying eyes, high enough to keep little girls inside. It completely surrounded the enormous lot and the brick colonial house on the lot's southern end.

Only the upper stories of the house were visible from the Subaru, a slate roof pierced by three attic dormers, five windows on the second floor. Foley's eyes jumped from window to window, half expecting a young girl's face to appear behind the curtains. None did, though Foley noted a pair of open windows.

If possible, Foley wanted to get into the house without being seen, to gain immediate control of an inherently unpredictable situation. The obvious alternative was to put the house under surveillance, maybe catch Carpenter as he came out. But Foley never considered this alternative. He was too busy fighting an urge to drive the Subaru through the gate, up the porch steps and through the front door.

Eventually, he parked the car beside a hydrant on Kappock Street, then made his way back to the Carpenter home. Moving as deliberately as possible, he circled the lot which occupied the whole of a small triangular block. From time to time, he peered between gaps in the fence, looking for the safest approach to the house, checking the cover, locating open windows on the ground floor.

Foley was at the narrowest end of the triangle, within a few feet of a locked gate, when he saw a woman come through a door on the side of the house, leaving it ajar behind her. The windows to either side of the door were covered with bright yellow curtains, and Foley assumed he was looking at the kitchen entrance. Though his eyes kept returning to the open doorway, he concentrated most of his attention on the woman who was walking directly toward him.

In late middle age, she wore a beige sweater over a tan skirt with matching pumps. A gold chain circled her neck and small gold hoops dangled from her ears. On her left ring finger, a diamond big enough to attract Foley's eye caught the slanting afternoon sun, winking merrily, mockingly.

Though the woman carried a plastic trash bag in her right hand, she was clearly not a servant. She was the mistress of the house, one of those enablers who provide a much-coveted veneer of respectability to pedophiles in it for the long run.

Or so Foley decided as he watched the woman make her way toward a row of plastic garbage cans laid out alongside a detached two-car garage. He did not consider the possibility that Toshi Matsunaga had warned Alfred Carpenter, that Carpenter might already have deserted the field, that he was about to scare the crap out of a completely innocent woman. He merely allowed her to come forward, waiting patiently until she lifted the lid of the garbage can farthest from the house. Then he took a step, grabbed the top of the fence and vaulted over.

52

U P   C L O S E ,   the woman was far less impressive. Her hair was dirty, her teeth a dark yellow along receding gum lines. On her beige sweater, a trail of encrusted stains appeared to be dried milk. Though Foley noted each of these defects, it was her utterly unreasoning look that commanded the better part of his attention as he watched her make the transition from slack-jawed shock to firm recognition.

After Patti's disappearance, Peter and Kirstin Foley had made the appropriate rounds, from network to network, and spoken the appropriate words: *Please give our child back to us.* The only measurable effects were Kirstin Foley's burgeoning depression and a celebrity that lasted just long enough for this woman to recognize Peter Foley six years later.

"You'll never take my baby," she declared. Her eyes were glittery with panic and she tugged at her lower jaw as though trying to free it from its hinges.

Foley unlocked the gate and pulled it open. Shielded by the garage, they could not be seen from the house. He recalled somebody—he couldn't remember exactly who—telling him that even the most psychotic human beings have some primitive instinct for survival. Foley tested that theory by drawing the Glock from its holster and training it on the woman's forehead.

"Time to go bye-bye." Foley jerked his chin toward the open gate. With no way to secure the woman, no handcuffs or plastic restraints, Foley's best bet was to get her away from the house. That she would use this opportunity to escape justice never crossed his mind. Given her state of mind, she wouldn't get more than a couple of blocks.

"No. Trish belongs to me." The woman smiled, her look at the same time demented and triumphant. "You will never have her."

Though she folded her arms across her chest, a clear act of defiance, when Foley cocked the automatic she flew through the gate as though released by a slingshot. He locked the gate behind her, scanned the backyard, then walked quickly to the open door through which she'd come.

The room before him (a kitchen as he'd suspected) was empty and there were no sounds at all from the inner house which did not surprise him. Strangers, especially live-in servants who often know more about a family than the family knows about itself, were always a danger. You excluded strangers from your life as much as possible. If you were in it for the long run.

The kitchen was large, a big country kitchen with copper-bottomed pots and pans hanging from a rack over a butcher-block table. From the wall behind the table, a framed sampler, red letters on a white background, announced JESUS IS LORD.

Foley stood in the doorway for a moment, looking through a second door into a formal dining room. The room was dominated by mahogany and crystal: a gigantic china cabinet, a monstrous sideboard, a table surrounded by twelve chairs. The chandelier over the table might have hung in the main dining room at the Plaza Hotel.

When Foley was reasonably certain there was no one lurking close by, he gave the outside door a shove, then crossed the kitchen to enter the dining room. The crash of the slamming door brought an immediate response from somewhere inside the house.

"Claire?" A man's voice, world-weary. "Was that absolutely necessary?"

Foley positioned himself against the wall beside a closed door. He did not reply.

"Claire?" Exasperated now, all those years with a deranged partner in crime apparent in his tone. "Claire? Are we having ourselves a little breakdown?" Another pause, then the voice, rapidly advancing, "I think you're going to have to spend some time in your room, Claire. Before one of your episodes attracts the attention of the neighbors. Again."

RECOGNITION DID not dawn in Alfred Carpenter's eyes when he almost literally ran into Peter Foley. It exploded. He took a step back, then stopped in his tracks as Foley raised the barrel of the gun and shook his head. Foley was not telling Alfred Carpenter to remain still. He was shaking his head in disbelief.

The years had been unkind to Alfred. His black wig formed an impossible contrast to the gray stubble covering his face and his muddy-brown eyes, rheumy at the corners, were filmed by incipient cataracts. Even in well-tailored slacks that minimized the twenty pounds he'd gained, it was obvious that he'd crossed that invisible line separating the middle-aged and the elderly. Not that Carpenter's advancing years inspired any softening in Foley's position. Far from it. The man's age was presumptive evidence of a successful life, an invisible life, a life outside the scrutiny of the law.

Shortly after Patti's disappearance, Foley had run a criminal records search on every male who worked within a block of the Little Kitty Daycare Center, bosses and employees alike. He was hoping to find somebody with a history of sexual offenses, but everyone had come up clean, including Alfred Carpenter.

Apparently emboldened by Foley's silence, Carpenter raised his head to reveal a narrow mustache as black as his wig.

"Who are you and what are you doing in my home?"

Foley called this bluff by cracking the barrel of the Glock into the left side of Alfred's skull, whereupon the man fell to the floor unconscious. This was not Foley's intention. The Glock's frame wasn't steel but some kind of plastic, and he'd half expected it to shatter on impact. Instead, unlike Alfred's scalp, the Glock was undamaged.

Though breathing normally, Alfred was clearly beyond rational conversation, at least for the moment. Foley took him by a limp arm, dragged him through the foyer to a staircase in the living room, finally handcuffed him to the banister post at the foot of the stairs. Then he sprinted up the stairs to begin a systematic search of the house with the five bedrooms on the second floor. The first three were devoid of furniture, guests at the Carpenters being apparently unwelcome. The next, the master bedroom, was cavernous, but Foley gave it no more than a casual glance before continuing along the hallway to the final bedroom. There he hesitated, forewarned by the fears that had rushed through him on the drive up to Riverdale, and took stock of himself.

He'd felt absolutely nothing when Carpenter's head split open. It was as though he'd been watching a movie he'd seen many times before, as though he were the projectionist, little more than a mildly interested bystander. He felt that same emptiness still. As if he weren't poised in front of this door, his right hand suspended a few inches from this doorknob. As if he were observing from a distance.

A thought caught his attention at that moment, a universally accepted cop truth. Human beings have three possible reactions to severe threat: fight, flight or fright. Door number one, number two or number three. But there was only a single relevant door at that moment, the door in front of him, and he was going to have to go through it. Obviously.

In fact, he had to will his hand onto the knob, to will his wrist to turn, his arm to push. He had to will himself to step into the room, to fumble for the light, to see what was in front of his eyes.

THE FIFTH bedroom had obviously been designed for a child, a much younger child than Patti Foley. The posters on the wall were not of Jennifer Lopez or Madonna, but of Mickey Mouse, Bugs Bunny and Cookie Monster. The furniture was undersized as well, the bed appropriate to a toddler graduating from a crib. But there was no toddler, no child of any age, to be found.

For the first time, Foley was afraid. He knew that pedophiles, though opportunistic by necessity, usually carry an idealized image of the perfect victim. It was possible that Patti had grown too old to fit this image, that Carpenter had moved on. Or that he'd finally cut his losses by shedding the primary evidence against him. Without doubt, given his relationship with Matsunaga, Carpenter was plugged into a pedophile network that stretched across the globe. What would the Thai pimps who ran brothels staffed by children pay for a well-schooled American girl? Or the Haitian pimps, or the Honduran. . . ?

The words spoken by the woman he'd stupidly sent packing returned to him then. *You'll never take my baby. You'll never have her.* He'd been encouraged by these assertions, had assumed them to mean that Patti was there to be taken. Now. . . .

THE NEED to escape from these and numerous other terrors, terrors still to be named, finally motivated Foley to continue the search. It was, after all, a big house. As he opened the closet door, then knelt to peer under the bed, he fought an urge to shout Patti's name. After six years with the Carpenters, he could not predict her reaction to a strange voice. An answering silence would mean nothing. Until (and unless) Alfred became responsive, a thorough search was all he had going for him.

Foley was more careful on his second pass through the upstairs bedrooms, opening closets and bathroom doors, pulling back shower curtains. When he found a staircase behind a door in one of the empty bedrooms, he began to climb into the attic, even though a layer of dust on the steps clearly indicated it had been months since anyone had made a similar climb.

He braced himself as he came to the top of the stairs, unconsciously thrusting his nose before him, unconsciously seeking the odor of death. But the attic was merely dusty, a repository for discarded pieces of furniture and boxes of every size. A wardrobe was packed with dresses. An artificial Christmas tree peeked from a narrow cardboard box. A tricycle minus its handlebars nearly tripped him as quickly walked the length of the attic before returning to the first floor and Alfred Carpenter. Hoping to rouse the man, Foley gave him an impatient shake, but Carpenter only began to snore softly, a baby rocked in his cradle.

Still with no option, Foley continued his search, moving faster now, throwing doors open as he worked his way from the living room back through the house into the kitchen where he found another staircase, this one leading down to the basement. It was at the bottom of these stairs that he slowed for the first time. He was in a large open space, perhaps sixty feet long and running the entire width of the house, broken only by a few wooden pillars.

A pair of in-line roller skates resting on a bench set against the far wall caught Foley's attention. The red skates were well-worn, the leather scuffed, the wheels chipped. A few feet from the bench, an open door revealed a utility room with a washer and dryer against one wall, a furnace against the other. Foley looked into this room, then picked up one of the skates and examined it closely.

The skate was obviously made for a child's foot, but a child of what age? Foley tried to imagine an eleven-year-old's foot as he slid his hand into the skate, but having missed the last six years of his daughter's life, was unable to do it. Suddenly, an image forced itself on his consciousness. A small girl, his daughter, skating all alone in a musty basement. Around and around and around she goes. Where she stops. . . ?

Foley emerged from the basement prepared to play what he believed to be his last card. That card was named Alfred Carpenter and he was lying where Foley had left him, on the carpet on his back. Foley grabbed him by the hair, intending to lift the man to his feet, but Alfred had no hair to lift. He was wearing a toupee which came off in Foley's right hand to reveal a naked scalp bearing three fiery stripes. The stripes were the direct result of the adhesive strips used to hold the wig in place suddenly tearing away.

Carpenter screamed once before opening befuddled eyes. "Claire!" he shouted. "Don't, don't, don't." Then he rolled onto his stomach and began to cry.

Foley again reached down, this time grabbing the collars of Carpenter's pinpoint oxford shirt and cashmere sweater before yanking the man to his feet.

"Where is she?" he said.

"Please."

"There's no please. And no maybe, either."

Foley pushed the Glock's barrel against Carpenter's mouth, slowly increasing the pressure until that mouth opened, until the barrel slipped inside. Then he twisted the automatic sharply and Carpenter began to choke on his own blood.

"Think I'm just fucking with you?" Foley asked. "You think I'm not serious? Well, it's do-or-die time, Alfred. Tell me where my daughter is or wake up in hell."

"Pete."

LATER ON, Foley would grow to believe that his failure to pull the trigger when Julia Brennan spoke his name was the result of a miracle. But at that moment, her voice brought him close to panic. He would be cheated once again, as he'd been cheated on the day Patti disappeared, and on the day he found his wife dead by her own hand, and by all the days since. His shoulders jerked upward as if to protect his head and he moaned like a wounded soldier deserted on the field of battle.

"He can't answer you, Pete."

Foley turned slightly to look behind him. Julia was standing ten feet away, Bert Griffith just to her right. Neither held a weapon and neither tried to approach him. Nevertheless, Julia repeated her assertion, adding just enough to make her reasoning clear.

"He can't answer you, Pete, unless you take the gun out of his mouth."

Foley turned back to Alfred Carpenter, then laughed. By God, she was right. Funny, he hadn't noticed before.

"These two people behind me," he told Carpenter as he followed Julia's suggestion, "they're both cops. If I kill you, they'll put me in jail. But I don't care, Alfred. I don't care about that. I want to know where Patti is and you're gonna tell me. And then maybe just for the fun of it, I'll kill you anyway."

Carpenter fell to his knees, his mouth opening and closing as he fought for breath. When he finally spoke, his words were accompanied by a fine spray of blood. "Oh, please God, don't shoot me. She's in the cottage."

"What cottage?"

"The garage, the garage. We had it converted. It's not a bad place. It's heated. It's got electricity and cable and. . . ." Carpenter looked from Foley to Julia Brennan. "You're a cop. You can't let him kill me."

"You think so, huh?" Julia responded. "Well, bottom line, if you're lying, you scumbag, I'll shoot you myself."

Foley closed his eyes for just a moment, in utter weariness, his endurance finally giving way. He'd been fighting for so very long it seemed obvious to him that he should have collapsed years before. Something had held him up. Or some things, one of which was standing behind him. He turned to look into Julia Brennan's eyes. To her credit, or so he later decided, he found not a trace of pity.

"Do you want me to go with you?" she asked.

Foley shook his head. He tossed his Glock to one side and walked directly through the kitchen into the yard. It was fully dark now and the unusual afternoon warmth was rapidly giving way to the realities of a March night. There was a breeze as well, enough to whistle between the needles of a white pine off to his left, to rattle the branches of the towering oaks overhanging the house.

As he approached, Foley examined the garage closely, noting for the first time that its walls were thickly overgrown with English ivy.

A light from within the garage was no more than a faint glow behind an ivy-covered window set high in the wall. To the left of the window, a narrow strip of light spilled onto a pair of flagstones arranged before a small door.

Foley held himself together as he crossed the lawn, telling himself that he must do this for Patti, that he must be strong for her sake. His resolve faded, however, when he came to the door and found it latched on the outside. It dissolved completely, now you see it and now you don't, when he unlatched the door, stepped through, and saw his daughter for the first time. She was seated in a ladder-back rocking chair, next to a small table. On the table, a lamp with an orange shade cast the only light in the finished room.

Apparently unafraid, Patti rocked in the chair, slowly, precisely, while she scrutinized Foley through hooded eyes, her gaze as penetrating as any cop's. As he watched her watching him, Foley admitted, to himself, that her eyes had changed. They were not the eyes he remembered. Otherwise, she seemed oddly unaltered. The auburn hair, the spray of freckles running across her nose, the full mouth, the button of a chin, the long curving neck—he recognized these features as if he'd last seen them only yesterday.

Foley wondered if he should introduce himself. He could find nothing in Patti's eyes, still fixed on him, beyond deep mistrust. Certainly, there was no hint of recognition. But then her eyes changed, all in an instant, and Peter Foley heard his daughter's voice for the first time in six years. It was at that moment he knew, absolutely, that some little piece of his heart must have survived, despite everything, because her words tore into that heart with the force of a thrown ax.

"Why," she asked, "are you crying, Daddy?"

53

A MAN and a school-age girl walking along East Sixty-Seventh Street toward Central Park on a cool day in early June. Tall and rangy, the man wears a canvas barn jacket, faded jeans and sturdy brown boots. The girl wears a red windbreaker and blue nylon pants that emit a distinctive swish as she marches forward. Though the man's stride is brisk, the girl has no trouble keeping up.

The man is Peter Foley, the girl his daughter, Patti. Their relationship is unmistakable, as both have dark red hair, a very unusual shade bordering on auburn, lighter red eyebrows and prominent assertive chins.

To the casual observer, they could be any father and daughter out for a stroll. It is, after all, spring. It is, after all, Saturday. They are headed, after all, for Central Park. But a closer inspection reveals several anomalies. First, they move forward with unnatural determination, as if late for an appointment, slowing only to avoid pedestrians and traffic. Though Patti's eyes hop over the land-scape, as restless as courting birds, she is never distracted, not even by children her own age.

Their relative silence is also telling. They have no small talk between them and long minutes go by without either speaking. Though naturally reticent, Peter Foley finds these silences uncom-fortable and he stops from time to time, as he stops now, to point out some item of interest. In this case, he chooses a limestone mansion with bowfront windows and a small portico supported by marble pillars. The mansion is home to the German Mission to the United Nations.

Dropping to one knee, Foley reminds his daughter of their visit to the United Nations on a previous Saturday. Then he tells her that this mansion, and many like it, were once owned by prominent New York families, but are now so expensive they can only be afforded by whole countries.

Foley monitors his daughter's expression intently as he goes on. By necessity, he has become a diviner of signs. He knows that his daughter will make no spontaneous comment on what he says. When he finishes, she will simply resume walking in whatever direction he should take. This is a bad sign.

Foley tells himself, as he has been told by Patti's therapist, Dr. Grace Carone, that Patti's silences arise predictably from her iso-lation, that the larger world is new to her, that she is struggling to make sense of it, an interrupted task that in the natural order of things would have been accomplished years before.

"Give her time," Dr. Carone advises, over and over again. "Be patient."

* * *

THERE ARE many things still unclear about Patti Foley's six years with Alfred and Claire Carpenter, and they will probably remain unclear. Absent her husband, Claire Carpenter (who was found wandering in circles, as Foley predicted, within a block of her home) has deteriorated rapidly and now resides at Creedmore State Hospital in Queens. As of yet, no dose of antipsychotic medication has found its way past her insistence that Trish Carpenter is her biological child. Alfred Carpenter, on the other hand, resides in the federal jail on West Street. Alfred speaks only through an attorney who proclaims his innocence despite the *Patti's Dance* tape and a drawer stuffed with photographs. As for Patti, she has yet to so much as mention her years with the Carpenters, to her father or Dr. Carone or anybody else. Nor has she spoken of her mother, although she has been told that Kirstin Foley is dead.

But Peter Foley does know this much. Patti spent the first three years of her confinement with Claire Carpenter on a ranch in central Idaho which Alfred occasionally visited. The ranch was owned by Claire Carpenter's now-deceased mother, and very isolated. In this way, the Carpenters managed to avoid the initial glare of publicity surrounding Patti's disappearance. A second strategy, generated by the fear that Patti would blab to a classmate or a teacher, was equally necessary. Patti was home-schooled throughout her years with the Carpenters.

Despite these precautions, upon her return to New York, Patti's isolation attracted the attention of the state. The Administration for Children's Services was the first to respond. Alerted by a neighbor who thought it strange that the Carpenters' daughter rarely appeared in public, ACS dispatched a case worker named Marie Pignatanno to examine Patti. Pignatanno's written report describes a well-nourished child, without sign of injury, who claims to be happy with her life.

The Board of Education arrived next, armed with a battery of tests designed to gauge the efficacy of Patti's home schooling. Once administered, these tests demonstrated only that Trish Carpenter, above grade in every subject, was a living reproof to the quality of public education in New York City.

As THE Foleys enter Central Park, Patti suddenly takes her father's hand. This is a very good sign and Peter Foley remembers his surprise when it first happened. Her moist hand was so frail, her touch so tentative, that he was initially afraid to close his fingers. At the same time, he was profoundly grateful for the trust she'd placed in him, however briefly, and for a sudden realization.

All those fears he'd entertained, that Patti wouldn't recognize him or he recognize Patti, evaporated the moment her hand touched his. The years had diminished neither his love for Patti or his nearly desperate need to protect her. He was as bound to his daughter as the clouds to the earth. If she was somehow broken, he would somehow fix her. Somehow.

Peter Foley and his daughter do not live together. Patti is in residence at the Kirkland Institute in Washington Heights, undergoing intensive therapy while her father puts his own life in order. They visit on Tuesday mornings at the Institute. On Saturdays he takes her for the afternoon, to museums, movies or the theater when it rains, on long walks whenever the weather permits.

As Foley has come to understand, he and Patti are preparing for each other, and though he has little knowledge of her efforts, his own have been systematic. They began with a trip to the 88th Precinct where he'd surrendered his weapon along with his license to carry it, for good and forever. Then he'd eliminated every trace of his search for his daughter, not only from his own computer but from the many web sites where he'd stored information. A few days later, the physical evidence, the tapes, DVDs and still photographs, were hand-delivered to a morose Raymond Lear who accepted Foley's retirement with great reluctance. Bye-bye, goose. Bye-bye, golden eggs.

That left Peter Foley with a pair of tasks. He needed a respectable job and a respectable home. The first, the job, was still up in the air, partly because Foley was a long way from broke, partly because he had yet to find a comfortable skin to inhabit after six years of obsession.

The home part, on the other hand, was quickly resolved when Julia Brennan formally requested his hand in marriage. They were sitting in the respectable living room of her respectable Wood-haven home when she'd dropped to one knee, then produced a small box covered in black velvet. The box contained an engagement ring which he'd refused to try on, much less wear. But he didn't refuse Julia's offer. They were mated for life and it was absurd to pretend otherwise. Besides, Julia wasn't offering Peter Foley a home. She was opening her home to Peter Foley's daughter. When the time came to present a respectable front to the Family Court judge who controlled Patti's immediate destiny, they would be ready.

A S T H E Foleys make their way into the park, Peter Foley spots a pushcart just ahead. "Do you want a hot dog?" he asks his daughter.

"Yes."

"How about a soda to wash it down?"

"Okay."

Good signs and bad signs. Patti never refuses an offer. Patti never asks for anything.

They are in an area of Central Park called Literary Walk, a long promenade that gives way to a wide plaza at its northern end. At the southern end, where they munch on their hot dogs, the promenade is graced by a series of monumental sculptures celebrating the literary life. A standing Bard, Robert Burns, Sir Walter Scott, Fitz-Greene Halleck. Thin and bearded, Halleck looks up at the sky as though demanding an explanation for his presence.

It is cooler in the park and Foley buttons his jacket as they walk through shadows toward the sunlit mall. Directly above, the branches of the elms to either side of the promenade have formed a bower. Hence, the light reaching the asphalt is dappled and constantly shifting as the a steady breeze flutters the leaves overhead. The air is filled with sound, with birdsong from the branches of the elms, with the conversations of passersby, with the distant thud of some fool's too-loud boom box, with the chatter of begging squirrels.

None of this is lost on Peter Foley who has learned to treasure these moments, but his daughter has neither eyes nor ears for the festivities. Patti's goal is far more specific and when she spots Corry Brennan sitting on a bench only a few yards from the mall, a wide, near-worshipful smile spreads across her face.

This is a very good sign. This is the best of the best.

SITTING ALONGSIDE her daughter, Julia Brennan cannot help but grin as Patti Brennan dashes up, red hair flying, then leaps onto the bench without so much as a nod in Julia's direction.

"Corry, did you bring my skates?"

"I did, squirt. You gonna put 'em on? Or do you want me to do it?"

"You."

"How did I know?"

Patti giggles as she extends a sneakered foot which Corry dutifully unlaces before retrieving a pair of in-line skates from the duffel bag she's hauled into the park. The skates, which Patti chose herself, are flaming red.

"You don't stop bouncin' around, squirt," Corry observes, "I'm never gonna get these laces tight."

When Patti instantly freezes, Corry reaches out to tickle her ribs, propelling the smaller girl into spasms of laughter which further delays the process. But then, finally, Corry is done. She gives Patti's foot a little shove, then puts on her own skates, pulling the Velcro fasteners tight across her instep.

Patti looks up at her father, hooded eyes silently questioning. She does not—will not—leave the bench without his permission.

"Go ahead," Pete says. "I'll be right here."

The transformation, when Patti's skates hit the asphalt, is nearly miraculous. Gone the hesitation, the sharp measuring glance, the composed wary expression. She glides onto the mall without a trace of self-consciousness, describing a lazy figure eight merely by leaning a bit to the left, a bit to the right, covering the length and breadth of the plaza while Corry Brennan struggles just to maintain her balance.

There are many other skaters on the mall, a favorite spot for skate dancers who work singly and in pairs. They are little more than moving obstacles for Patti and she swirls around them, as unaware of them as they, inspired by the music pouring through their earphones, are of her.

Or so Julia thinks as she takes Peter Foley's hand and pulls it onto her lap. These days, Julia is oddly content with her life, a temporary condition, of that she is sure. Julia has been transferred without loss of rank to Internal Affairs where she sits behind that dreaded desk, supervising a bevy of lieutenants who supervise sergeants who supervise field investigators.

It would have been far worse if not for Betty Cohen. After turning Craig Whitmore, Betty had suggested that Lily Han accompany them to Liebman's apartment, then urged Lily to personally apply the cuffs to an enraged Liebman's bony wrists. Assistant District Attorney Han was still recounting the details to anybody willing to listen.

You should've seen his face. The man didn't know whether to cry or spit.

AT THE western end of the mall, two busts, of Friedrich von Schiller and Ludwig von Beethoven, rest on marble pedestals. Properly Teutonic, they do not look to the heavens for inspiration. Instead, they glare down at Patti Foley as she swirls around them, skating backwards, grinning at Corry Brennan, who misses a turn and has to grab at a low fence for balance.

"You're tryin' to kill me," Corry declares. She is panting and drenched with sweat. "I'm gonna take a break."

Patti stops short, dragging the toe of her right skate. She watches Corry's retreating back until Corry settles onto the bench next to her mother. Then Patti is off, arms flying, bent forward from the waist as she gathers speed.

She heads toward the limestone band shell at the eastern end of the mall where four skateboarders take turns negotiating the steps leading down to the plaza. The task preoccupies them and they fail to notice Patti Foley until she whips into a turn that carries her to within a few feet of the steps. Then the tallest of the four, a blond boy in a grimy Knicks cap, pumps his fist into the air.

"You go, girl," he proclaims. "You go."

If Patti Foley hears him, she gives no indication.

Fifty feet away, Julia Brennan watches Peter Foley watch his daughter. Idly, she runs the ball of her thumb across the hairs on the back of his hand. Though she has not spoken of it, not even to her uncle, Julia was profoundly moved by the little girl in the rocking chair. For weeks afterward, she'd dreamed of her own childhood, of her alcoholic parents, of the chaos and the fear. How had she survived? By pluck, certainly, and perseverance, and by a pure refusal to submit. But there was another factor as well, this one far closer to the heart, and only when Julia finally stumbled upon it did her nightmares cease.

Julia feels this now and applies what she feels to everything around her, to Corry Brennan as she drinks from a bottle of green tea, to the dappled sunlight at Corry's feet, to a skating couple who break into a hot-step boogie in the center of the mall, to the quizzical smile playing over Peter Foley's lips, to a long trellis covered with flowering wisteria on a hill behind the bandstand, to the clop of a horse's hooves and the rattle of a hansom cab, to this candle flame of a girl with her red hair and her red jacket and her red skates, weaving, weaving, weaving.

Julia Brennan calls these things hope.